DRACO SANG BOOK 2

WOLF PACK

MARY BEESLEY

MONSTER IVY
PUBLISHING

DRAGON'S GATE

NOGARD'S PASS

Azure Lake

SHI CASTLE

R

DANBE CANYON

DRACO SANG CAMP

LION'S CAMP

KIPTOS

ABADDOON

ZEPHA

High
Sea

Scorpion
Sea

To Ann Crompton of Lancashire, England, who lost three sons in World War I. And to all mothers everywhere who have sacrificed a child to the great cause of freedom.

ONE - HUNTING

THIRRO

*T*hirro swooped low, inhaling the sweet scent of humans as a warm southern breeze ruffled his wings. His scouting loop complete—nothing new in the Elysium camp—he circled north to cross the Rugit River and return to Skotar. The fox canine that hung on a leather ribbon around his neck skittered over his sternum and clanked against a knife handle in his baldric. Instead of landing at camp and giving another boring report to Captain Ferth about the inactivity of the humans across the river, Thirro crossed the border and flew east, the waning moon and laughing stars silhouetting the dense forest.

With his eagle-sharp vision, he spotted a black beast stalking through the trees far below. He tucked in his long wings and dove, pulling up barely in time to alight with aching gracefulness onto a thick tree branch. The scent of blossoms clogged his sensitive nose. Spring was here. It had been a long winter of waiting, but with the Draco Sang reinforcements almost arrived, they would attack Elysium within days. It didn't feel like soon enough. Impatience revved through his veins, fluttering his wings as he crouched, his focus riveted on his prey.

Inky black scales covered a body the size of a ram. Poisonous horns glinted in the moonlight as its narrow head swiveled back and forth. An iron-toothed crosk on the hunt. A rare sight. Had it sniffed out the Draco camp? Thirro's heart hammered in eagerness at the same time his skin chilled. He palmed the tooth that hung around his neck. He wore the canine to impress the great chief, Laconius. And Laconius had not even noticed Thirro's prize. Laconius would take note of this. Only the bravest, fiercest Dracos could take down an iron-toothed crosk. At least in a fair fight.

Thirro lifted his bow off his back and pulled an arrow from the quiver between his wings. The crosk's scaled skin was virtually impenetrable, the weak spots being underneath, at the joints. From above, there were only two tiny targets for Thirro. The wind shifted, and the beast stopped and sniffed. It turned and padded toward Thirro's tree. Thirro set his arrow and pulled on the string. He whistled. The iron-toothed crosk looked up, and Thirro released. The arrow sliced into the crosk's right eye. He grinned as his prey let out a bone-chilling howl. It kicked and screamed and clawed at the tree trunk. Blood squirted down its face.

Thirro fired another arrow. The Dracosteel tip hit the thrashing creature's brow and bounced off. He cursed. Braced against the tree trunk, he waited for the crosk to weaken and slow. It didn't. Its claws cut deep groves in the tree harboring Thirro. The beast looked up with its one good eye and snarled out a promise of death. Thirro ignored the fear in his belly and took aim. The arrow struck true, burying deep into the skull. Blinded, the crosk flailed and screamed. Thirro tucked his bow into the case between his wings on his back. He waited. And waited.

Red sprayed the tree trunk and dribbled down black scales. Thirro was hungry. He swallowed as he thought of the warm meal that awaited him back at camp. He yawned and leaned against the tree while down below the beast cried and tore out chunks of earth. It was deep night by the time the iron-toothed crosk slumped into the jagged grave it had dug.

Thirro slid his dagger free. Scanning the trees for company, he glided down. The fearsome face came into focus. Blood crusted over dead black lips. Thirro pulled another knife and squeezed the handles tight. His pulse rang louder than the war horns as he crouched by his motionless prize. He jabbed a blade into the weak spot underneath its forearm. The crosk didn't move, and Thirro let out a sigh of relief. He pulled his arrows free with a sickening *pop*. The eyeballs came too. He tasted one, didn't like it, and cut the rest off, flicking the pieces onto the dirt. He wiped his arrows clean on the brown grass. He'd helped the steelsmith make the weapons, using his own feathers as fletching.

Now for his prize. He couldn't pry the jaws open without anchoring the body. Talons curled at the ends of Thirro's half-human feet—he hadn't worn boots since his transformation into an eagle Draco. The crosk's scales were cold against the bare pads of Thirro's foot as he stood on its neck. Panting, he sawed through jawbone and muscle. Grateful for the strength and sharpness of his Dracosteel, he cut out the largest tooth, a serrated barb as long as Thirro's finger. He held it up to the starlight, a victorious grin spreading over his face.

Fleeing the scene, he flapped up to a high branch. Congealed gore stained the tooth. He left it. Blood splatter was a good look. He untied the fox tooth from the leather around his neck and tossed it to the wind. Carefully he secured the deadly beauty so it hung at his sternum. While he flew back to camp, he imagined the look of pride the crosk's tooth would bring to Laconius's face. Ferth would be so jealous.

Not quite ready to leave his realm in the sky, Thirro circled camp, savoring his treasure. Below him, a few night-loving Draco Sang crisscrossed the paths. The fools didn't look up. They never did.

A familiar fox Draco crept up to Ferth's tent. There was only one reason Dara would visit their wolf Draco captain in the middle of the night with her vest unbuttoned, revealing cleavage velveted in short amber fur. Now that Ferth's slave had left him, Dara was making her move.

Thirro grated his teeth, hating Ferth. Even after Ferth had been whipped raw yesterday, humiliated in front of the entire army, the females still flocked to him. Tasting the pain of Ferth's punishment on the cold air and hearing the music of the crop had been a sweet pleasure.

Dara disappeared inside Ferth's tent. Seconds later she stalked back out. Satisfaction warmed Thirro's feathery chest. *Rejected again.*

He tilted his wings, intent on landing next to her, but storming footsteps kept him airborne. Directly below Thirro, Ferth sprinted past, his sword drawn, his wolfish face hardened into threatening lines, and his golden eyes bright with fury. Thirro flinched, then cursed his cowardly reaction and forced his chin up. He was *not* afraid of Ferth. Coming out of the shadows, Dara turned to follow their captain. Thirro landed in front of her. She jerked to a halt inches before walking into his chest. She narrowed her honey eyes and scrunched the fur on her forehead in a scowl.

"What's that?" Her gaze dropped to his chest.

"An upgrade from the little fox trinket."

Her frown deepened. So sensitive, always taking it personally when he mocked foxes. She moved to walk past him, but he flared his wings.

"Come with me. It will be easier to follow Ferth from the air."

She hesitated. Then, to his pleasure, she nodded. His nerves hummed as he wrapped his arms around her back and pulled her waist against his own. The scent of fox and female tickled his nose and warmed his blood. As he spread his brown wings, he held her closer and tighter than necessary, but she didn't need to know that.

With all the elegance he could muster, he lifted her into the night air, into his domain. She let out a low gasp that sent a secret thrill through him. Her head rested against his neck. Her hands held tight to his shoulders. Flying was pleasure. Flying with Dara's body flush against his was ...

"He went that way," Dara said, interrupting his fantasy. She craned her neck and pointed with her nose.

He lifted a wing and tilted south.

Twenty feet below, three Draco soldiers, swords drawn, followed Ferth into the forest south of camp. Thirro's pulse hitched. Had the humans attacked? He was itching to fight, put his training to the test.

Through a gap in the skinny spring treetops, Captain Ferth came into view as well as a white wolf, a woman in Elysium uniform, and an injured man lying on the ground. The scent of blood and wolf and human rose on the wind. Thirro inhaled, racking his brain for memories that came with that smell. He flashed back to the night of Captain Jobu's murder. This was the human with a wolf abomination that had killed their previous captain. And Ferth was going to kill the assassin before he could escape.

Ferth would get all the praise.

Forget that Ferth let a slave escape. Forget yesterday's lashing. Forget that Ferth still had human patches of skin on his face and chest. Ferth would be the hero. Again. Killing an

iron-toothed crosk was nothing to killing an enemy abomination. Thirro swallowed bitterness.

He and Dara watched Ferth rise to meet the three Draco
soldiers as they approached, but instead of directing them to
take the humans prisoner, Ferth held up his sword. Moonlight glinted off Dracosteel as Ferth brought his blade down
against his own soldiers.

Thirro reeled back, squinting in disbelief as Ferth
attacked his Draco brothers. Dara let out a strangled cry as
the white wolf abomination joined the fight, helping Ferth
kill the last two soldiers. Thirro sucked in air. He exhaled.

Ferth was a traitor.

His oldest friend. A traitor. Thirro blinked, but it didn't
change the scene unfolding. Ferth had turned on his Draco
Sang soldiers. He'd murdered them.

Ferth and Thirro had grown up together at Shi Castle,
sharing a room in the nursery and moving to the hatchlings
floor at the same time. They'd pulled pranks and stolen
things out of the citadel before they were old enough to
enter. Inevitably, every teacher and trainer had compared the
two boys. And Ferth always came out on top. He was the son
of Laconius—what sharper edge could a boy ask for? Thirro
had to fight, beak and talon, for everything he had. His
parents were lawless ones. They'd given him as tribute to
Mavras when the queen had begun planning this war all
those years ago. When the humans had put in their irrigation
canals, weakening the Rugit River, Queen Mavras had
responded by demanding children from her subjects all over
Skotar. Growing up as an orphan trained for war, Thirro had
to prove himself to the officers at Shi Castle every minute.
But not Ferth. Ferth, the last to transform and still the first to
become an army captain, had been given everything.

And he'd just thrown it all away.

Dara's heart pounded a frantic beat against Thirro's chest,

and her claws dug into his arms. He'd unconsciously risen in the air as the shocking scene had unfolded. Thirro forced a deep inhale, relaxing enough to fly closer for a better view as Ferth set his treasonous sword in the mud and knelt by the injured human again.

On silent wings Thirro stayed out of view behind the figures on the ground. The human woman at Ferth's side tilted her head, the moonlight catching familiar lines. Dara hissed at Ferth's runaway slave, Shale. Thirro knew her name because Ferth had made everyone in their unit learn it. He should have realized Ferth was a traitor long ago.

Thirro's eagle eyes narrowed as gray fog rolled off Ferth. The mist coalesced, darkening and taking shape. Thirro's body went rigid with shock as a gray wolf appeared from the swirl. *Abomination.* Ferth sagged as his body shrunk to its weak human form. Laconius's son, the captain of the camp, Thirro's lifelong rival and friend, *Ferth*, had lost his birthright, had failed so spectacularly that his beast abandoned him.

Dara gasped. Thirro forced himself to breathe, air rushing into his aching chest. His mind churned. Horror and glee clashed through him. Ferth was an abomination. Dracos hunted failures like Ferth. Thirro should bring him in. This was his chance to prove himself. If he brought Ferth, the human assassin, and the runaway slave to Laconius, Thirro would finally be the hero. He meant to move, to land with a flourish and draw his blades, but he didn't. His body failed to obey. Maybe it was the shock, maybe it was the grief painted on Ferth's familiar face, or maybe it was the pain tearing through Thirro at the thought of losing the closest thing he had to a brother. But instead of flying down, Thirro shot toward the moon.

He ignored Dara's protests, climbing higher and higher. The wind blasted away his cowardly emotions, his hesitations. As he touched the clouds, Thirro laughed. All that Ferth was, all that he had, was now Thirro's to take. Wicked cackles pierced the stars. He looked down at Dara in his arms. Buzzing with delight, he kissed her. He ignored her blanched face and watery eyes as he pried her lips apart with his tongue.

Anger flared when she punched his jaw. His head snapped back, and he almost opened his arms to let her go. He tipped forward and dove toward the ground like one of the arrows in his quiver. To her credit she stayed silent, but he grinned at her hammering heart and shallow breaths.

The forest was empty and quiet. Ferth, the wolves, and the humans had fled. Thirro was glad to give Ferth a head start. Let him live in fear a little longer. Thirro would enjoy this hunt. And *he* would be the one to kill the traitor. After years of living in Ferth's shadow, it was Thirro's turn to step into the light. How sweet his revenge would taste.

He shot over the first row of tents. He flipped upright and slammed into the ground in front of Ferth's door. Dara's knees buckled. He let go, and she fell. He left her sprawled in the dirt, trembling and whispering Ferth's name, as he waltzed into Captain Ferth's private tent.

Thirro's tent now.

TWO - CROSSING

FERTH

*B*lood-piercing fear powered Ferth forward as he carried his brother's dead body up the southern banks of the Rugit River and onto Elysium soil. Shale and the gray wolf—*his wolf*—flanked his sides. Through their mental connection, Ferth felt the animal's shock mirror his own. They followed dumbly, too confused for thoughts of rebellion or escape.

The white wolf, Lyko, led them through rows of sharpened timbers, a paltry defense against the Draco Sang. A three-toned horn sang through the night, and shouts reached them before Ferth crossed the camp boundaries.

Soldiers approached, weapons at the ready. Confused eyes darted between him, the two wolves, Shale, and Cal's corpse.

"I'm taking him to Captain Titus." Shale wrapped a steady hand around Ferth's elbow, fueling him forward, past the silent humans. A group of soldiers fell in around him like prison guards.

Her fingers tightened on his arm. *Shale.* His escaped slave. The reason his back was on fire from his father's crop. She'd made it here, to freedom—at least she'd be free until the Dracos arrived. Why had she risked her life to follow Cal back to Skotar? He couldn't make sense of any of it. He wanted to sink to the mud and give in to the overwhelming pain and confusion, but adrenaline kept him staggering forward, kept him from buckling under his twin's dead weight. Blood trickled down Ferth's spine where his wounds had reopened from the whipping. Was that yesterday? It felt like a lifetime ago. A different life completely.

Ferth could not meet the surrounding soldiers' eyes, not when he carried their fallen brother in his arms.

Not when Ferth had killed him.

No. He couldn't think like that. It was Laconius's horn that had gouged Cal's organs, torn a hole in his side. Their father had killed Cal.

Ferth had a brother. An identical twin. If he kept thinking it, would it start to seem real? Ferth didn't want this to be real. He wanted to wake up and have Cal alive. But it was Ferth that had blocked Cal's knife, saving his father's life and dooming Cal. The burden of grief and regret slammed his slumping shoulders and snatched his breath away.

Gray fur rubbed against his thigh, the shared sorrow drawing them together like lost children. *"This is not your fault."* The wolf spoke in Ferth's mind.

"Are no thoughts my own?" The mental connection to the two wolves shocked and excited him despite the circumstances. He'd lost his beast. He was an abomination to the Draco Sang. But he did not feel broken, at least not in this thing. His mind was clear and sharp. Free.

"I didn't have to hear you to see your guilt. Our father killed him. Laconius separated us from Cal and kept us from our mother." The gray wolf's voice in Ferth's head was the same low gravelly tones as Ferth's own.

"I killed him too." Ferth thought back to the chase, when he'd hit his brother's injured side. That's when Cal had dropped. *"I'll spend the rest of my life atoning, and it won't be enough."*

The wolf didn't reply.

Ferth held the cooling body closer, his chest caving in.

Shale stepped nearer to his side. He leaned into her strength as she guided him along the path to camp. The same path Ferth had taken only days ago. He'd been going the opposite direction, toward Skotar, fleeing the scene of his crime after kidnapping the baby. Had the little girl made it back to her mother? He could only hope.

A man came forward, and the soldiers parted. Judging by the wild directions of his graying hair, he'd been roused from sleep moments ago, but he held himself with authority and steel, like Ferth's father, but *different.*

His cobalt gaze cut into Ferth. Two scars striped his face, across his eye. His focus shifted to Cal, and pain crumpled his expression. Ferth stood paralyzed, clasping the corpse, as a muscled lion padded up behind the man.

The Lion. This was Titus. His father's enemy. Ferth's enemy—not anymore.

"Callidon." Titus's low voice was a whispered plea. Tears welled in his eyes as he laid his hands over Cal's neck, feeling for himself the silent pulse. Stony seconds ticked by. "My son."

Ferth's gaze shot up to the man's scarred face.

Blue eyes held his stare. "He found you. He brought you home. Our lost son."

Warmth spread across Ferth's icy heart as those powerful words struck deep. Titus gripped Ferth's shoulder with a wiry hand. He didn't hate the impertinent touch. In truth, Titus seemed to be feeding him courage.

"He vowed to kill his father and leave the Draco Sang

leaderless," Titus said. "Did he pass in the peace that he had avenged his ma?"

Ferth shook his head, pain shooting from his tight jaw to his cold feet. Ferth had destroyed Cal's mission. He eked out the confession. "Cal's blade went wide of Laconius's heart. The chief will heal."

Titus's eyes hollowed out in grief.

"But I do not think Cal realized that. He found peace in the end." Ferth could offer that slight hope.

"Because he found you."

Heat swelled behind Ferth's eyes. He held the stiff body closer to his heart.

"Your mother ..." Titus's voice trailed off. Tears dripped down. He tilted his chin to look at the heavy body in Ferth's arms. "Your mother," he whispered to Cal, voice soft and full of anguish.

Ferth ached with hope and want, his hidden dreams suddenly appearing on the horizon. Hearing of her spoken with such love rocked him. Desire rose painfully within him. Could he finally meet her? Where was she?

Titus's hand left Ferth's shoulder to cradle Lyko's narrow head. The wolf whimpered and nuzzled his palm. Titus dropped to his knee and drew the wolf against his chest, his arms wrapping white fur. The wolf who had lost his master, his human half, seemed to melt into the shared grief.

At Ferth's side, Shale's breath hitched. A quiet sound, but he was aware of her even in his trauma. Ferth flicked his focus to her weeping face and followed her gaze to a newcomer. He hadn't thought his heart could hurt any more, but it throbbed as Shale soaked up the broad-shouldered, dark-haired soldier who came forward.

"Uriah." She whispered his name like a prayer.

Had she found love so quickly?

His muscles coiled, wanting to fight the man. He flung the

thought away. *Not now. Not ever.* He tore his gaze away from the swooning Shale.

No animal followed Uriah, but he exuded prowess. His gaze bore down on Cal as he came forward. Without a word, Uriah scooped Cal out of Ferth's arms. Ferth sagged as the weight lifted. This was Cal's *real* brother. The thought crumpled him further. He had no right to be here, to bring back the body of their fallen comrade. He'd killed their friend. He'd kidnapped their child. He'd been their enemy moments ago. Was he still?

Every face had turned away from him to follow Cal. With smooth steps, Uriah carried the body into camp, Lyko close at his heels.

Ferth thought perhaps he might disappear into the shadows. Forever. But Shale tugged him forward by the elbow she still gripped. Her touch was a lifeline, the only thing keeping him from drowning. The gray wolf slunk along at Ferth's side, his tail between his legs.

A slow horn rang out. Sleepy humans stumbled out of tents to line the path. Each person stood with their fist on their heart as the procession seeped through. Grief rolled across camp. He wished again he could trade his brother in death.

Uriah carried Cal into a large tent. Ferth stopped in the shadows a few yards away. Shale let go of him and turned familiar green eyes up to look at his face, now furless and human. He wanted to draw her to his chest, hold her, smell her. Never let her go.

Without a word, she turned and went into the tent, no doubt anxious to be away from him and his shame. Cold isolation dropped over him like a cage. Rooted to the spot by exhaustion and indecision, he and his gray wolf went largely unnoticed. Except by the lion sitting in the darkness. Torchlight glinted off the blue gaze that guarded Ferth.

Men and women poured forward to see the body and share their grief. One woman with tears already washing her cheeks passed Ferth, and his wolf's head shot up at the same moment Ferth saw the baby in her arms. The baby he'd stolen. He could not face that mother. He had no hope of forgiveness.

Her wail rent the air as she crossed into the tent. "Callidon!" Her cries pierced the thin canvas and cut into Ferth's heart. Now he had taken Cal from her as well.

Still as a statue, Ferth watched and listened in horror as the night ebbed away.

Uriah and the mother left the tent. They stood together, the dawn basking them in pale colors as she wept into his chest. A panther glared at Ferth as it padded up to the mother. It was the one he had fought, and Thirro had injured. It hissed. Ferth almost wanted it to attack now. Standing here waiting for his punishment was torture on his nerves.

He needed to leave. He didn't belong here. He didn't belong anywhere. Except in hell. This was misery. Ferth eyed the lion still watching him. Maybe it would kill him when he tried to escape.

Titus left the tent and put his arms around the grieving couple. "Come."

Dismay rose in Ferth's chest as Titus led them forward to where he stood with his wolf. He wilted under their sad faces and heavy stares.

Titus stuck out his right hand, palm open and held vertically. "Captain Titus."

Ferth eyed the human hand. What was he supposed to do with it?

Titus lowered his arm to his side. "What is your name?"

Ferth decided he'd better start learning the ways of Elysium. In Skotar, Dracos greeted each other by lifting their elbow out and holding a fist over their heart, above their Draco Sang brand. Or among friends, punching eachother's chest marks with varying degrees of aggression.

Ferth stuck out his hand as Titus had done, holding the fingers straight. "Ferth." He let his hand fall as Titus had, but Titus was bringing his arm back up as if to grab Ferth's palm. Ferth quickly tucked his hands behind his back.

The woman's brows rose at the exchange.

"It's custom here to shake hands in greeting," Titus said, voice calm. "You are meant to take my palm in yours."

"Hold your hand?" Ferth's voice rose in surprise.

Titus's lips curved up, the hardness melting off his features. "I suppose you could say that."

He held out his hand again, and Ferth reluctantly brought his up and touched his palm to the stranger's. As Titus's wiry fingers wrapped around his, squeezing Ferth's stiff hand, warnings flared through him. This didn't feel romantic; it was aggressive. Titus was expressing his dominion. Ferth should never have surrendered his sword hand. He ripped his arm free as his wolf rose to a stand at his side and took a threatening step forward.

Titus tilted back, his palms flying up in surrender. "We'll work on that later."

Ferth's breath sped. This was it. They were going to kill him now.

He didn't want to die.

At least he wasn't alone, even if it were only he and his wolf against the world.

"Ferth," Titus said. "Callidon's brother. Mira's son. It's been nearly nineteen years. I'm very glad to see you again."

Ferth blanched. *Again?* But before he could stutter out a question, Titus turned toward the broad-shouldered soldier.

"This is Uriah."

Uriah didn't extend a hand. His bronze eyes blazed as he

looked over Ferth's face, the face that matched his dead friend's almost exactly. Ferth swallowed.

"And this is Zemira," Titus said.

The woman looked as though she might speak, but a fresh batch of tears washed her face instead. She shifted the swaddled baby and wiped at her cheeks.

Titus put his arm around her shoulders and pulled her close.

"I'm deeply sorry I wasn't able to save Cal." Ferth's voice held steadier than he'd hoped.

Uriah's scowl deepened.

Ferth wished his face wasn't going to remind them how much he was *not* Cal. "I didn't know who he was. I went to stop him from killing Laconius." *My father. His father.*

"I blocked Cal's knife from hitting the chief's heart." Ferth took the blood-crusted knife from his belt and handed it to Titus. "Cal wounded our fath—Laconius, but the chief gored him in the side with a horn. Once I realized …" Ferth's voice faded. Could he say the words? Claim brotherhood in front of these people who had earned the title? *No.* "I tried to save him. I became human in the process, but I failed. I'm sorry. I was your enemy and behaved as such. I understand if you kill me. But I swear on my blood and my brother's blood that I will fight with you. For you." Ferth's voice was iron, as was his promise. He looked at the baby and then up into the woman's eyes. "I was the Draco that took your baby. I don't expect forgiveness." The look on her face told him not to. "But my life is yours." He turned to the other grim faces. "All of you. Kill me if it will begin to pay the debt."

Ferth expected them to. That's what they would have done in Skotar. That's what his father would have done. Make a celebration out of his killing. Boost the army's morale. That's what it looked like Uriah and Zemira wanted to do.

Titus's voice cut through the heaviness. "I accept your offer to help us defeat the Draco Sang."

Uriah bristled. "How can we trust him not to stab us in the back?"

Lyko appeared, dragging his sunken shoulders out of the tent and over to the group. He nuzzled his head against the gray wolf. Guttural groans sounded as the two wolves sniffed and licked at each other, their faces rubbing along furry necks and sharp jaws.

Titus studied the animals. "Lyko is not as destroyed as the hewans without their humans I've seen in the past. He has not run off in a grief-stricken rage, turning wild."

Uriah squatted down and held a hand out to Lyko. Lyko licked the gray wolf's nose before turning and trotting up to Uriah.

"He has me," Uriah said. "I can't replace Cal. He can't replace Poe. But, we will take care of each other. Together."

Lyko turned pain filled eyes on Ferth as Uriah ran strong fingers along his fur. *"Just when I thought I couldn't feel worse."*

Ferth's tongue felt heavy. "He's linked to me and to my wolf."

Uriah's face tilted toward the ground, and his hands fell away from the animal. What more could Ferth take from him? The surrounding air seemed to burn away, leaving him without breath. His heart shattered at the extent of the destruction he'd brought to these people. In silent agony, he watched the slumped Uriah.

Titus looked at the wolves, thoughtful. "What is your wolf's name?"

Ferth's mind blanked.

"Rom," Lyko said in Ferth's head.

"Yes," the gray wolf replied.

"Rom," Ferth said.

Titus nodded a greeting to the gray wolf at Lyko's side. Rom nodded his sharp head. "Lyko," Titus said.

The white head turned, and golden eyes blinked at Captain Titus.

"Ferth is your master now? You accept him? Trust him?"

The wolf nodded.

The scars on Titus's face gleamed in the first rays of daylight. "I trust you, Lyko, and if you trust Ferth …" Titus turned to Ferth and extended a hand. Ferth gritted his teeth, not wanting to give up his right hand to this man again, but knowing he had to. "Then so shall I." Titus's grip tightened, and this time Ferth squeezed back. "You will honor your fallen brother and your mother." It was a command.

"Yes, sir. To my last breath." Ferth had sworn all sorts of things in Skotar, but never did he say it with every fiber of his being as he did now.

Uriah grunted as he stood. With a glance at Zemira, he marched away.

"I hope you and Cal share more than just looks," Zemira said, her voice colder than Azure Lake.

"So do I."

She scowled as she left.

"Let's see about breakfast and rest," Titus said, his voice somber.

THREE - GONE

THIRRO

*T*hirro paced. Ferth's stink clung to the tent, but Thirro grinned at the open space, the privacy, the stacks of uniforms, and pile of weapons. The fool had given it all up. Thirro couldn't quite process it. Couldn't be sure it was real. He hadn't touched anything in Ferth's tent for fear that the captain would come through the door as fearsome and wolfish as usual. He hated that a part of him wanted that. Wanted to see Ferth's familiar face and infuriating grin. Thirro's parents had abandoned him all those years ago. Now Ferth had left him too. Thirro chided his own weakness. He forced himself to take a bite out of one of Ferth's persimmons. He set in back on the table, bite mark facing away from the door. Heart pumping, he snagged one of Ferth's throwing knives and stuck it in his baldric. He froze at fast footsteps outside.

Keal stuck his ape-like torso through the door, the fur on his head matted on one side, eyes frantic. "There was an attack. The chief is injured. Six soldiers dead." Keal looked around. "Where's Captain Ferth?"

Thirro let out a tense breath. Ferth was truly gone. Time

to step up. He whipped past Keal and out into the dawn. Camp buzzed with activity. Slaves carried the dead Dracos out of camp, toward the burn site.

"Are we attacking?" Thirro overheard one soldier ask another.

"No. The chief is unconscious."

What had happened to Laconius? Thirro marched to the command tent, Keal close on his heels. A guard barred his entrance. Thirro's nostrils flared.

"Only officers allowed in this morning." The mole-ish Draco folded his arms. His haughty eyes might have been more impressive if he hadn't been two feet shorter than Thirro.

"I have important information to deliver."

"What is it?"

"I'm not telling you. Let me in."

"I can't do that."

Thirro's hands flew up, and he shoved the surprised guard to the side. When the mole Draco tried to draw a weapon, Keal put a massive palm on the guard's skull and threw him back into the dirt. Thirro nodded his approval, and they stormed into the command tent.

Dara was there. *Officers only, huh?* Her blood-shot eyes and ashen cheeks made her look sick. Ferth didn't deserve her grief. Like a mouse, she stood timidly near the wall, behind the unit commanders. Tense silence blanketed the room. No one acknowledged the new arrivals. No one moved. A grim-faced slave slipped in and out of the back room. Thirro's mouth watered at the smell of the food laid out on the table. He wanted to sit and eat, but he remained standing with the rest, as if their discomfort might somehow help the chief.

A healer stepped out of the back room.

Blood coated her hands up to her elbows. Her gray hair

flew wildly around her exhausted face. "He's awake. He should be sleeping, but he refuses. He is asking for Captain Ferth. He insists on speaking with him immediately." The healer slumped. "I'll be back after I wash." She shuffled out of the tent. A petite Draco Sang slipped in before the door closed.

Jade.

She'd arrived with Laconius and his small advance party ahead of the main body of troops. He would not soon forget the girl who Ferth had helped in the hunger pits, whom he had defended from Thirro's playful hazing. Now she was a jackal Draco Sang, top of her class. Vicious and deadly, and one of the youngest ever claimed by the beast. Mottled fur coated her pointed ears, scalp, and neck, but her face remained shockingly human, not a strand of fur on it. He studied the attractive sharpness of her nose and cheekbones. Her transformation had darkened the skin around her purple eyes to black. Her freckles ranged in color from gray to amber. Her lips were a deep maroon.

"Who let you in here?" His voice was sharp with annoyance.

"Hello, Thirro." Her pretty features twisted into a mocking smile.

He pointed to her face. "Looks like you're missing some fur."

"Where is Ferth?" Commander Mina asked.

"I've looked everywhere." Keal threw up big hands.

Dara's fear-filled gaze found Thirro.

"I know where he is." Thirro failed to keep the thread of eagerness out of his voice. "Best tell everyone at once."

Thirro led the group into the back room where the chief lay on a wide bed, his torso wrapped in cloth. Laconius's usually flushed face was deathly gray. He opened blood-shot eyes. His frown deepened.

"Where is my son?" His usually resonant voice was weak and airy.

Thirro stepped forward as if he could claim Ferth's inheritance. He wasn't going to let Dara take this moment from him. "He's gone."

"Dead? The human killed him?"

Thirro was surprised at the grief that darkened Laconius's features. Horror flooded every face. Thirro forced his voice to stay somber despite his excitement. "No, sir. It's worse. I was in the sky early this morning when I saw him in the woods with the human who attacked you. I was coming to his aid."

Dara shifted at the lie.

"Three warriors on the ground got to him before I did. Instead of having them help him defeat the humans, Ferth killed them."

Laconius's black eyes narrowed.

Thirro breathed in the thick air, smelling of blood and herbs. He would have feared the chief's rage, but with the buffalo bed-ridden, Thirro plowed ahead heedlessly. "Ferth is a traitor." Oh, the sour sweetness of saying that. "He turned on his own soldiers. He aided the human in attacking our camp. He lost his heritage. He is an abomination. The Dragon cursed him, and he lost his beast. He's *human*."

His heart hammered against the stunned silence. He chewed on his lip to keep back the smile that might reveal the perverse pleasure he took in Ferth's destruction. Keal looked like he'd been punched in the gut. Jade's furless face was bone white.

"No," Laconius said. "He fought the assassin in my tent. He saved my life."

"Maybe Ferth was too cowardly to kill you in the end, but the dead Dracos ... He killed them."

Rage rippled over Laconius. "You think my son is a traitor? You think my son plotted to kill me?"

Thirro hated himself for the tiny step back he took. "We were all deceived by Ferth." Except Thirro. He decided that he had always known Ferth was a coward in wolf's clothing.

"Is this true?" Laconius's beady red eyes scanned the group.

Dara looked down. Thirro scowled. How could she mourn Ferth now? She couldn't even admit the truth to herself, let alone the chief. Keal slid to her side and put a long arm around her shoulders. She nestled into his chest—as if their brother had died.

"Clearly he hadn't completed his transformation. He harbored a traitorous soul from the beginning," Thirro said. "His runaway slave was with him. He must have helped her escape as part of his plan to attack you."

Laconius shifted in pain—whether from his son's betrayal or his chest wound, Thirro couldn't tell.

"And you let him get away?" Commander Mina asked.

Thirro knew he'd made a grave mistake, and he didn't appreciate her bringing it up. He'd suffered a moment of weakness. He wouldn't hesitate next time. "I pursued, but he had human help and was already beyond the river before I could capture him."

"Time to rest," the healer's voice rang out as she entered.

"Mina, order extra flyers to scout the human camp tonight. I want confirming reports of this story by the time I wake up again."

"Yes, chief."

His onyx eyes bore into Thirro. "If you've lied to me ..."

Thirro's throat bobbed as he suddenly imagined the chief's axe slicing through his neck. "I would never."

"All of you, get out." Laconius's voice was a broken whisper.

Silently Thirro followed the others out. He squinted against the sunlight and breathed in air no longer tainted with iron and poultice. He needed to tread more carefully next time. He would not take any of the blame for Ferth's fall because he was the messenger.

A tight fist slammed into his jaw. Anger flaring, he rocked to the side. He grabbed at his weapon belt, but a thick palm jerked his arms back, wrenching them against his folded wings. Keal held him immobile. The big gorilla-man's face was somber. Jade wound her fist back and struck again, and this time Thirro's ribs sang with pain.

"What in the—"

"We'll ask the questions," Jade said. "And we want the truth."

Thirro spat. Blood and phlegm globbed on the amber fur carpeting Jade's arm.

She slapped his face, sending a zing up his big nose. "Where's Ferth?"

Venom and steel laced his voice. "If you hit me again, I swear, I will kill you." He might anyway. His skull was ringing, and he wanted nothing more than to douse the lights in her insufferably bright eyes. He'd just gotten rid of Ferth. This arrogant child was not about to take his place. If only Keal would loosen up. The brainless ape had no concept of how sensitive Thirro's wings were.

Jade kept her first clenched, but she didn't hit him again. "Did you kill Ferth?"

"Not yet."

"Putting an arrow in his back isn't beneath you."

"No. But this time I'll make sure he sees my face and knows that I've finally won."

"This isn't a game," Jade said.

"No. I'm dead serious." He chuckled at his little joke

before turning his voice hard again. "He's human now, Jade. He is a traitor. He's gone."

"You're gloating."

Coppery spit rolled over Thirro's smiling lips. Jade scowled. Dara watched impassively from across the path. She owed him big time for this.

"You're disgusting," Jade said.

Keal relaxed his grip and threw Thirro down hard on his folded wings. He hated smashing his wings.

"Training in thirty," Keal said. "Don't be late."

"Who put you in charge?"

"I did," Commander Mina said, stepping out of the tent and approaching with her spotted arms folded. "You think *you* should be a commander after you failed to bring Ferth in?"

A large crowd had gathered. Thirro swallowed his retort. Gingerly he got to his feet. "You'll see when the flyers return."

"Yes, we will." Jade's voice was low and missing its usual softness.

FOUR - HUMAN
FERTH

"Come. Sit." Captain Titus motioned to an empty corner of the long dining tent. The tables stood in straight lines and no feathers or spit littered the braided carpet flooring. Ferth sat with his back to the wall, for protection and so he could return the stare of hundreds of eyes. Lyko followed Titus to scout the food, but Rom stayed at Ferth's side.

Tentatively, Ferth reached out a hand and rested it on the wolf's fur—the fur that had once coated his neck. A shiver ran down Ferth's spine.

"Is this home? Can we ever belong here?" he asked Rom through their mind connection as his gaze drifted over the tables full of human soldiers.

"It feels good here. Smells better too," Rom said.

A young woman with a pitcher in each hand moved between the tables. Warriors smiled and thanked her as she poured drinks. No one pawed at her body or snapped at her.

"Think if we could have started out here. Fresh. Untainted."

"I intend to," Rom said.

Ferth's past clung to him as painfully as his bloody

bandages to the stripes on his back. He found it nearly impossible to keep his spine straight and his chin off his chest. He hadn't slept since the night before last.

Titus returned carrying two plates. He looked to Rom. "Lyko is outside with a fresh gopher. You'd better go if you want any of it."

Golden eyes flicked to Ferth briefly before the wolf whirled, and his sleek form streaked through the open doors.

Ferth thought his body and emotions too frayed to eat, but when Titus set down a steaming plate of eggs, turnips, and sausage, Ferth picked up the fork. Besides, eating gave him an excuse to avoid those searching blue eyes. Thankfully, Titus let him eat in silence.

When his plate was clean, Titus said, "You'll have the day to rest. Tonight we'll send Callidon's body on. Tomorrow you report here for breakfast, and I'll assign you a squad."

"Yes, sir." He was grateful the man had adopted a military tone. No more emotion, no more tears. Business. Good.

Titus led Ferth outside and over two rows of tents. The twin wolves trotted around a corner and up to Ferth's side. When Titus opened the door of another tent and led them inside, Ferth knew immediately whose home this was.

No, no, no.

"I'd feel more comfortable somewhere else." He looked at the crisply made bed, Lyko's mat, the table holding papers carrying Cal's words on them.

"Maybe you would. But this is your tent now. This is still Lyko's tent. All the hewan soldiers live in this section, and this tent is now available."

Available because his brother was dead. It hit like a fresh punch to the kidney.

Titus's expression softened. "You will not hide in the shadows of this camp. You will start over. You are Mira's son. You are no longer a Draco Sang."

Mira's son. No longer a Draco Sang. When would that sink in? His heritage, his life. Gone. What did this new one mean? Waves of nausea rolled through his gut.

"Do not carry that brand with you," Titus said.

His brand. Was it still there, etched into his chest?

"You are now one of us. You have overcome your beast." Titus breathed out. "In a situation that I'd have deemed utterly impossible." The man cracked a small smile and laid a hand on Ferth's shoulder. "I look forward to getting to know you, Ferth Mirasson. You are undoubtedly a man worth knowing."

Ferth didn't breathe until Titus left the tent, because the moment the flap closed, he doubled over. He sank to his knees. Did they think that he could ever replace the man they'd lost? He was *not* his brother.

But hearing those words, those words of comfort, of respect. *Ferth Mirasson.* Could he ever be that man? He clutched at his waist.

Two wolves—brothers—stood before him, amber eyes seeing to the darkest parts of his soul.

"Lyko," he said. *"You'll share your tent with us?"*

With Ferth on his knees, the wolf's face was level with his. *"We are blood. I will serve you and protect you."*

The words sent a chill through Ferth. He straightened his spine and vowed, *"I will serve you and protect you."*

Rom echoed the commitment.

"Go to sleep," Lyko said. He brushed past Ferth toward the door.

"Where are you going?"

"To spend the last day with my heart."

Ferth's body couldn't fight off sleep anymore, and he laid down where he was on the floor. Rom dropped next to him as he closed his eyes. He woke briefly when Lyko returned, head down and tail limp, and curled up with them.

Heavy drums woke Ferth. The pounding accompanied the throbbing in his chest. He squinted at the dying sun waving from the western window. He shifted out from underneath a tangle of paws and fur. His Draco Sang uniform was splattered with blood, sweat, and Rugit water. He couldn't wear this to the funeral, but how could he wear the dead man's clothes?

He stripped. His skin was soft and pale, nearly hairless—except for the mane of chestnut hair that fell past his shoulders and a straggly beard. And there it was—his brand—bright white scars against his pectoral. *LF09285. L for Laconius. F for Ferth. 09285 for his birth.*

Just because the scar is visible doesn't give it power.

Hissing, he pulled the soiled bandages off his back where Laconius had beaten him after Shale's escape. His hands, arms, and legs were peppered with the marks of his violent past. Dried blood flaked off his right arm where Lyko had bitten him, protecting Cal from Ferth's attack.

How much had changed.

Ferth hated that his torso felt thinner and his shoulders smaller. Flat nails adorned his fingers instead of the claws that he'd come to depend on. He ran a tongue over straight, square teeth. He shook his head. He would *not* mourn the loss of his claws and canines, his scent and sight. His powerful presence. Regret tried to push in, but he glanced at the wolves. He still had all those things in abundance at his side.

Keturah's voice whispered in his head, *never mistake humanness for weakness.* He missed her. He could almost imagine her elation if she could see him now. He'd done what she'd always hoped for. This was what she wanted for him. And now he'd never see her again.

He picked up a large bucket of water and tipped the wooden edge to his mouth.

"*That's washing water,*" Lyko said. He thumped a tail across the room at a pewter pitcher on the table.

Ferth set the heavy bucket down and took a long pull from the fancy water.

Moving back to the bucket, he lathered up. Using Cal's soap, he scrubbed at his wounds and hissed at the sting. It was so much harder to inflict the pain himself. How had Shale managed to tend to him without causing him to flinch or tremble? He tried to imagine she were here. It didn't work. He grit his square teeth and soaped the bite marks on his arm. Blood and dirt darkened the water with each pass of the washcloth. He couldn't reach his itching back. Far from truly clean, he dropped the towel. He found a brush on the table and tried it on his tangle of hair. The muscles in his arm complained and so did his scalp. Defeated, he lowered the brush.

With a clean linen he found by the wash basin, he wrapped his bloody forearm. It wasn't as tight as he wanted it. It wasn't as tight as Shale would have done it. He didn't see another cloth he could use for his back, and he didn't know where to get bandages. Again, no slave to send for it. No Shale. With a drawn-out sigh, he sat naked on the chair. For the first time, he thought maybe he should have never followed his brother into the forest. He wanted to wake up back in Skotar, with his fur and his slave and his title.

The drums continued to beat, long and sad, calling to them.

"*Clothes are in the chest,*" Lyko said.

"*I can't wear Cal's clothes.*"

"*Then let's go.*" Lyko stretched.

Right.

Ferth gingerly opened the trunk and selected what looked like the most basic training uniform. With no dressing for his back, he put on an extra tunic to protect it and hide it should he bleed. The clothes fit too perfectly.

He scratched at his beard, knowing it didn't hide the face that matched his brother's, but hoping anyway. He'd better try again to tame his hair, anything to help him appear less feral. He found a bone comb on the table next to a cleanly folded letter.

Mira Closdaut was written in bold letters on the front.

Mother. Ferth fell into the chair as he stared at the name. Cal's last words to his mother lay on that crisp parchment.

Careful not to touch the letter, Ferth sucked in a few deep breaths and picked up the comb. After a few painful yanks on his tangles, the comb stuck. He groaned as he tugged at it.

"Let me help."

He jumped in his seat.

The soft light of sunset through the open door tinted Shale's face in pink and gold. She'd changed into a white Elysium dress with a red sash cinching her waist, accentuating the curves that Ferth had admired for so long. Long chocolate tresses flowed over her shoulders and breasts.

Ferth stared.

Shale smiled.

Ferth's throat bobbed.

He shrank back into the chair as she approached. Like a fantasy and a nightmare. She was his master now and he her slave.

The two wolves headed her off. She stopped and ran a hand between their ears.

"Hello, Lyko," she said. "Who is your brother?" Her voice was like honey, her presence like wine. Ferth failed to steady his pulse.

Three faces fixed on him.

"Oh, yes. Um. Rom."

Shale's lip tweaked up as her gaze danced across Ferth's

face, and then her focus mercifully drifted to Rom. "You're beautiful, Rom, just as I imagined you would be."

He purred. The disloyal wolf *purred*.

"Traitor," Ferth said to Rom.

"Jealous?" Ferth felt the pleasure Rom took in the woman rubbing his skull.

He scowled. "Let's go." He stood, the comb still tangled in his hair. He'd cut it out later.

Shale stepped past the wolves, looking more like her lap dogs at the moment. "Just a second, soldier." She pointed to the chair.

He sat.

She looked over his beard and tangled mane. "I see you're still trying to hide behind fur."

He had no answer for that truth. She stepped behind him. His vision blurred, and his heart galloped as her gentle fingers worked through his hair. He folded his arms and scowled. Her presence was a comfort and an anguish. He hadn't had human hair in Skotar, but plenty of times he'd made her brush his fur—and not just the fur on his scalp— until it had gleamed. Why would she help him now?

She worked in silence, but her touch was louder than the Gamply Falls crashing through his mind. He shuddered when her fingers brushed his neck. She still smelled of jasmine and salt. She still made him ache with want.

She carried with her the memory of so many past pains. He'd been her master, her owner, her tormentor. It had not seemed so wrong at the time, not when she was human, and he was Draco Sang. But now, here, in this new world where Shale walked with her hair unbound and her eyes up, he felt the monstrosity of it like a knife in his chest. How could he ever make restitution? How could she stand to be here with him, touch him, serve him?

With a voice raspy and low, Ferth said. "I'm sorry, Shale."

Her fingers stilled for a moment, then she took a leather thong off her wrist and tied his hair together at the base of his neck.

"There," she said.

Ferth turned in his chair, but stayed sitting. If he stood, he'd be looking down at her—as he had for months. He contemplated getting down on his knees.

"I'm sorry, Shale. For everything. I'm sorry I hurt you." Without thinking Ferth took her hand. When the touch woke every nerve in his body, he quickly dropped it again.

She looked as if she might speak, but her brow pinched, and tears fell instead.

Ferth shifted forward, not knowing what to do, wanting to cradle her, but feeling like he could not touch her again. Not without her permission. Never again.

Lyko stepped to Shale's side and leaned his warmth against her thigh.

With her fingers gripping Lyko's fur, she turned and walked out of the tent with the wolf.

Every rib in Ferth's chest cracked as he and Rom silently followed them out.

The drums called them south of camp to a rolling field. Seven blaring fires burned around an army of soldiers, all facing the center, where Cal's body lay clothed in white silks above an altar of sticks.

This would be a good time to attack. Even as he thought the words, Ferth cringed. He was not a Draco Sang captain anymore.

Shale and Lyko glided between a company of soldiers toward Cal, but Ferth stopped on the edge with Rom.

Shale reached the cluster of a dozen warriors with their hewans. A small moat of space separated those with Draco Sang blood from the rest of the army.

Zemira embraced Shale. Good. She had made friends here.

A hawk soared down and landed on Shale's shoulder.

Realization hit like one of Keal's punches. Ferth reeled, clutching at Rom's back to keep from toppling.

He blinked. *"How did we not see it? How did I not know?"* His legs shook. *"She was my slave. And she was Draco Sang."* The horror of it rose like bile in his throat.

"She hid it well," Rom said. *"But it makes sense now. She did not seem like an ordinary slave."*

"No, she is no ordinary woman." Ferth thought of her strength, thought how her fertile blood had called to him, still called to him. *"How many more slaves hiding their hewans do you think there are in Skotar?"*

"More."

The thought didn't chill Ferth as much as he expected it to, not nearly as much as his next thought. *"She will never forgive me."*

"You were a good master."

"There is no such thing," Ferth said.

"She came back to Skotar to save your brother."

Ferth needed time to think on that. What had Cal meant to her? Why had she done that? *"And she returned with me instead."*

Across a hundred heads, Captain Titus approached Shale and they turned. Both faces found Ferth over the sea of soldiers.

Titus motioned them forward. When Ferth shook his head, declining the invitation, Titus strode over.

"Come, soldier." His voice was hard. "You will stand as you are assigned."

"Yes, sir."

Titus led Ferth to a space behind Uriah, Zemira, and a large man holding the baby. With a start Ferth realized he was the same man Ferth had fought with when he'd stolen the baby. It seemed a world away, a life separate. The man eyed him pointedly, but the rest ignored Ferth. Uriah didn't lift his gaze off the pyre.

A raven, perched on an older woman's shoulder, turned around and trained its glossy eyes on Ferth. Ferth nodded an acknowledgement, but the creepy bird didn't blink or shift its stare.

The music changed and the assembly dropped to one knee. Ferth knelt on two. Captain Titus stood and with a booming voice, praised their fallen comrade. Praised Callidon for his strength, for his sacrifice, for his humanity. Callidon was loved, honored, revered. Callidon had died for Elysium. Callidon died for freedom. Callie Poe bore his name, but may they all bear his errand in this fight. Let no Draco Sang find victory here.

Vomit rolled up Ferth's throat, coating his mouth in acid. He swallowed bile and bit down hard on his tongue. He gagged, but sealed his lips and swallowed it all back down. Down. Down.

A bone-jarring cheer rang through the night as Titus finished his rousing tribute.

When silence fell, Zemira stood. As she got up, Shale came into view. Ferth thought for a moment Shale looked to him, but his chest crumpled when he realized she stared at Uriah. Jealousy flamed through him at the look she sent that man. And Uriah didn't spare her a glance. Didn't even notice the longing in Shale's eyes. No, Ferth was left to watch it. Ferth wanted the ground to devour him, but it was hard and unyielding.

Zemira opened her mouth, and her song rent the night. Powerful notes rang over the army, piercing and clear.

When we fall into the pit and darkness swallows us whole,

There we find that the Great Ones descend below.
They rise up and carry us on.
Though the road is grim and bleak,
They go before our feet.
Carry him home.
Raise me up.
If they leave us on the brink, for them we will not sink.
Let us carry the sacrifice on. Carry it on.
Grant us their mantle of honor that we might carry it ever onward.
Ever forever onward.

Firelight reflected off the tears streaking Zemira's face. The Warrior's Rite ended, but the music seemed to linger in the air and in Ferth's soul. The raven cawed. Zemira extended a hand to Uriah and pulled him to his feet. One of the commanders passed them each a torch, giving one to Captain Titus and keeping one.

The drums rocked Ferth's bones as the four took their places surrounding Cal.

Captain Titus set his flames against the pyre first, leading off the commander and Zemira. Flames licked the sky before Uriah finally threw his torch in. He stood so close, Ferth thought the fire might claim him too.

As the inferno devoured the face that matched his own, grief embraced Ferth. He thought of the time he never had with his brother. If only he could go back and save Cal instead of bringing him death. Death by the horn of their father. Their father who was now his enemy. The exquisite pain of regret overwhelmed Ferth's mind. The fire burned through him as it did Cal. Ravishing, destroying, purifying.

Ferth sank lower on his knees. The heat hollowed his insides. His raw heart pounded with the rhythm of his brother's death drums. Hazy darkness engulfed him. The world disappeared.

When Ferth could finally peel his soul away from the embers of what had been a mighty fire, a mighty life, he knelt abandoned in a grassy field, the dawn approaching. Everyone had left him alone with his sorrow and shame except Rom and Lyko, who slept nearby.

Lyko lifted his head as he sensed Ferth's attention returning to this world.

"He lives on in you," Ferth said to Lyko.

"And in you." Floating ash landed on a white nose.

"Let's make him proud."

The wolf nodded, and Rom nudged his head against Lyko's neck.

"We've got work to do." Ferth turned his gaze north, toward the training yards, toward Skotar, toward the father who had killed his son.

FIVE - CONFIRMED
THIRRO

The weary scout landed heavily outside the command tent, near where Thirro loitered in the shadows. Thirro slid closer, ears perked, as Commander Mina approached the flyer.

"Confirmed visual of Ferth," the bat Draco said to Mina. "He's human and has a wolf abomination with him, the second wolf in the camp. He is not treated like a prisoner. He seems to have joined their army, along with the escaped slave, Shale."

Exactly as Thirro had said. Satisfaction warmed his feathers.

"Come in." Mina motioned the flyer toward command. "You will report the details to Chief Laconius."

Thirro slunk to Ferth's tent—his tent now—and dropped his bow and quiver on the table. He picked up one of the traitor's books—a ballad. What a waste of time. Thirro dropped the book when the door of the tent peeled back. Dara marched inside. Shadows circled her puffy eyes.

"Still weeping for our lost comrade?" His voice dripped with scorn.

"It still smells like him in here."

"Regretfully."

"You truly feel nothing? What we saw wasn't right. It wasn't normal." Dara looked at Ferth's things. "What happened to him? How?"

"I wasn't surprised."

"Yes, you were."

Thirro didn't appreciate being reminded of how he'd reacted that night. He hated that Dara had witnessed his hesitation and shock. And since then, he'd had plenty of time to remember how Ferth had protected underlings. How he'd snuck food to slaves. "He's always been weak."

"He could beat you in a fight." Dara's voice rose.

Resentment flared in his breast. "He couldn't even beat his beast."

She rolled her eyes, but her shoulders slumped. She turned away. Defeated.

"You're welcome for covering for your cowardly silence. I could have told them you were with me. You saw it too."

Her face hardened as she whirled back. "And I could have said you lied about several important details."

"And you're too late to speak up about it now."

She glared, her orange eyes like twin fires. "I don't owe you anything."

He cracked a crazed grin.

"I certainly don't miss you in our tent." With that parting blow, she waltzed out.

He muttered curses at her under his breath, marched over to Ferth's bed, and sprawled across, claiming it. The tooth around his neck slid over his chest, shaving off small feathers in its path and cutting into his arm as it came to a stop. He was going to look like a molting hen if he didn't do something about this stupid trophy. Careful not to let the tooth cut him again, he got up and left.

Laconius was resting alone when Thirro entered command. Perfect.

"You look to be healing up nicely, my chief." Thirro executed a beautiful bow.

Laconius closed his eyes with a sad sigh and leaned back against pillows. "You were right, Thirro."

Beautiful words. Warm pride gushed through him, bringing tears to his eyes.

"My son is a traitor and an abomination. I have no son."

"You have me. I will not fail you."

Laconius opened his terrible eyes and studied Thirro. Thirro leaned so the treasure on his chest would swing forward. Laconius's focus shifted to it. Thirro gratefully lifted it off his neck and held it out.

"A token of my devotion to you."

The chief accepted the giant tooth, crusted with rusty black blood. "An iron-toothed crosk."

Thirro swelled at the awe in Laconius's voice. "Yes, sir. While scouting last night, I found one outside of our camp. I couldn't risk it harming one of our own."

Laconius turned the tooth over and over in his thick fingers. "You took it down yourself?"

"Cutting that out of its jaw was the hardest part." He grinned.

Laconius laughed. "Well done." He sobered. "I see I have underestimated you."

Thirro's ribs expanded nearly to bursting. The tent flap rolled back, and Jade sauntered in. He deflated.

At least she couldn't worship that traitor Ferth now. A smug smile crossed his lips. He had enjoyed telling Jade of her hero's tragic fall. He'd seen the horror in her eyes, the utter devastation. He hated Ferth more after seeing Jade's broken-hearted reaction.

"My chief." She smiled at Laconius before giving Thirro a

curt nod. "Thirro." She turned her delicate face back to Laconius. "I'll be brief so you can rest. I found an iron-tooth crosk carcass one mile northeast of camp."

Thirro smiled.

"Yes." Laconius held up the jagged tooth. "Thirro here is telling me how he brought it down."

Pale purple eyes narrowed on Thirro. "How did you get your blade under its arm before it killed you?"

His grin broadened. "Skill."

"There was blood everywhere." She looked at the hanging tooth, her brow furrowed in thought and her emotions unreadable.

"We'll leave you to rest, chief." He swept his arm, motioning Jade to leave in front of him.

She darted out. He ducked the low door, unable to move as fast. He caught a glimpse of the deep purple sash she wore tied to her weapons belt as she slipped around the back of the tent. He followed. He jumped around the corner and caught her elbow before she could disappear. He pulled her close as she jerked at her arm. He didn't let go; his sharp fingernails dug in. She swung a blade at his chest with her free hand, but he'd anticipated her move. Using his strength and size advantage, he grabbed her wrist and squeezed until she released her weapon.

"Going somewhere?"

"Away from you."

He chuckled, bringing his face closer to hers. "Ah. You don't mean it."

She tugged at her arm, and he wrenched it behind her back, drawing her front against his chest as he secured her other wrist in his long wiry fingers. He brought a blade to her belly. Her breath hitched.

"You hit me." His voice was as soft as a lover's caress. "And in public."

The flash of fear in her eyes set his pulse singing.

"Do you think because you've got fluff on your scalp, you're my equal?"

"I was very upset about Ferth. I reacted poorly."

"Is that an apology?" He licked his lips as he looked over her enticing face. Was she ever going to grow fur on that freckled nose? He found it hard to believe someone with a heart as stony as hers might still have that much human weakness in her.

"Is that what you want?"

"I want a lot of things, but I'll start with retribution." He thrust her back, making sure his blade sliced through skin.

Violet eyes burned with hatred above gritted teeth. Her pointed canines gleamed. One of her hands went to her weeping waist, the other to a short sword. Before she could draw, he backhanded her across the jaw with all his strength. She flew, landing on her side with a *thump*.

He straightened his vest and marched away, grim but determined, paying no attention to the murderous look she directed at his back.

*F*erth's back hummed a harrowing hymn. He'd taken his dressing off himself yesterday before the funeral with no replacement. After this morning's training exercises, Cal's undershirt had become the new bandage. He couldn't move without feeling the stuck linen pull at his stripes. He wouldn't be able to get the shirt off alone without making things worse. Checking over his shoulder like a fugitive, he worked his way to the healers.

"Don't let Shale in here," he said to Rom when they reached the low building.

Rom curled up at the door. Lyko was on the other side of camp with Captain Titus and his lion hewan, Eio.

Satisfied that Ferth hadn't been seen by anyone he knew —the list was short—he slipped inside. Three rows of cots ran down the length of the long room. Rectangular brick fireboxes dotted the spaces between the rows. Only the first few beds had occupants.

"Morning, sir," a woman said as she approached. She smiled kindly and the skin around her eyes crinkled up. Gray hair twisted into a knot at the top of her head.

Ferth's knees buckled at the sharp memory of Keturah—the slave woman who'd raised him, nursed him, tended him, *loved* him. He'd left her in the slave quarters at Shi Castle. Far from this freedom.

The healer stepped forward in concern. Sturdy fingers gripped his forearm. "You're ill." She motioned toward the first open bed.

He straightened. "No. I'm not ill."

Her brows lifted.

"I'm fine actually. I just need. Um. I just need a bit of dressing. For a wound."

She scanned his upright frame, clearly confused. "And how much dressing does the *wound* require?" She grinned.

"Quite a lot."

"I see." She clasped her hands over her apron. "Actually, I don't see."

She was teasing him. Ferth shifted his feet. "I guess I'll have to show you."

"I guess you will." She spoke as if sharing a joke.

"Over here maybe." He strode past the other patients, several of which had taken an interest in the conversation. He stopped halfway down the building, in the shadows. The fires had not been lit this far down. He faced the front, making sure to make eye contact with each curious face until they turned away. He did not want anyone to see his stripes. He did not want anyone to talk about his whipping. He did not want Shale to find out. He slowly peeled off his jacket.

The healer, standing in front of him, watched with matronly amusement.

He unbuttoned the shirt and let it hang open, revealing healthy skin. Her eyes locked on the stark Draco Sang brand above his heart.

"If you could help me get this shirt off?"

She stepped behind him and lifted her short arms high to

his shoulders. Ferth grimaced as she, none too gently, started to tug the linen down.

She gasped. "Oh, my." Her voice was sorry, not a trace of her earlier cheer. Achingly slowly she peeled away at the rest of the cloth. Warm liquid dribbled down his back in itchy rivulets. "Best lie down." She kept a comforting hand on his arm as she invited him onto the bed.

"Please," he said before moving an inch. He looked over his shoulder to stare in her eyes. "Not a word to anyone."

Her sad gaze flickered over his back. "Who did this to you?"

His voice hardened. "Not a word."

She exhaled and nodded.

With a tired sigh, he lay face down on the bed.

"I'll be right back." She returned three times with supplies and set a torch near her tray. She picked up a wet cloth smelling of witch hazel and herbs. "Ready?"

"Yes."

She brought the rag down.

Not ready. The acid burned. His back arched. His jaw clenched. His eyes watered.

"I'm sorry, dear. I must clean them properly. They've festered and somehow you've gotten gray fur stuck in here."

Somehow. He wondered what fun it would be to tell her that it was *his* fur, but a whimpered acknowledgment was all he could eke out of his tight lips. Was it only two days ago that he was a feared Draco Sang wolf?

"Incoming," Rom said.

Ferth jerked his head up, and the healer reeled back.

"Just a bit more," she said.

"It's Shale, and she'd headed this way."

The healer pressed Ferth's head firmly back into the cot, but her touch was kind, more tender than he'd ever deserve.

"Stop her," Ferth said to Rom.

Rom's bark carried through the walls. Through their mental connection, Ferth sensed him pacing in front of Shale as she tried to step past him.

"Let me in, Rom," Shale said. "Xandra saw him go in. I know he's in there, and I will find out why."

Rom barked.

"I'm going in there."

He leaped in her path, using his bulk to block her legs. He nuzzled her waist back with his head. His meaning was clear.

She shoved him away. "You'll have to fight me to stop me." She pushed past.

Rom snarled low and deadly, flashing her razor-sharp canines.

She ignored him.

"No respect," Rom said to Ferth.

Shale opened the door to the healers' building.

"Cover me," Ferth said to the woman.

"I'm not finished."

He got to his elbows and looked up at the terrifying woman charging through the tent. Shale's gaze locked on him and slid down his back.

Too late.

Rom heard Shale's horrified gasp all the way from his station outside.

Ferth turned his face away from Shale and sank to the cot.

The healer resumed her work.

Heavy minutes ticked by in silence. Ferth could feel Shale's gaze stinging across his skin. He could almost hear her thoughts turning. His heart sank.

The healer spread cool balm over his lashes. "On your hands and knees while I do the wrapping."

He obeyed, face tilted sharply away from Shale's direction as the healer wrapped gauze around and around his furless torso. He didn't dare look over. Was she still there? He wouldn't blame her if she'd left. He sank back to his stomach, feeling weak as a baby and heavier than a full-grown magu.

"Rest as long as you like," the healer said. "Come back tonight, and I'll replace the balm."

"Thank you." The words didn't adequately express how much her compassion had healed not only his back, but his heart.

The healer took her tools and padded away.

Silence reigned.

Ferth sighed, telling himself it was better that Shale left. He did not need to see her gloating—enjoying his lowliness.

Tender fingers traced his jaw. His eyes flew open and locked on her face. Green eyes were inches from his. Her voice was a whisper. Her breath caressed his neck. "They did this to you because of me." There was no triumph in her face. Fat tears brightened her eyes and rolled down her pink cheeks.

Why wasn't she celebrating this? "Shale, no."

"I'm so sorry, Ferth."

His own eyes watered. She was sorry? How?

She put a hand on the back of his neck and rested her forehead against his. He didn't move a millimeter. He couldn't. She smelled of gardenias and girl—of Shale. "We're free now."

He wasn't sure that was true for him. But she was free. That was what mattered. Chills carpeted his skin when she let go. She turned and ran toward the door, wiping at her face. Ferth lay on that bed for a long time. When would he stop hurting her?

SEVEN - FOUND
SHALE

*S*hale couldn't wait anymore. She'd watched Uriah for three days of mourning.

If he would just look at her. See her.

But he'd hardly glanced her direction, even when she'd had to report every heartbreaking detail of her return trip to Skotar and Cal's death to the commander. Uriah had been there, but he'd kept his face in his hands and his eyes down.

She'd suffered to give him space to grieve, in which time he'd sunk into a dark abyss. She would wait no longer.

As she stepped up to Uriah's tent, her excited heart spun.

"Hello," she called at the door.

After waiting through a breath of silence, she slipped through the stiff flaps.

The tent was big, too big for only one bed, even if the man heaped on top of it was large.

"Hello, Uriah."

His head lifted from the mattress, and he trained chocolaty eyes on her.

Oh, those eyes. They warmed her heart and raised goosebumps along her arms.

"I brought you some dinner." She held out the plate in offering.

His eyes narrowed. "Who sent you?"

"No one sent me." Her tone carried a slight bite. Did they send women to soldier's tents around here too? She refused to believe it, refused to acknowledge that she might not have escaped all her demons, that the humans could be so much like the Draco Sang.

"Cal would have," he said.

Cal didn't seem like the sort of man who sent women to bed his friends. No, he would not. She refused to taint the dead man's memory. She had looked into Cal's beautiful eyes, and she'd never forget the goodness brimming there.

Uriah slumped back onto the mattress as if the mention of Cal sent a fresh wave of physical pain through him.

Shale sighed. His anguish was real, and she sorrowed too, but she didn't want his sulkiness now. Not when she'd fantasized about this reunion for twelve years, when she never thought she'd see Uriah again.

Hands shaking, she set the food down and strode over to the cold fire pit. She deftly lit the kindling as the last daylight leaked away with the setting sun. She built up the fire until golden warmth chased the shadows away.

He hadn't moved from the bed, and she'd had enough. She marched over to his side, put her hand squarely on her hips, and with a tone she'd learned from their mother, she said to his back, "Uriah Granadine, get up right now. I need a good look at my brother." She tried to be stern as she said it, but the last words were slurred by her tears. She bit into her knuckles. Her lips trembled.

In one shocked movement, he flipped over and sat up as he swung his legs over the bed in front of her. The color drained from his face as his eyes, deep as the Danbe Canyon, took her in.

For a heartbeat, fear stabbed through her. What if he didn't remember her? What if he didn't care?

"Suzaena?" He said her name as if it were a prayer, a hope, a dream.

She nodded, unable to speak as her shoulders shook. Her heart swelled so large she thought her ribs might crack, and then he was there, standing with her. His arms went around her shoulders, and she melted against his chest.

"Suza." His voice was thick with emotion. "You're alive. You're *here*. You're ..." He pulled back and touched a calloused thumb to her cheek.

Human.

She smiled at the look of awe in his face.

He drew her into his embrace again, holding so tight she could barely breathe. But she didn't need air when she had him. Warmth permeated her whole body. In all her longings for home, never once in her dreams had it felt like this.

Time stopped as they stood encircled.

Finally, Uriah's voice cracked the spell. "Mother?"

Suza shook her head into his shirt. "No."

He pulled away and looked over her face again, as if studying it carefully. She tried to do the same but was hindered by the grimy skin, shaggy hair, and unkempt beard.

"Tell me."

She nodded, and he led her to the chairs by the fire.

What could she tell? How could she burden her already grieving brother with her past?

Her gaze shifted from his face, the face of a man acquainted with sorrow and eyes that had already seen too much death, features that mirrored her own. Near their feet, flames danced destruction on the logs.

"I need to know," he said. "Tell me the truth. All of it."

Their dinner grew cold as Suza dug up memories she'd buried deep in the fields of her soul.

The last time she'd seen her brother had been when their mother had hidden him in that ditch moments before the search party found them. He'd landed in a rosemary thicket, the scent helping mask his presence.

"When they found us, they dragged us back to Gristle-cove." She wasn't going to mention how they'd whipped their mother senseless. "They kept asking her about you. You were too valuable to lose. Mother insisted you were dead. Killed from a fall during our escape attempt. Finally, they believed her, I think that's because she actually believed it herself." Suza hesitated. "We thought you were dead." She looked at her brother then, soaked him in, afraid she'd lose him again. Pressure built behind her eyes. Here he was, strong and beautiful and human and alive.

He reached out and gripped her hand with a thick palm.

"Mother saved me. I wish I could tell her. I wish I could see her again." His voice was hoarse.

"Gristlecove must truly have cared for her." Suza paused remembering the black stare of the hyena Draco. "In his own way, at least, because he didn't kill her. They brought her back and added to her duties and left her. I think that might have been worse for her. Her escape fruitless, her son left for dead, and still the Draco lord controlled her."

Uriah's grip tightened around Suza's fingers.

"She got sick. Every month she withered. By the time I turned ten and joined the hatchlings in training, she was a wisp. I buried myself in training, pushing hard and planning how I would one day save her. I didn't realize as I learned to fight, I was becoming more like ..." *Our father.* "Them. I tried to bring her stolen medicine and food, but Mother continued to die a little more each day. Only in her eyes could I find our mother. As if they housed her whole soul. As if she'd already left her body." Suza looked at Uriah's eyes and saw their mother again. He had the same brown orbs she'd missed so much. "She got pregnant and tried to hide it. I didn't even know. Not until the baby came." Her body shook as she remembered what came next. "The baby was born dead. Mother tried to bury the body in secret, but the smell was too strong to hide from Lord Hyena. He found her as she dug a grave in the Trimp Forest."

"But that's just outside the gates."

She nodded. "I don't think she had the strength to go farther." She sucked in a breath as she remembered the scene. She'd woken in haste, somehow knowing something was wrong. The image of Gristlecove dragging her mother into the courtyard was scarred into her mind. The sun's early rays had lit up the blood painting her mother's dress crimson and running down her pale legs. She forced herself to share the memory. "She had just given birth. She should have been in bed. Gristlecove himself bore the whip. He yelled at her, waking the world. Sleepy Dracos waded out of the buildings at the commotion. Gristlecove told her that she'd taken all his babies from him. Destroyed his heirdom. He pointed at me then, his mottled face festering with rage. 'You left me with a girl too weak to become a Draco Sang!'" Suza's voice lowered. "I was only fourteen. Many in my class hadn't yet shown signs of the beast. I was ashamed of what he said. I knew I was growing strong and would make a good fighter one day. As Gristlecove brought the whip up, mother rolled over so he would be forced to strike her front. She was covered in blood already, her shift soaked from the waist down. Her face was gray. She tilted toward me and with a voice louder than I thought her lungs could manage said, 'I hope she never does. She's too good for you.' Something broke inside me then. A gate or a wall or whatever had held me up gave way. Gristlecove hesitated for a moment at her words, and then I saw the whip rise higher. He would kill her. I dove. I landed over mother as the whip came down on my back."

Suza shuttered, and Uriah inched closer, but stayed silent, his face intent on her every word.

"She looked at me, and for a heartbeat there was life in her eyes. I can still see her in that brief moment. Her horror was replaced with hope. She looked at me with so much love. And then. Right there under me, she left. She died at my chest." Suza wiped at the tears that refused to abate. She'd never shared this with anyone, and the flood of emotion would not be restrained.

"It's a blur after that. The whip fell, but I've no idea how many times. You might be able to tell by counting the stripes on my back. But I remember pain. They threw her body and the baby's body in a shallow grave, didn't even give her the respect of a funeral fire. They put salve on my back and told me to be ready to train the next day. That night my beast emerged. But not in me. No. Next to me. A hawk."

Uriah glanced around.

"She's been on your roof. Xandra doesn't like confined spaces. She's lived so long in hiding."

She strode over to the tent and pulled back the door. Xandra glided in and landed in front of Uriah.

Uriah's eyes lit up with pride, and his lip curved. "Impressive, Suza. She's exquisite."

Xandra puffed up, as did she. She sat by her bird and stroked a few feathers before continuing with her harrowing story.

"I'd seen it happen to another underling. Another abomination. A girl and her horse. They killed the horse. She went mad, attacking the Dracos and screaming all the time. They killed her too, in the end. I was terrified."

Uriah's face fell back into grim stone.

"For days I lived in fear, hiding Xandra in the forest and

failing to think of a way out. When it came time for Lord Gristlecove to send his tribute to Queen Mavras, I made a plan. I snuck out after the wagons left and followed from a distance, knowing that the guards would recognize me. I stole a slave's shift from the wagon, and the night before we reached Shi Castle, I gave myself the brand."

Uriah gasped, and Suza flinched. He glanced at her sleeve, and she pulled it back, revealing the stark scar on her forearm. He drew her arm forward and tenderly traced the brand with his thumb.

She'd seen it done by Dracos before: when an underling had lost their beast or when human babies were born. And her life had depended on it, but still, bringing that knife to her skin had been harder than she'd ever imagined. She'd lit a small fire and thrust in her blade. When her knife glowed, she sliced the barbed triangle and crescent of the slave mark into her right forearm. Her left hand wasn't nearly as good with a knife, and she'd had to go excruciatingly slowly to get it correct. She had intended to cut away the Draco brand on her chest until it no longer read, *GS10285*. But she hadn't been able to go through with it. She'd plastered marl on it instead and kept it hidden under long hair when in the slave baths.

"You did this." Uriah's fingers tickled the damaged nerve endings around the scar. "My little sister did this. You're tougher than any warrior I know."

She smiled, her chest expanding at his praise and his warm touch on her arm. "The next morning, I tied the dagger to my thigh." She unsheathed the knife from where she now kept it within easy reach on her belt.

"Dracosteel. Nice. The humans can't make anything like it." Uriah turned it over in his hands, noting the G on the end of the handle. He lifted a brow at her. "Our father's favorite, if I remember."

"I took it before I left." She smirked, delighted when he chuckled at her. She'd always wanted to impress her brother. He handed her back the knife and nodded for her to continue. "I left my other weapons and gear hidden in the forest and slipped into my stolen shift. I think it was better I didn't have too much time to think about what I was doing. I snuck in with the cluster of Gristlecove's slave tributes just before reaching Shi Castle. The scar was red, raw, and blistering. I should have cut the brand the minute I left Gristlecove, but it ended up being fine. The attendant didn't even look for my slave brand before assigning me to the kitchens. The kitchens are the best place for a slave to hide."

She shrugged. "I told them Gristlecove had shaved my head as a punishment. It was odd, as that was never done at Shi Castle—slaves were banned from cutting their hair—but they believed me. It did not benefit them to doubt my story. That's about it. Slave there for three years under the name Shale, and then I came south with the Dracos' advance half company and made my escape when baby Callie finally gave me the courage."

Uriah looked at her in awe.

She smiled and poked him with her elbow. "Your turn. Tell me everything."

And so he did. She laughed and cried when he told her about his grizzly bear hewan, Poe, who had died saving Zemira and baby Callie *Poe*. He told her how Captain Titus had found him starved and scared in Kiptos after he'd managed to survive the crossing into Elysium. Titus had become like a father to him, but no one had come close to replacing Mother. He told her how he'd been in the middle of Mitera when he'd conquered his blood. He hadn't even done anything momentous. It had seemed like a normal spring day. He'd sat to rest by a fountain while Titus was buying himself another hat—the man *loved* his hats. Uriah had been watching a toddler trying to pull coins from the water, and he'd thought how much he'd enjoy being a father one day. He'd be the antithesis of Gristlecove. And the next thing Uriah knew, Poe was there, helping the little girl fish for bronzes.

Uriah hadn't meant to join the army, but he was exceptionally good at fighting, and Elysium needed good soldiers. He shuddered. Oh, how they needed good soldiers. So he was doing his part, but he hoped this wouldn't be his whole life. He wanted to find a woman and make babies. At some point in his story, Suza had nestled against his side, and she poked his ribs at the way he said *make babies*.

He laughed. A real laugh that drew a satisfied sigh from his little sister.

The moon went to bed while they talked and talked. Dawn found them asleep atop pillows near the cold fire.

EIGHT - ALONE
FERTH

"*W*ant me to go in there and break them up?" Lyko asked. Ferth caught the mocking undertone as the wolf thumped down in the dirt.

Ferth deserved to be mocked. Shale had gone into Uriah's tent hours ago, and still Ferth watched for her to leave. And still she hadn't. Why was he torturing himself? Let. Her. Go. She wasn't even his to let go of.

"*Shall we take shifts?*" Rom's voice was all seriousness.

Ferth turned on a booted heel and strode away. Lyko's chuckle grated at his brain. "*Go home,*" Ferth ordered. "*Get some sleep.*"

The wolves peeled away as Ferth marched to the training fields. The area was deserted and dark. He didn't want light. Titus had returned Ferth's Dracosteel sword and long dagger.

"A man should fight with his own weapons," Titus had said.

Ferth pulled his blades free and set his feet.

And then he danced.

He closed his eyes and discovered the way his new body moved and flowed. Satisfaction swelled at the power and precision in his movements. Over and over he struck and moved and sliced and cut.

NINE - WOUNDED
THIRRO

Thirro edged a fraction closer, still well out of range of the raging chief. In the week since his stabbing, Laconius had healed just enough for his fury to be dangerous.

The bull Draco sat on an enormous pile of pillows in the command tent. Four slaves hovered around him, flitting in and out of range of his grasp as they tended to his whims.

"I will go," Thirro said. "I will hunt Ferth. I will bring back your son."

"He is not my son!"

Thirro flinched. He should have known not to use that word.

"And no." Laconius's black eyes bulged. He leaned forward in pain as a slave removed the bandages. She cowered for a moment before hurriedly returning to her work. She spread green paste over the wound. He hissed. "That hurts."

"Yes, sir." Her voice trembled. "You're healing remarkably well, sir. This will help, sir. I'll get you whiskey, sir."

Laconius's fingers twitched as if to strike her, but instead he focused his attention on the room full of his top leaders and warriors. "Commander Mina."

The cheetah slunk forward. Thirro raked his gaze over her long torso and thin legs as she bowed. She left her taut belly exposed, wearing only a cropped leather vest over her small breasts. His body stirred.

"You are now captain of Jobu's half company." Thirro noted Laconius didn't say Ferth's half company, though his son was the last leader. Stricken from history, a fate worse than death. "Serve well and you shall lead a full company into battle."

Mina's dark eyes sparkled as she dipped her head. "Yes, my chief."

A slave walked in front of Laconius, and Laconius shoved the man aside with a quick blow that knocked him hard on his butt. The chief's gaze never left Mina. "You'll appoint your unit commanders."

Mina nodded.

"The rest of my army is still a week out." They'd been held up by a rockslide in the Danbe Canyon. "But we strike now."

The room stirred.

"At the heart." Laconius touched his chest, a fraction to the right of his wound. "And we won't miss."

The tent silenced.

"Thirro. You will go hunting, but your prize is not the weak-hearted abomination erased from my bloodline."

Keal, the Ferth-loving ape, let out a small sigh of relief. Thirro's lip curled in disgust as he sent Keal a condescending glance.

"No," Laconius said. "You shall kill the king."

Thirro's pulse soared.

"Fly to Mitera and put one of those arrows you're so fond of through Andras's heart. Do you accept?"

It wasn't a question. His voice came out as flint. "With pleasure, Chief."

"You shall be Skotar's Arrow." Laconius smiled, and Thirro swelled. "You may suggest a team."

Thirro opened his mouth, but a voice from the back of the room cut him off.

"I volunteer."

Thirro turned to see Jade. Deep purple bruises marred her jaw and cheek—courtesy of his fist.

"Do you accept her help?" Laconius asked.

Thirro frowned. Not ever. "No, sir. She'll be a hindrance to the mission. I'll go alone. Fly swiftly and silently and strike from the sky." She wasn't going to get credit for his success. And he didn't want to have to watch his back every second.

Jade's eyes narrowed into sharp points.

"Permission granted. You leave tonight," Laconius said.

Thirro dipped his head.

"Return victorious."

"Yes, Chief."

The meeting disbanded, and the Dracos left Laconius to his slaves. Thirro had only gone a few feet from the tent when Jade accosted him, glaring up at him from chest height.

"I would not hinder the mission." Her facial features were still remarkably human. Her childlike eyes and nose bore no resemblance to the killer Thirro knew lurked below the surface. She snarled, showing razor-sharp canines. He stopped.

"I'm not taking an underling with me. You'd wet yourself just flying over the river."

She didn't flinch. Didn't take the bait and state the obvious—she was most definitely not an underling anymore.

"Besides, you'd slow me down, and I'd have to worry about you getting yourself killed."

"You'd like that."

"Yes, I probably would, but not when it would endanger my mission. Why do you want to come anyway? Falling for me?"

The hate and disgust on her face said no to that impossibility. Too bad.

"I don't want this mission to fail because of your arrogance," she said. "You could use back-up, and I'm good. I can help. I can get in places. I can stay hidden."

Possibly all true. "No, thanks. You're too green. You're small. And your skill with the bow isn't close to being trusted." A lie. He'd seen her practicing yesterday—not as good as he was, but still deadly accurate. "And if I were to take someone, I'd pick a companion I'd at least let warm me at night."

Her face contorted. She balled her fists and rolled forward on her toes.

His muscles tensed, but he kept his face calm. "So eager for round three? I'm ready whenever you are. This side ..." He motioned at her pale cheek. "... is just begging me for matching color."

In a heartbeat, her face calmed, and her body relaxed. "Don't die until *after* you kill the king." She smiled.

He lifted his chin and strode past her. He went into his tent. If only it would stop smelling like Ferth.

A slave man threw logs into the fire pit before darting out. Thirro sat on a stool, thinking about the mission. Flying into the heart of Elysium. Alone. He shook off the sudden chill. He was a Draco, afraid of nothing, certainly not weak humans. He rolled his shoulders back, stood, and stretched his wings. Soon. Soon he would fly. Soon he would win power and glory.

The tent flap flew back and Captain Mina slunk in. Her sharp gaze darted over the room. "Yes. This will do nicely."

His belly dropped. She already had a private tent. "What's wrong with your tent?"

She shrugged. "I like this one better." She dropped her weapons belt on the table and stalked over to stand in front of him. She tilted her head, looking him over. "Bold move, claiming it for yourself, soldier."

"Make me the next commander of unit five."

"Why?" She ran her fingers down his downy chest. "So soft."

He shuddered under her touch. "Because I'm good."

"Keal's better with a sword. Dara's better with a knife. What are you good at?"

Thirro reined in his annoyance. "I'm the best archer in camp." Archery wasn't an impressive skill to the Draco Sang so he added, "I'm Skotar's Arrow."

"Not yet." Her hands slipped around his narrow waist, skimming the top of his pants.

She was teasing him. He didn't like to be toyed with.

She chuckled at the look on his face. "I'm going to need some more convincing." She tugged her bottom lip between her teeth. Cat eyes taunted him.

He wrapped an arm around her spotted waist and brought his mouth down on hers. As she drank him in, he thanked the dragon again that his mouth had remained soft and human, unlike so many other beaked flyers. When his body had turned warm all over, she bit down, hard enough to draw blood. He jerked back, tasting copper and salt. Mina licked the drip of red smearing her lip. He recoiled. She laughed, high and staccato.

"I like you, Thirro. I'll consider it." She turned away. "Now get out of my tent."

Thirro slunk to his old tent where Keal greeted him with a punch to his brand, and Dara smirked as she watched. She could laugh all she wanted. He *was* going to be made commander when he returned.

It was with determination that he took to the skies that

night. He flew above the clouds, following the emerging stars south and a little west. He was looking to the lights of Kiptos when a pelican hit him in the face. He raked at the bird, grabbing it by the neck. The bird snapped at him, its sharp beak nipping his jaw.

"Stop."

The bird only flailed more.

Thirro chucked the dumb animal at the flock of pelicans now surrounding him and squawking. They flapped and honked and pooped in a mad swarm of fright.

"Stupid birds." He disengaged from the tangle of brainless feathers and beaks. "I'm embarrassed by association."

But as he moved on into open sky, anticipation made him eager. Flying unhindered with nothing but clear night air to conquer, his hollow bones filled with joy. For hours he lost himself in the freedom, the wind, the thrill. When dawn approached, his wings ached, and exhaustion pulled at his eyes. He dropped below the clouds, searching the semidarkness for a safe place to hide. He plunged toward a rocky outcropping. Wearily he drank from his canteen and pulled a meal from his pack before dropping to sleep.

The next three days repeated the same. The deep ache in his wings lessened as they gained strength and endurance. He flew higher as the populations increased, diving low only to look for landmarks previous scouts had mapped out for him. His anxiety increased as his daytime hideouts became riskier, and he was forced closer to civilization.

The landscape tamed as he moved south. Rocky cliffs and tangled forests gave way to rolling hills and fragrant foliage. The scents of flowers and fertility washed him each night as he flew, whetting his appetite.

This land, tasting of luxury and promising pleasure would soon be his. Thirro flew with a grin on his face.

TEN - PLANS

FERTH

*F*erth shifted around the side of the command table, hiding his scowl from Shale and Uriah, who sat together. Very close together. He needed to stop looking at her.

"You sure you want to expose your back to that woman?" Lyko said.

"Uriah looks more likely to knife you," Rom said.

Ferth ignored the wolves, ignored the tingling target he felt on his back and forced his attention to the stacks of maps, reports, and battle plans spread before him. Shale's hawk, Xandra, had reported this morning that Laconius's forces had made camp and their swelling numbers matched Ferth's previous statements, but the confirming report seemed to do nothing in the way of earning Zemira or Uriah's trust.

Zemira paced next to Captain Titus. Ferth could hardly believe she was the same sorrowing mother he'd met on his arrival. She wore twin blades on her hips, a black leather body suit that was hard not to stare at, and a haunting look in her eyes.

He thought back to his last encounter with Zemira three days ago, when she'd sent her baby to safety. A small party had prepared to go south with news and baby Callie Poe. Ferth had arrived as the group was leaving, intending to send Cal's letter south with the hundreds of curious letters Captain Titus had prepared. Zemira was there, kissing her baby and fussing over the tiny girl.

Ferth hadn't dared approach. Zemira tucked her precious bundle in the arms of a wet nurse seated on a horse. A guard held the lead rope as they plodded away. Cal's words to their mother stayed in Ferth's pocket.

Zemira had watched her baby disappear over the ridge, and then she'd whirled around, her gaze latching onto Ferth among the dissipating crowd.

She'd stalked up to him, her panther on her heels. Zemira's words had come down like a whip and they still stung days later. "I cannot feed her. Since you stole my baby, I have no milk. You have shown me I cannot keep her safe. I feel as though she is ripped from me again." The mother's pain had lashed across the space between them. Ferth could think of no comfort to give. "It is my greatest hope that I might see her again." She marched away, her footsteps heavy.

Titus's voice brought Ferth's focus back to the command tent. "Twenty-five hundred Draco Sang warriors to our six thousand," Titus said, more to himself than the others.

Dreadful odds. "How fast can you get more soldiers?" Ferth asked. "A ten to one ratio would be a more even match."

No one scoffed. They'd seen Draco Sang. They knew. Good.

The scars on Titus's face crinkled as he frowned, and Ferth wondered if they'd come from a Draco Sang long ago.

"Two companies of two thousand each are being organized and outfitted to join us within the next two months,"

Titus said. "I've sent requests to Mitera pleading for more, but nothing has been promised or mobilized."

They wouldn't get here soon enough anyway. "Laconius will attack as soon as he's strong enough to wield his axe."

The river, standing only a foot deep at the deepest part of the delta was no barrier now. Foolish humans.

"Their army is a mix of Dracos from all around Skotar," said Ferth. "They won't have had much time training together, but that won't be necessary. Their only commands will be to attack here or there. My ..." Ferth choked on the word. "... half company, the five hundred wintered here, have trained hard and are a cohesive cohort. Much deadlier than the larger army." His success would be costly. A chill skittered down Ferth's spine as he thought about Keal, Thirro, and Dara, each capable of shredding through humans. What did they think of his disappearance? His traitorous defection? They would know about his failure from the scouting reports. He hadn't tried to keep himself hidden, although he found himself constantly checking the sky for familiar wings and the whistle of an arrow. They would hunt him. And now he found himself on a fool's errand. Trying to keep these humans alive and protected from the hammer about to fall. A hammer he'd helped forge.

Ferth continued, his voice flat. "That half company is the tip of the spear. Mina might be captain by now or possibly Emil if Mina managed to get on my father's bad side." A twinge of longing for his old station flashed through. He cleared his throat. "They'll attack quickly and move south into Kiptos, establishing a foothold in the valley. Queen Mavras promised reinforcements by end of summer for the march to Mitera. We—*they* know all the details of this camp. Numbers, provisions, etc. Surprising them would be impossible. Once they arrive it will be a swift destructive march to the capital. That is the goal."

They would slice through this country like a fresh blade through worms. And now he was on the losing side. "Humans will be slaves." He couldn't help it; his eyes flicked over his shoulder to Shale. Her ashen face was tilted down at the floor. *No.* He would not see her a slave again. She would be free. Free to love that man. "The Draco Sang will be the elite rulers, and the continent will bow to Mavras." *Laconius.* For he would kill her before that day.

Ferth flattened the map of the delta over the table. He jabbed a finger at the Draco camp. Commander Asvig had relaxed in a chair, watching and listening without comment, but now he heaved his protruding belly out of the chair and came forward. Zemira, Uriah, and Captain Titus leaned over the map as well. With his fingers, Ferth traced the paths and aid stations the Dracos would use, dredging up minute details from the plans he'd helped create. Heads popped up from their bent-over position when the tent flap pulled back.

A raven perched on her shoulder, Pelussa waltzed into the tent unannounced and unaccompanied. "You've done a good job with those guards." Her milky eyes were unfocused.

Ferth shifted a fraction in surprise at her voice. She'd spent the last week silently stalking the camp with her uncomfortable stare. The guards hadn't stopped her from entering anywhere.

"It'll be like your worst nightmare," Pelussa said. "Soldiers attacking with no pattern, no formation, each with their own individual strengths and forms."

"Hello, Pelussa. Are we now allowed to acknowledge your presence?" Titus said.

"I have seen much these past days."

"And?" He didn't comment on the irony of the blind woman's statement.

"And the Draco Sang must not cross the river."

"And when they do?" His face hardened into a rare display of impatience.

Silence.

The raven cawed an eerie, chilling toll.

Not helpful, Ferth thought. Who was this woman?

"You must kill The Dragon." Her voice was raspy and far away. "Kill Prince Nogard."

She was a lunatic.

Titus's stoic mask slipped slightly. He recovered, squaring his shoulders and focusing back on the map.

"Join us, Pelussa." Titus said, his voice calm. "We'll gladly welcome your *practical* advice on how we can break this invasion. You and I can have a conversation about Nogard The Ancient over dinner, shall we?"

Ferth bit his tongue, impressed with Captain Titus's civility in the face of such idiocy. The Dragon, the father of all the Draco Sang, had died nearly three hundred years ago in the north reaches of Skotar, far from this time and place.

"I think Pelussa is right, though." Titus smiled at the woman as if she could see his face.

The raven tilted his head.

"We do need to stop them at the river." He looked down. "The chains will go here." With his finger, he drew lines on the map across the water at the western points of assault.

Ferth had been impressed and a fraction hopeful when he'd seen the barbed links. Stepping on one of the hooked razors would seriously damage a foot, even through a thick boot or heavy hoof. But it would not be enough. They would not win a head to head battle. They needed more trickery, traps, decoys, and baits.

Not having real battle experience to draw on, he thought back to his training. He fell into a chair as an idea formed. Every head turned to him. He met Titus's eyes, then his focus shifted to Shale. Her green eyes held his gaze.

"The calls," he said.

Her face brightened, and her lip curved up a hair.

"We'll mess up their communication," he said. At least what little the Dracos had of it.

Shale nodded, and Ferth grinned at her. It took a force of will to break away from her eager face, the moment of connection with her, the shared understanding. He turned to the gathered warriors and explained the horns the Draco Sang army used and the battle calls they issued.

They began to form a plan—a risky tentative plan, but one with a ray of hope.

ELEVEN - STRIKE
THIRRO

Thirro nestled in a skyscraping crimsonwood tree, the dense leaves providing cover. His keen eyes scanned the sprawling city of Mitera as the morning sun lit up the jewel of Elysium. Thirro filled with awe at the size, expanse, and wealth. The humans had claimed every inch of these flatlands. Homes spilled out of the city gates and into the unprotected valley like disgorge out of a giant mouth. Farms and pastures bumped into the surrounding hills and forests on all sides.

So many humans.

The Vasil River flowed directly toward the city, splitting at the northern gates and curving around the sides, encircling the city walls before converging again as it rushed south.

Legend was the first queen placed her staff in the center of the river, and the water split, creating an island for Queen Vasil's castle.

To Thirro it looked more like a lot of slave labor had built the city.

Twin drawbridges spanned the river. Scouting reports had informed him there were two more bridges he couldn't see to the south. The castle, made of marbled green rock, sat not at the center of the city, but at the eastern edge, butting up against the black walls. A gift to a single winged assassin. The palace towered over the city, shading it from the sunrise.

Last night at sunset, Thirro hadn't been able to tear his eyes off the green castle as the fading sun had lit up the fortress like a torch.

The walls were much higher on the eastern side, almost as if to encourage an attacker to cross on the western edge and cut down the entire city before reaching the great green heart. The boy king would watch in helpless fear as the Dracos crashed over his city like a wave, coming for him, like Thirro was coming for his father.

Thirro breathed the eagerness out, settling deeper into the branches. He rested his wings, slept for a few hours, and watched the humans live out their day in peace and ignorance. As darkness fell, the bridges stayed down, and the gates remained open.

To his shock and delight, the guard outposts along the top of the black wall appeared unmanned, and no soldiers walked the ridge. That night, when a passing cloud crossed the moon, Thirro dove from the tree and shot over thousands of sleeping heads onto the wall. Rocks shifted beneath his taloned feet.

Whipping out his dagger, he ducked into a tiny stone hut. Thirro's head brushed the ceiling, and he had to tuck his wings to fit. Empty. He sheathed his blade. It looked like it'd been forsaken years ago. The fuel to light a warning fire had dried to a black sludge. The wood in the corner was decayed. No water, no food, no weapons, no chair. *No fear.*

Mitera did not watch for enemies. When was the last time

they'd been attacked? Had this wall ever done more than get in the way of its citizens? Would Thirro's attack serve only to alert this placid place and increase their vigilance? Would this be a warning to prepare them for the forthcoming invasion?

Something told Thirro, yes. Mitera would wake. But he mocked the thought of aborting his mission. He'd enjoy his first enemy kill, and he'd return to his army as Skotar's Arrow. Let the humans taste fear. Let the humans know what comes.

Thirro peered out of the open doorway. Mitera lived not only in perpetual peace, but in prosperity. Sturdy homes and shops of timber and stone edged the curved streets that ribbed the city, rippling out from the castle in concentric circles. Fountains and flowers punctuated courtyards. Statues staked intersections, and lanterns lit corners. The few people who walked the streets at this hour did so with their purses out and their heads up.

A couple spilled out of a warmly lit shop. The smell of spice and meat wafted up the wall. The woman threw back her head and laughed, revealing her neck to the sky, and Thirro. The man pulled her closer as they ambled on their way. Thirro salivated.

As the streets quieted and the night darkened, he moved southeast across the wall until he occupied the abandoned guard station nearest the castle.

When the sun broke up the dark, he watched King Andras strolling through his private gardens. Thirro checked the string on his bow and ran his fingers through an arrow's fletching. A king who pranced about without protection deserved to die. Such an idiot was not fit to rule.

Thirro did not shoot, suddenly unsure if he had the correct man in his sights. Could it be this easy?

He cursed when the man went inside still breathing. Wings of the castle jetted off from a tall central building. Glass panels dotted the walls and ceilings and black buttresses rained over the entire complex.

A fitting home for the Draco Sang.

Through massive glass windows, Thirro saw several people approach the king and bow before they were lost again to his sights. He had targeted the correct man. He took satisfaction in that thought while he waited for his mark to step outside again. He tore at a stringy piece of meat as he watched the royal court with mocking awe. Richly dressed men and women crisscrossed his vision for hours before King Andras showed his face again.

The king had changed into a soldier's training uniform and carried his sword in hand. He walked with another man similarly outfitted.

For a heartbeat, Thirro feared he'd been discovered, but he relaxed when the king and his partner began to spar. The training was tame and choreographed as if for show and exercise.

Members of the court watched and mingled and ate from silver plates.

Thirro's blood heated. This splendor was meant to be his. With a jolt of pleasure, he stepped out of the hut atop the wall and into the light. No one looked up as he cocked his arrow.

When the king shook hands with his opponent, Thirro let the arrow fly, wiping the smile off Andras's face.

The king stumbled as the Dracosteel tip lacerated his throat, cutting off his air supply and tearing through his neck. Thirro waited as the shock wave hit the humans. He waited until a dozen heads turned their blanched faces from their dead king to the wall. To him. A woman screamed.

He let out a dark victorious hoot. Then he coiled and shot

into the sky. He tore at the air, his strong wings flinging him out of sight. Above the clouds, he flew north, but he did not fear any retribution.

He returned to Skotar unhindered. He returned as Skotar's Arrow. He returned hungry.

TWELVE - PARALLEL
SUZA

*S*uza entered the command tent. Lyko lifted his head at her approach. Ferth did not move from his position standing bent over the piles of reeds and rope on the table. He and his wolves were the only ones here. She halted, remembering only a few weeks ago when he, as her Draco master, had pinned Shale to his bed, ripping through her dress, his mouth on her skin, his hands desperate. He'd stopped himself, shredding his mattress apart instead of her. But Suza felt a remnant of the same fear trickle up through her belly at being alone with him again.

Ferth raked a hand, a hairless human hand, through his long brown hair. The tip of his pink tongue was wedged between his lips as he focused. No—she might not know this new man well, but she knew he was not the same creature who had attacked her. She surprised herself and then chided herself for wanting to get to know this new Ferth.

Striding into the tent, Suza greeted Lyko with a scratch behind his ears. When she reached the table and Ferth still hadn't acknowledged her, she picked up one of the completed pipes and blew over the top.

"Yeah." He didn't look at her. "I cut that one too short." He snipped a piece of twine. "Try this one."

He handed her another set, careful not to touch her, the same smooth handoff she had used every day as his slave. A knot twisted in her belly. He was giving her space; why wasn't she happier about it? She lightly blew on the horn. It still wasn't quite right.

Ferth grunted in frustration as he tightened another two hollow reeds together.

Suza picked up an untrimmed reed and a small knife and started carving.

They didn't talk, but it wasn't the same working silence they'd grown accustomed to as master and slave in Skotar, when she'd tried to be invisible. Today she wanted to ask him about his healing back. She wanted to tell him her real name, hear "Suza" in his low voice instead of Shale. She wanted to share her joy at finding her brother, talk about his grief at losing his own. And what about Lyko? Why did Cal's wolf follow him as loyally as Rom? She wanted his focus to turn to her. If he would just look up at her, let her see his golden eyes.

But he never did.

His gaze stayed trapped on his work. Her words stayed trapped on her tongue.

THIRTEEN - DEFENDING
FERTH

"*D*rop," the warrior said, his voice a puff of air under the strain of Ferth's crushing blow.

Ferth released his hold and stepped back. The young man stood gingerly and bowed.

Ferth dipped his head in return. "Well fought. Thank you."

The soldier snorted. "I seem to be getting worse."

"You're improving, I assure you." Just not as quickly as Ferth was. He'd spent every available moment on the training yard for the past four weeks. Fighting to rid himself of his feelings for Shale, his festering guilt, his homesickness. He tried to focus solely on honing his body and mind into a weapon of penance. The blade of his brother's vengeance.

The soldier shook his head. Ferth joined him for a drink before returning to the sparring arena.

"Who's next?" Ferth grinned.

The soldiers laughed. Ferth had found some camaraderie here, where skill with the sword and respect for your comrades was honored. He worked hard and fought cleanly, and they welcomed him with a tentative friendship. He clung to it.

"I'll have you warm me up for a bit," a warrior said.

Ferth turned his head to see Guap stepping up.

Ferth smiled and twirled his practice sword.

Guap was one of the best swordsmen Ferth had found— the best one willing to spar with him. One of the few that could even keep up with him for longer than a couple blows. The Draco-blooded soldiers had all refused to practice with Ferth. He tried not to let it bother him.

The mid-summer sun burned overhead. Guap removed his clean white shirt, revealing bulging muscles under his dark skin.

Sweat drenched Ferth's shirt, but he refused to remove it, refused to reveal the Draco Sang brand on his chest, the strips on his back from his whipping when Shale escaped, the arrow scar on his side from an Elysium arrow, the mark on his shoulder from Zemira's sword when he'd kidnapped baby Callie Poe. He'd finally surrendered his beard to the heat and shaved, revealing the face that matched Cal's in full, but he kept his hair long. Today he wore it in a braid down the back of his neck.

Ferth attacked first in a quick series of strokes, putting Guap on the defensive, but not for long. The solider warmed up quickly, starting his own attack. Ferth ignored the sting of sweat dripping in his eyes and the ache of tired muscles as he focused solely on this fight.

Lyko yelped in Ferth's head, *"Raptor attacking from the sky."*

Ferth stumbled back in surprise, and Guap struck his side with a painful whack.

Ferth grunted.

Guap retreated a step. Shock spread over his face along with worry, as if he feared Ferth's retribution.

Ferth glared at the wolf lounging outside the sparring ropes.

"You're dead," Lyko said with a lupine grin.

He rubbed at his side. *"That hurt!"*

"You should have blocked it."

"You surprised me."

Rom cut in. *"You can't ignore the rest of the battle and only focus on one man."*

Ferth growled out loud at the wolves watching from the sideline. They were right. *Bleeding skies.*

Guap looked from Ferth to the wolves, discomfort written on his face. The wolves tended to have that impression on everyone, even when they were acting as docile as lambs. There was no hiding their lean strength, sharp teeth, and cunning eyes. Skies, they were beautiful.

"Nice hit." Ferth rolled his shoulders back and lifted his wooden sword. "But you're going to need to do better than that."

"Allow me." The deep voice, edged with anger, came from Ferth's right. He whirled, bringing his weapon up defensively.

Two wolf heads jerked. Their bodies coiled at the threatening undertones.

Uriah stepped over the ropes and into the arena. He held an open palm out to a wide-eyed Guap.

"May I *cut* in?" Ice formed on Uriah's words.

Guap hastily handed over his practice sword and hopped over the ropes.

Ferth wanted to do the same when Uriah turned eyes festering with rage toward him.

Lyko snarled a warning at Uriah.

"Stay out of this, Lyko."

Lyko and Rom rose to their feet, standing side by side but not moving forward.

The atmosphere of playfulness around the training yard died like a pixinettle blossom in winter. Soldiers shifted uncomfortably on their feet, but they all stayed and watched.

Ferth had been hoping to spar with Uriah, but not like this, not when Uriah's face promised death.

Uriah's jaw rippled, and then his sword slashed forward.

The pain in Ferth's side and the ache in his legs were forgotten as he fought against the impossibly strong blows.

Uriah was good. Really good.

This was the sparring partner Ferth had been looking for.

The crowd thickened as they traded strikes and blows at galloping speeds.

Without the adrenaline-fueled rage that seemed to power Uriah, Ferth weakened.

Finally, muscles burning, he slipped under an attack, allowing Uriah to step in close. Uriah's sword locked on Ferth's. He pressed down, looming over Ferth.

"She was your slave." Uriah ground out the words, his face inches from Ferth's.

Ferth froze. His heart pumped ice to his limbs.

"Your *slave*." Uriah's voice was a venomous hiss.

Dread filled Ferth. What could he possibly say in the face of stark ugly truth?

And as if to counter Ferth's heinous past, Uriah's face bore the pure truth of his love for Shale. Ferth's heart collapsed and with it so did his fight.

He gave way, and Uriah threw him to the ground. His back barked as he slammed into the packed dirt. He dropped his sword and lifted himself onto his elbows, chest exposed. He looked Uriah in the eye.

"I'll never hurt her again," he promised.

"You'll *never* have the chance." Uriah turned away. Handing his sword to a gaping Guap, he stormed out of the training yard.

Goodbye, Shale. You deserve to be happy with a man like him.

Ferth sank to the dirt and stared at the azure sky. Uriah had every reason to loathe him. So did Shale. So did Zemira. So did ... *Stop doing that.*

He'd given them all as much space as possible these last weeks, staying away and staying busy. When would he ever stop bringing pain to these good people?

With your future. The voice in his mind sounded like Keturah.

That future seemed impossibly far away.

FOURTEEN - WRONG
SUZA

*S*uza marched into Uriah's tent. He looked up from tying his belt and smiled when he saw her.

Her pulse soared, and her voice betrayed her anger. "Please tell me the rumors of your scene in the training yard are unfounded."

His smile fell, and a hint of red stained his cheeks. "Was I wrong?" His voice was hard, aggressive. "You told me he was your *master.*"

She stabbed a finger at his chest and tilted her neck back to face him. "Don't you tell me what I said. I know perfectly well what he was, and I know much better than you what he is. That man over there is the best Draco Sang I've ever met. That man saved me over and over again. He protected me from every prowling soldier who wanted to take advantage of me. He even protected me from himself." Her voice unexpectedly caught on the words. When had her feelings for Ferth grown so strong?

And now he avoided her.

The color drained from Uriah's face as Suza plowed on.

"Can you even imagine what it would take to overcome

your beast after having nearly completed your transformation? Have you ever once thought what kind of man could do that under Laconius's tutelage? As a captain in his army? Do you ever think?" Her voice rose in volume as she spoke.

Uriah opened his mouth, but she cut him off.

"And now the entire camp knows I was his slave. And they will think the worst. Can the man never start over?" Heat flushed her face as she laid bare the depths of her feelings for Ferth.

Warm hands wrapped around her shoulders, silencing her.

"Suzaena," His voice was gentle. "I'm so sorry." Her muscles relaxed at the sincerity in his voice. "You're right, I didn't think. I only thought of the pain he caused you. I was never there to protect you. I was never there, Suza. I'm here now, and I want to protect you."

"You did it wrong." The fight left her voice, replaced by the warmth of having a brother who would protect her so fiercely. Who loved her.

"You made that clear."

She huffed out a sad breath.

"You're right." Uriah drew her against his chest, and she rested her face against his broad shoulder. "But don't get used to it."

She pulled back, her lips pursed.

He smiled. "I'm sorry I mucked it all up."

"You'll apologize to Ferth."

He scowled. "Yes."

"You'll try to make friends."

"I need time."

She folded her arms.

He sighed. "But I'll try."

She nodded, satisfied. "Now, take me to dinner."

He held out his elbow, and she took his arm. Together

they exited the tent to find Xandra swooping low over the camp, a rare sight in broad daylight.

"*What is it?*" she asked her hewan.

"*Six people arriving from the south. The horses are exhausted and so are the travelers, like they've been chased by Laconius. I don't know what's happened, but it can't be good.*"

Suza dropped her brother's arm as a chill spread through her veins. "Something isn't right." She ran toward command, Uriah close on her heels.

*F*erth sat with Captain Titus and Commander Asvig in the command tent, filtering through every detail of Skotar's operations, *again*. The man was thorough. Ferth would rather be patrolling the camp with his wolves. His stomach grumbled—or eating.

"The slaves live here." He pointed. "But they're often found in soldiers' quarters at all hours. The water sources are here." His words trailed off as Rom spoke to his mind.

"Riders on horseback from the south. They look travel-worn. Four men and two women. Three in uniform. Dismounting at the stables."

"Rom reports six human arrivals at camp," Ferth said.

Titus raised a scarred eyebrow.

Ferth swallowed. Humans never referred to themselves as humans. Only Draco Sang did that.

Titus straightened from his position bent over the table. "Forerunners for reinforcements, I hope." He righted his uniform.

"The guard is bringing them here," Ferth said.

Moments later the door flung open. The six people who

stumbled into the tent were exhausted, their clothes filthy and their faces unwashed. One woman wore a wide-brimmed hat with a veil hanging over her face and hair, hiding her features. Ferth tried to piece the unexpected group together, guessing the three soldiers were the veiled woman's guards, the remaining male and female possibly her servants. A short-haired black and brown dog a head shorter than Rom followed them in. The dog's keen eyes held his. Another hewan? Questions queued up in Ferth's mind.

He looked to Titus, who had stopped mid-step as if paralyzed. His blue eyes froze as he focused on the woman, glaring as if he could see through her covering to her face. She straightened her spine and gripped the fabric as if to pull it off.

"Don't," Titus said.

Ferth could sense the woman's focus shift to him as if questioning, *why not?*

"Not here." Titus's voice was strained. He raked graying hair back in a frustrated gesture.

Who was she, and why couldn't Ferth know?

A man in his prime, wearing a green tunic and brown riding pants stepped forward. He stuck out a hand, and Captain Titus gripped it.

"Raja Darius," Titus said.

Ferth vaguely remembered learning a little about the human ranking system. A raja was a ruling member of the king's inner circle and a wealthy landlord. The Draco Sang didn't put much value on studying a system they intended to destroy.

"Captain Titus." Darius affected a half smile, but it quickly died, setting his face back into thin sharp lines. "Our proper greetings will have to wait. King Andras was killed by a Draco Sang assassin."

Titus's face paled, but he spoke with icy calm. "Come in.

Sit." He gestured to the seats and pillows set in a circle around the maps. "Rourke!" His voice cracked.

A young man stepped into the doorway. "Sir?"

"Gather my officers. Have them report here immediately." Titus paused and looked at the wall. In a low voice as if talking to himself he added, "The king has been murdered."

"Yes, sir." The boy stepped back, eyes wide.

"*After* you gather my officers, have food and drink brought here."

The boy fled.

"How long ago?" Titus asked.

"Eight days," Darius replied. Despite the sunken eye sockets and wild hair, the man sat up straight in his chair. "I might have gotten here faster if—"

A stern woman's voice from below the veil cut him off. "I did *not* slow you down."

Darius's thin lips tweaked up as he glanced at the figure hidden behind fine cloth.

A shadow passed over the tent door as Eio and the wolves entered the tent. The three soldiers stiffened, and their hands went involuntarily to their weapons. Darius, to his credit, did not flinch. Rom and Lyko padded over to Ferth and stood at his sides.

Eio, to Ferth's shock, went directly to the veiled woman.

"Eio." She squealed and threw her arms around his thick mane. A jolly rumble issued from the golden beast. The dog yapped a happy welcome and wagged his thin tail at the big cat.

Titus narrowed his eyes at the scene, but when he turned away, Ferth caught the smile that spread over Titus's face.

"The Draco-blooded woman is hidden. Why?" Rom asked.

So, the dog was her hewan. Interesting.

"Maybe she's horribly scarred," Lyko said.

"Or to hide her identity," Ferth said. *"Which I intend to find out."*

Zemira shot into the tent, her fighting leathers tight over her lithe form.

Ferth's chest cramped when Uriah and Shale entered right behind Zemira's panther, Opal. Ferth didn't meet their eyes. The training yard scene was hot in his mind and in his muscles. Several more warriors and commanders entered.

"Come, Kira," the veiled woman said to the dog. "Come. Sit." A gloved hand stroked the narrow head. "Good girl."

Ferth's eyebrows rose. *"Is she pretending that dog is an ordinary pet? Who does she think she's fooling?"* he asked his wolves.

"Probably every human," Rom said.

Ferth itched to rip off the woman's face covering, unveil her secrets.

Pelussa and her raven arrived last. With everyone seated, Titus spoke. "Raja Darius has just arrived with alarming news from Mitera." Titus nodded to Darius.

"Eight days ago, King Andras was assassinated in his own gardens," Darius said. "A Draco Sang with dark brown wings and a white-feathered head stood on the city walls and shot an arrow through our king's throat. One shot. One masterful shot."

Ferth's blood drained from his limbs as he listened to the report. *Thirro.*

"I was there." Darius's long fingers gripped his sword pommel. "Three other members of the raja circle and many more courtesans were all standing targets. Including the heir. Thankfully, for whatever reason, the Draco Sang left after firing a single shot. The raja met that evening. Abner has been crowned king. He is only fourteen years old, but six rajas remain in Mitera with him. Messengers were sent to the five rajas not in the city, and I elected to bring the message here myself. Two thousand troops are four days' march behind us."

As the news sank into the silent room, food arrived. Servers set down platters of cheese, bread, fruit, and cut meats. Despite the alarming news, Ferth wasn't the only one who took a large serving.

"Raja Darius, who are your traveling companions?" Uriah looked pointedly at the veiled woman.

Raja Darius turned to Captain Titus instead of answering.

Titus shuffled parchments on the desk as he answered, his voice crisp. "This is Imanna. She's my ..." He hesitated as if looking for the right word. "... daughter."

Titus's daughter. Ferth blinked in bewilderment.

"She brings a healer for our camp with her." He indicated the middle-aged woman. "Imanna covers her face to protect the healing burns on her skin."

The veil twitched.

"I win," Lyko said.

Before Ferth could make sense of that curt explanation, Titus had moved on.

"Two thousand soldiers will strengthen our battle tactics greatly." His gaze flicked to Shale and Ferth. "How are the calls?"

Shale waited for Ferth to speak, but he didn't. They were equals here, and she was indescribably more liked and trusted by the group.

"We crafted four horns that work properly." She held up a circle of pipes.

They'd made a dozen more that didn't sound right. It had been easier work before she'd joined him, filling his mind with her scent, reminding him of what he would never deserve.

"Ferth and I both know the calls," she said. "And I've taught six others them as best I could."

Titus nodded. "Well done. You'll be heading that effort. You'll call out the orders from my command station. I need Ferth and the wolves leading a squad on the ground."

"Yes, sir." Pride flickered in her emerald eyes.

Good. She would be safest at Titus's side and away from the front lines.

An alarm rang out across camp, followed by another piercing cry and another. Ferth fled the command tent with the others.

A soldier ran forward, panting. "The Draco Sang are on the move. The army marches south in battle gear. They're a half-mile from the river."

Ferth's pulse hitched and his nerves crackled. His Draco army was finally attacking Elysium.

He would stand against them.

Father, Thirro, Dara, Jade, Keal, Mina. Names and faces flashed across his mind in a blink. His family. His clan. He felt betrayed and a betrayer. Ice seemed to form over his heart and spread through his limbs.

Around him, the human camp came alive. A camp full of strangers.

"Armor on," Titus yelled. "To your squadrons! Skinny formations."

Fight.

Kill.

He did not want to do it. His hands were too bloody already.

Ferth pictured his brother's ashen face. Dead before battle. Cut down before they … before even … He gasped in pain, his ribs like a clenching fist around his heart.

War drums cut through the warm air.

He harnessed his tidal wave of grief, channeling it into battle fuel as around him the human commanders sprinted away, hands on hilts. Ferth was about to follow, to collect his leathers, his weapons, and a drink, but Titus's hissing whisper stopped him.

Ferth glanced over his shoulder. Captain Titus's hand gripped Imanna's elbow as he spoke to her. "You promised to stay in Mitera. You *promised* me."

"The king was not safe in Mitera, so neither was I. And here I can help. I can fight."

"Absolutely not." His voice was firm and rough.

"You need fighters." The more she spoke, the younger she seemed.

"I need you to live. I need you safe. I don't have time for whining. You will stay in my tent, and I will post a guard with the sole instruction to keep you from leaving."

"Don't waste a guard on me." Her voice was resigned.

"It's not a waste." Titus let go of her elbow and wrapped a loving arm around her shoulders.

Her fingers gripped his back. "Stay safe."

He let her go and turned to Ferth, who shrank back, embarrassed to be caught eavesdropping.

"Ferth, take her to my tent on your way. Get Tomark and give him instructions. Make sure he knows the privilege and importance of his duty to keep her safe during this battle. If things go poorly, I trust him to take her south. She must escape."

Chills rolled along Ferth's arms. "Yes, sir."

Titus's daughter turned to Ferth, and he imagined all sorts of faces hiding behind the veil, but never once did he imagine one covered in burns.

"And Ferth." Titus unbuckled a thin leather knife belt from around his waist. He held it out.

Tentatively Ferth wrapped his palm around the beautiful bone handle and unsheathed the blade. Dracosteel. Expertly crafted. Cal's knife. The knife that had killed Captain Jobu and had nearly ended their father.

"It's yours," Titus said.

Ferth opened his mouth to decline the generous gift. He didn't deserve this. But no words came. He wanted the knife. Another piece of Cal. And he wanted to someday *deserve* to bear it. He closed his lips and sent an uncertain glance at his new Captain.

"It cannot be easy to fight on this side of the line after spending your whole life on the other. It is no small thing to lift arms against your friends."

Ferth swallowed, grateful for the acknowledgement. His guts were a torn-up jungle. "You have no reason to trust me after I already turned against the Dracos, but I won't turn on you today. Elysium is in the right, and I will fight for you."

Titus nodded grimly. "When this is over, I'll tell you how Cal came to own that knife." By the glint in his blue eyes, it was a story worth hearing.

"Deal."

Titus jogged away. Ferth belted the treasure on his waist, feeling defensive and exposed because the strange girl had heard such a personal exchange. His wolves circled closer to Imanna's dog. Kira bared her teeth aggressively, her short fur on end as the predators inched closer.

"Beautiful wolves." Imanna's voice held steady, but her shoulders tensed.

Ferth didn't answer, letting the wolves flank the terrified dog instead.

A deep taunting growl rumbled from Lyko's chest.

"They're not allowed to eat my pet."

"They're just making friends with your *hewan*. They must really like her."

Imanna didn't respond, and Ferth wished again he could see her face.

In the privacy of their mental connection, Ferth spoke to Lyko. *"You know Tomark?"*

"Yes."

"Get him. Meet us at Titus's tent."

Lyko's tall shoulder bumped Kira's nose as he bolted off.

"I'll take you to your father's tent." Ferth strode out.

"You have two hewans." She nearly jogged to keep pace.

"I do." His voice was curt.

"I've never heard of that." Her inflection invited him to elaborate.

"I've never heard of Captain Titus's daughter."

Imanna didn't respond.

They arrived at Titus's tent, and Ferth pulled the door open. She ducked inside with Kira, but he stopped at the threshold. They waited in awkward silence until Lyko returned followed by a confused-looking soldier.

"Tomark," Ferth said. "Your battle orders from Captain Titus are to guard this woman. She is very important to him."

He peered inside the tent at Ferth's gesture. He'd been strapping on his armor, but his thick hands paused.

"Who is she?"

"Imanna. Captain's daughter."

Tomark's eyes widened.

"If the battle goes poorly," Ferth didn't add that it most surely would, "you are ordered to escape south with her and keep her safe."

"Yes, sir."

He thumped the man on the shoulder and left. He threw out all thoughts of the captain's daughter and focused on the approaching battle. The drums had settled into an eerie rhythm as they rang out the enemy's advancement. The Draco Sang were a quarter mile from the river now.

His friends.

He shook his head. His father would have ordered his son killed on sight. Today, he could not think of the Dracos as anything more than enemies.

Inside Cal's tent, he tied leather vests on Rom and Lyko, before letting the waiting attendant help him into Cal's fighting gear. The trio then headed outside to meet the gathering army.

He'd been training with his new squad of three hundred humans, and a flash of pride hit his chest when he saw them filing into formation and adjusting armor and weapons. The Elysium troops operated at an impressive level of order and efficiency. But that would only go so far against the Draco Sang.

Not far enough.

SIXTEEN - CHANGE
SUZA

*S*uza tore off her dress and dropped it in a heap on the ground. With Zemira's help, she'd had a custom suit of fighting leathers made. Where Zemira was sinew and length, Suza was curves and brawn.

She hadn't worn her body-hugging suit outside the privacy of her tent. She still wasn't used to having control over her own skin. She'd felt awkward and strangely presumptuous with the soldier gear on, a lingering effect of having a submissive slave mindset for so many years.

But she was free. She was a soldier now.

And Suza wasn't going to battle in a skirt. She buttoned up the black leggings and bent her knees a few times to loosen up the stiff leather. She secured her breasts with a tight band before pulling on a cotton undershirt. Overtop, the leather jerkin molded to her torso.

She gripped twin Dracosteel short swords, each the length of her arm. Her pulse settled as she slashed through the air, feeling the familiar comfort of her favorite weapons. She'd practiced with them every day since her escape, since she'd stolen them from the enemy's armory. With determination, she'd returned to the drills and sequences she'd learned as an underling at Gristlecove. She sheathed them at her sides and slung her call horn around her neck. Striding out of camp to the northern battlefields, she felt powerful and free. Until Ferth saw her.

He stood at the head of his squad, handsome and fierce. His wolves flanked him in an intimidating display of force. He appeared to be about to make the signal to lead out, but his hand froze when his eyes met hers across the dirt. The dirt destined to run red.

Suza's heart hammered against her fitted suit. Ferth's piercing gaze raked over her, taking in her swords and curves. Her skin burned with what she tried to tell herself was *not* pleasure.

Would she see him again? Would she ever get to tell him her true name? Regret washed through her like soured mead. She should have gone to him, forgiven him when she'd had the chance. She'd wanted to run to him now. Hold him for a moment before losing him to this hopeless war.

Ferth's focus stayed fixed on her as he formed the Draco Sang blessing. Her breath hitched as she recognized the sign. His fist circled his head and hit his heart before jetting out to her. It should have been out of place here, traitorous, but instead, it hit her like a tidal wave of warmth. She felt her hand ball up, returning the salute of their fathers back to Ferth.

A grim smile split his full lips, and he nodded before turning back to his command and giving the signal for battle.

Please live.

Ferth's unit marched forward.

She darted behind their formation to check on the three callers she had stationed around the field. Then she ran to the command unit on the hill. She skidded to a stop next to Captain Titus.

From this vantage point, Suza could see the Elysium soldiers forming up behind rows of sharp timber. The muddy riverbed ribboned in front of a cruelly large mass of Draco Sang. They accelerated when they reached the water. Terrifying roars, screams, and shrieks poured across the terrain as the Draco army spotted the waiting Elysium troops.

Arrows rained down on the enemy at the same moment the front line of Dracos hit the barbed chains hidden in the river. A spurt of hope hit Suza as the Draco Sang began to fall. It was squashed away a moment later as the main body of Dracos surged over the chains and through the hailstorm of death.

"Three flyers hovering high to the northwest," Xandra said.

"Stay safe, stay hidden," Suza reminded her hawk. Pointless commands, but ones she still begged of her hewan every day.

"I'm circling east now."

Eio looped away from Captain Titus to join Uriah's squad, his golden fur a gleaming target.

Suza searched the horizon for a white wolf and a gray wolf. She spotted them as Ferth gave the command to engage. His troops clashed against the Dracos weaving through the timber fencing. Clanging iron and death screams filled the air as the armies slammed together.

"Thirro incoming," Xandra shrieked.

"Thirro," Suza whispered, her voice inaudible, papery thin with fear.

The Draco raptor landed in front of the command unit on the hill. A bow and quiver were strapped on his back between his wings. Armor plate protected his chest. He held a lasso.

"First to the prize." Thirro's eyes fixed on Titus. "The

chief wishes to have you alive. I will give him the pleasure of tasting your death."

"Lucky for me," Titus said, crouching and swinging his sword.

"*Un*lucky for you," Thirro said.

Commander Asvig, his sword held up like a skewer, lunged at the flyer. Thirro tilted his chin and with a flash of his wrist sent a knife Suza hadn't realized he held into Asvig's chest.

The brave, foolish commander slammed into the ground. His sword rolled away, still clean. The red pool of blood expanding from the man snapped something inside Suza. Her paralysis broke, and her focus intensified. She harnessed her fear into a spear as she steadied her grip on her swords.

Titus's ten guards inched forward. Thirro crouched and rolled forward on misshapen feet, a crazed grin on his face as he surveyed his next prey.

"Get back," Titus barked, his gaze glancing to his fallen commander.

The soldiers halted.

Titus leveled his sword at the bird, a challenge.

"I know better than to engage you with a sword." Thirro threw out the lasso. It snapped around Titus's shoulders.

Titus twisted. He dropped his sword as he groped for a smaller blade on his belt. He ripped a knife free from his waist and brought his hands up to cut the rope. Thirro coiled his strong legs and launched into the sky. The rope snapped taut and jerked Titus off his feet. He roared as he lost his grip on his knife.

Suza lunged. Her fingers brushed her captain's boots as he sailed overhead.

"*Help,*" she cried to Xandra.

She picked up Titus's fallen knife and cocked her arm back. Xandra dove in, scratching at Thirro's wings. Suza let the dagger fly on a prayer. It struck Thirro's leg. The eagle dropped a few precious feet in the air. Suza jumped for Titus, grabbing his ankles. He cried out, and a moment later she fell back, landing hard on the earth. Titus crashed into the ground next to her, the rope slapping to the dirt.

"Slave." Thirro's voice was venomous.

He had his bow in his hands now. He trained his arrow at her chest. Blood rained from his leg.

Xandra clawed Thirro's arm, and the first arrow flew wild. Thirro slammed a fist into the bird, and Xandra spiraled through the air, agony surging through their mental connection.

"No!" Suza yelled, scrambling to her feet.

Thirro paused, his head cocked. "Your little abomination, is it?" He trained his next arrow at the lump of chestnut feathers now heaving on the ground.

Titus hurled a rock at Thirro, distracting him for a heartbeat. The captain hadn't gotten up, and Suza worried about his injuries.

Elysium arrows followed Titus's rock as a small unit of archers had finally come within range.

Fast as the wind, Thirro shot higher into the sky and out of range.

The guards rushed to Titus as Suza darted to her hawk.

Xandra breathed, but was otherwise unresponsive. Suza couldn't see any breaks, but as tenderly as possible, she tucked in Xandra's limp wings and lifted her hawk into her arms.

Titus used a guard as a crutch as he stood, keeping his weight off his right leg.

"The calls," Titus said, his tone hard despite his ashen face.

Suza's hands shook as she groped for her horn. The scene

in front of her iced her chest. The Draco Sang had torn apart their lines.

This was it.

She brought the pipes to her lips and blew with all her strength.

SEVENTEEN - STRIKE
FERTH

Finally, Ferth thought when he heard the counterfeit call echoing across the battlefield.

He tried not to think about how many of his squad littered the fields, how much blood caked his sword and his hands.

Pick it up. Pick it up, Ferth begged. And then they did. Enemy horns began echoing the call. *Form up. Form up. Center strike.*

The Draco Sang fought strung-out across the south banks. They'd passed the chains and timbers and stood firmly on Elysium soil.

The Draco soldiers Ferth and his squad fought against disengaged and stepped back. Slowly the Dracos began to move, clustering together in one central mass. Their vicious attack subsided for a blessed moment.

Runners sprinted up, and Ferth accepted a cup with hands caked in blood, sweat, and viscous. He stiffened when he brought the pungent drink to his face, but thirst compelled the cup the rest of the way to his lips, and he gulped down the creamy blend of nuts, honey, and herbs.

Excluding the distinct vinegary medicinal aftertaste, it might have been palatable. He shuddered as he handed the empty cup back, but he did feel better.

"The wolves need some." He motioned to Rom and Lyko, who had formed up at his sides. Their fur hung limp and matted, and their eyes shone maniacally. Blood dyed their heads and paws red.

The boy trembled as he refilled the cup from the pitcher he carried on his shoulder. Ferth rapidly whipped his sword against a whetstone as the brave boy held the drink out to the beasts. Rom and Lyko lapped at the greenish tan liquid as the boy struggled to keep hold of the mug. Ferth thanked the skies for the heavy clouds, sweet relief on a hot day.

They'd been fighting for nearly three hours, and already the Dracos' victory was nearly won. Ferth had caught glimpses and flashes of familiar faces and members of his old unit. He'd cowardly focused his efforts on unknown Dracos.

The enemy calls changed, ordering the forward attack to resume.

Ferth waited. The Elysiums holding the center lines sprinted back. He counted to ten and then, *boom.*

The boulder smashed into the thickly packed Dracos. The second catapult launched, landing squarely on the enemy.

And that was it. They wouldn't be able to reload the catapults in time to relaunch. Both boulders hit home, causing maximum damage, but the Draco stormed forward again like an angry swarm of wasps. Elysium's doom approached.

"Form up," Ferth yelled to his tired squad. With a thrust of his fist, he propelled them toward a rapid death.

After the catapults, the Dracos fought hard to earn back their long front. Ferth joined his unit up with Uriah and Eio on the eastern edge. They could not let the Dracos break through and spread out.

Countless Dracos fell beneath Ferth's Draco-made sword.

In the far reaches of his mind, he wondered if he killed his soul as he killed his blood brothers.

Ferth ducked a slash from a thin weasel soldier. A hyena joined the weasel, and Ferth fell back, defensive. He looked for his wolves, but they were engaged in heavy battles of their own. Exhaustion and discouragement swept over him as he barely blocked the two Dracos from landing a killing blow. He couldn't hold off this concerted attack for much longer. He slipped in mud and gore, landing on his backside, his blade locked with the weasel. The hyena hitched back for the killing blow. Panting, both hands trapped, he watched his death swing down.

Ferth blinked as the hyena's head severed completely from his body and thumped to the ground. The weasel jerked back, and Ferth thrust his sword into her belly before looking over to see Uriah looming above the decapitated hyena. Uriah's eyes were coal chips when they met Ferth's.

"I hate hyenas." He turned away, his dripping sword tilted up.

Gasping, Ferth scrabbled to his feet. He blocked out all thoughts of his fragile mortality and joined Rom and Lyko. Together they ended three more Dracos before Ferth looked up and froze.

His father fought ten yards away. A blood-soaked bandage wrapped his chest wound, but he swung his battle axe with healthy speed and power. With each stroke, one or two soldiers fell. He moved forward in a deadly rhythm.

Laconius had already killed one of his sons.

Ferth adjusted his stiff chest plate and wiped an arm over his grimy face. Killing Laconius might be the only chance Elysium had left.

Mind bleak and heart grim, Ferth stepped forward to finished Cal's mission. *"Let's go,"* he said to Rom and Lyko. They knew exactly what he meant.

Before he got halfway to his father, two familiar faces barred his way.

"Dara. Keal." Their names jumped off Ferth's tongue.

"Captain Ferth." Keal's long ape arms hung at his sides.

"Traitor." Her fox eyes were sad as she said it.

"My fight is not with you." Ferth felt as if he'd been thrown in a pool of molasses, his body heavy and reluctant.

Dara cocked her furry head back and laughed, a hollow sound. "Such a pretty human. When this is over, I shall enjoy having you as my slave."

Ferth had already feared that fate once before. He would not again.

Keal held up his sword. "The chief's honor guard cannot let you past."

He opened his mouth and yelled as loud as he could. "Father. Laconius. Fight me!"

Keal and Dara stepped back slightly and glanced over their shoulders. The surrounding battle paused as if frozen, as if taking in a collective gasp.

His father's broad shoulders turned, revealing the familiar bullish nose and horns. Had his face always been so cruel? Laconius's black eyes locked on Ferth. He scanned the twin wolves, and then in a low voice that cut across the field, he said, "Kill him. Kill them all."

The spell broke, and the sound of death clanged again.

"I am sorry, my friend." Keal brought his sword forward and bent his legs.

Ferth tried to step back, tried to fall behind his squad, tried to escape this fight, but Dara leapt forward, twin daggers appearing in her hands.

"This is no knife fight," Ferth said.

"Do your worst," she said.

Deep sorrow swelled in his chest as he remembered sparring with her a lifetime ago, teasing her, kissing her.

One of Ferth's soldiers stepped up to fight at Ferth's side. Dara stuck a blade in the brave man's throat. The rosy filter on Ferth's past cleared away, and his resolve hardened. He had only one path forward—through the cruel valley of death.

Rom circled left, and Lyko circled right. Lyko's fury rippled across the connection like searing flames.

"Keep your head," Ferth said to the broken-hearted hewan.

Lyko's blood-chilling growl was the only reply before he leapt at Dara, fangs gleaming. Ferth brought his sword up to block the stroke that Keal aimed at Lyko's back.

"Two," Keal said as he whipped his sword toward Ferth. "I would not expect less from my captain." Metal clanged. "I am sorry to kill you."

"I had a brother." Why did he say that? Why did he talk to Keal as if they could still be comrades?

"I had a brother too," Keal said.

Ferth faltered at the ape-man's words, and Keal's sword split open the leather on Ferth's shoulder.

Rom howled as Dara's dagger cut open his ear.

"Payback," Dara yelled as she held her red blade high, circling Rom.

Ferth sucked in a panicked breath as Keal came forward. This wasn't a game. He had only one option now. Flashes and memories of their many sparring matches flooded his mind and muscles. With his agile human body, he danced to Keal's weaker left side and inside the ape's long reach. He slashed his blade across Keal's waist. Pain blasted across Keal's face and a look of deep anguish pierced his dark eyes. He fell to his knees, his sword still drawn.

"Keal!" Dara screamed.

Ferth slashed his sword across his friend's throat, ending the Draco's torture.

Keal fell silent and still. Distant thunder cracked as if in tribute of his death.

"You killed him." Her orange eyes were frantic.

Ferth nodded, his face harsh, and his gaze promising her the same fate. Her hands shook. She turned, fleeing into the ranks of Draco Sang. Ferth took grim gladness in her departure. He would not have to kill her—yet. But he'd still killed his friend, one of the best Dracos he'd ever known. Regret and sorrow crashed like an avalanche over his heart. Rom came to his side. Careful of the severed ear, Ferth rested his hand on the gray head.

"May the Dragon keep you," Ferth whispered. They honored Keal for another moment, then, sword heavy in his palm, he inched past Keal's silent mass.

The battle had moved Laconius west, and progress toward the chief slowed. All around, Elysium soldiers fell and with them, Ferth's hope.

Was Shale safe? It wouldn't be long until they were all dead. Ferth had known they had no chance of victory, but still the sour reality shocked his core.

He rubbed a bloody hand over Lyko's skull. *"We'll take as many down with us as we can."*

The wolves snarled. It was the right sound for this moment, and it fed Ferth strength. He held up his weapon for the thousandth time, for the last time.

He had wanted to meet his mother.

And then the rains came, as if his sword had slashed open the sky, spilling its watery guts.

EIGHTEEN - RETREAT
THIRRO

Thirro hovered fifty feet above the ground, swearing into the wind. He'd wrapped his thigh where that slave viper had knifed him, but the pain still seared up and down his leg. Blood bubbling, he scanned the battle from the sky, his bow in hand. Every arrow he sent was an enemy dead.

He could taste the victory, like fine liquor and human woman. And then the storm hit and washed the sensual flavors away.

Water weighed down his clothes and his wings. Visibility diminished. Every flap of his wings was a struggle against the torrent. He knew he should land, but he didn't want to join the melee of blood and mud on the ground.

He'd tilted, intending to fly into the human camp and take ownership of a tent. The rest of the slow-legged Dracos could join him when they got there.

A call rang out, and Thirro halted his southern dive. He cocked his head to listen. Had he heard that right? The call rang out again, this time echoed from several horns.

Retreat. Retreat. Retreat.

Baffled, Thirro lost altitude. The battle was won. Why were they retreating?

Thirro squinted at the storm. Under the darkening sky, the Draco Sang army ran north. They crossed the rapidly swelling Rugit River and back into Skotar.

Elysium soldiers stood as statutes—the ones that could stand. No cheering, simply silent stares as the enemy disappeared into the mist. The humans were exhausted. Defeated. Thirro could not make sense of the retreat. What had happened?

An arrow struck his butt, narrowly missing his tender wings. Furious, Thirro scanned the enemy troops. He couldn't tell who'd fired the shot. He blinked rain from his eyes and sent two arrows at drooping humans before following his army north.

Back at the camp he'd hoped never to return to, he tried to land gently, but with the pelting rain and his injuries, his legs gave out, and he landed in a painful heap.

Nearby, a slave startled. She snapped her gaze away and made for a tent entrance.

"Slave," Thirro yelled.

She stopped. Her shoulders slumped as she turned and rushed through the rain to his side. When he extended a hand, she gripped it and pulled up.

"Careful!"

"Sorry, sir."

On his feet, he leaned heavily on the woman. She groaned as he shifted his weight over her shoulders. Grime from Thirro stained her dress and coated her hair. With her assistance, he limped into one of the two medical tents. Slaves and healers lined the walls, waiting. He pointed to a healer before falling forward onto a cot. A gust of wet wind heralded the arrival of more wounded. Within seconds, the tent came alive. He took a long pull from a cup of spiced wine and closed his eyes.

When he opened them again, his wounds were cleaned and dressed. He sent a slave to fetch him fresh clothes and then ordered her to help him change. When he stood, she offered him a crutch, but he waved it away.

"I have wings." Of course, he couldn't spread them inside the busy tent, so he hopped ungracefully on his good leg outside. Thankfully, it only took a few flaps of his exhausted wings to get him to the door of the command tent. By the time he entered, his fresh clothes were soaking wet. Water beaded off his feathers when he shook them dry.

At the head seat, Chief Laconius received treatment for the weeping chest wound he'd torn open during battle. Captain Mina sat at his right. Thirro deserved a seat with the dozen unit commanders on the right, but since he *still* didn't have the title, he took his seat on the left with the other soldiers brought here to report. He couldn't sit properly with the arrow wound in his butt. He slid to the side of his stool, letting his injured cheek hang off. He hated humans. They would pay for this.

"Report," Laconius said to Captain Mina.

"Numbers are still rough. The storm has affected our eyes on the field. We estimate five hundred and twenty Draco dead and close to thirty-five hundred human dead."

"The Lion?"

"We do not have a confirmed kill, and Thirro's kidnapping attempts were unsuccessful."

Thirro bit his tongue, hating that Mina had said his name. He had failed in his mission.

The disappointed flick of Laconius's gaze on him was a punch to the throat. "And the traitor?"

Captain Mina shifted uncomfortably. "It's believed he still lives."

Laconius's horns trembled. "Queen Mavras deserves better of her army. We bring dishonor and shame." Spit gleamed on his lips. "Who gave the center strike call?" The fuming chief's black gaze scanned the room. "Who gave the call?" The slave at his side flinched. A dozen callers stood in a line against the wall of the tent. Laconius pinned them with a glare. "Well?"

After another ten heartbeats, a frog Draco spoke in a croaking voice, "I echoed the call after hearing the master tone, chief. As directed." The boy's hands shook on his pipes.

The remaining callers nodded their agreement.

"And the retreat call?" Laconius asked. "Who started that?"

Silence.

"So," Laconius said. "No one knows who gave the center strike attack, and no one knows who gave the retreat call?" The chief's voice hardened into an ice pick. "And yet, they cost us—Mavras—her swift victory." He scanned the room. "Someone tell me how!"

Thirro flinched as Laconius's gaze passed over him. Cold blew in from the open door as Jade sauntered in. Thirro ground his teeth at the bounce in her uninjured step.

"I can tell you." She threw a set of call pipes down on the table in front of Laconius. They were green, though, instead of brown. "The humans started the calls. I took this set of fake pipes off a girl after I killed her." She said that last part with a smile.

A horrible silence stretched over long moments.

"Well done, Jade," Laconius finally said, his voice barely containing his rage. "Such promise for one so young. Join us. Captain Mina will assign you a unit to command."

Thirro bit on his tongue so hard he tasted blood. That was supposed to be his promotion. If that stupid slave hadn't gotten in the way, he would have been the one to bring Titus in. He would have received his just reward. Instead, Jade was a unit commander instead of him. He seethed, his teeth complaining at the tension in his jaw.

Jade bowed deeply. "An honor, chief, thank you."

Laconius's focus returned to the pipes on the table. His fist came down, splintering the reeds and startling them all.

NINETEEN - HELPLESS
FERTH

*R*elief warmed Ferth when he entered the medical unit. Shale was alive. She sat in a chair cradling a bundle. Rain drummed on the roof.

She looked up, and Ferth's step faltered. Red rimmed her sparkling green irises. Tears streaked her filthy face.

"Shale." He rushed to her side and dropped to his knees.

Did she flinch when he said her name? He pulled back, giving her space.

Xandra lay inert in Shale's lap. The hawk's wings hung limp, and her tiny head rested on her feathered breast.

"What happened?" Ferth hated his helplessness. Dozens of his unit lay in the dirt with empty gazes.

"Thirro came after Titus." Shale's voice was a rasp. "He knocked Xandra out. I keep expecting her to wake up." The words came out warbled. "It's been hours."

Uriah appeared in the door, his eyes snapping to Shale. With a voice full of relief, he whispered the name, "Suza."

Who?

Shale's eyes flicked to Ferth, but he couldn't read the

expression there. She turned back to Uriah, her own joy at seeing the soldier evident on her face.

Ferth took another step back.

Uriah swept forward. He grabbed Shale's hand and leaned down to kiss her brow.

That's not where Ferth would have kissed her if she were his. Especially not after today's dance with death.

"Well fought, Ferth," Uriah said, turning.

Ferth's eyes widened at the unexpected compliment. "You as well." He rubbed blood-stained hands together, failing to clean them. "And thank you." His thoughts flashed back to Uriah beheading the hyena that was about to deliver a fatal blow.

Uriah gave a short nod. He motioned Shale to stand. "I have someone to help Xandra." With an arm securely around Shale's shoulders, he led her away. Her head tilted to rest against him as they retreated.

Ferth let out a hard sigh. *"There's a line for healers,"* he said to Rom. *"I can sew that ear, or we can wait."*

Lyko licked furiously at Rom's wound, pausing only to take a turn cleaning his brother's face and then back to the wound. Lyko's own fur hung dirty and neglected.

Ferth's chest pinched, right above his heart, grateful they had Lyko, but mindful of the cost. If only Cal were here. If only Cal were here.

"I'd rather you do it," Rom said.

"You'd probably scare the healer into poking your eye out," Lyko said.

Ferth helped himself to a needle and thread.

Dara had sliced half of Rom's right ear off, leaving an uneven triangle of skin to be repaired.

After cleaning the wound, Ferth braced Rom's narrow head on his thigh. Rom held still as stone, but a mist of pain crossed the threshold of their connection and into Ferth's thoughts as he stitched his wolf. Pride filled Ferth's chest and oozed back across the link. Rom closed his eyes and settled more comfortably against his master's lap.

When Ferth finished, exhaustion clouded his vision. When had he last slept? Before he'd sparred with Uriah at the training grounds? A lifetime ago. Ferth staggered to his feet and padded out into the rain with his wolves.

"Food or sleep?"

"Both," Lyko said.

"Sleep." Rom's head drooped below his shoulders.

"Go," Ferth ordered. *"I'll bring food."*

They looked as if they might protest, but then Lyko turned, leading Rom to their tent.

Ferth stepped up to the door of the dining hall.

"Whoa there, soldier." The pot-bellied man at the door held up a hand. "What are you doing?"

"I'm here for food." Ferth looked around in confusion.

"Not with Draco blood on your shirt." The man looked him up and down.

Ferth had battle juice from his brown hair to his black boots. His stained sword hung limp in his hand. He hadn't had time to clean it so he hadn't put it back in its sheath. "Why not?"

The man snorted in disbelief. "Where did you grow up, lad? Skotar?"

Ferth's eyes narrowed.

The man stopped laughing mid-burst. "I'll have someone bring you a plate. By the look of you, it's the least I can do. What's your tent?"

His tone was flat when he said, "I live in H3. I'll want meat for my wolves."

The man's face blanched, and his mouth fell in an "O" shape as he realized exactly whom he addressed.

Ferth whirled on a heel, a satisfied grin on his face.

The walk in the rain revived him somewhat, and he realized he might not be ready to receive the dreams that would repaint Keal's death and the abominations of this day.

He climbed up a watchtower and looked over the river, now swelling and frothing. He cleaned his sword as he watched the dead and wounded being carried toward camp. The clouds wept, washing away the horrors of the killing field. Ferth tilted his face to the sky.

Wash away my crimes.

When the dangerous cold of wet exhaustion started tightening its grip, Ferth climbed down. He stopped at Captain Titus's tent. A hearty fire burned in the center of the large room. The smoke drifted up and out a hanging vent. He hesitated on the threshold, feeling like he'd interrupted a party he wasn't invited to. They were all here without him. Pelussa and Shale sat hunched in the corner with Xandra. Uriah hovered over them. Eio, Opal, and a few other hewans tore at chunks of meat off to another side. Zemira conversed with several soldiers near the fire. Imanna and her dog sat near the bed, the only ones clean and dry, except for the irritated-looking soldier assigned as the veiled woman's guard standing behind her. Raja Darius slumped in a chair, his battle armor dented and filthy. The man had fought despite his exhausted arrival here moments before the battle. Impressive. Captain Titus lay on the bed, a healer tending to his leg. He opened his eyes and lifted his head.

"Ferth." Titus's voice rang through the tent. "You're here. Thank the stars. Are you well?"

Ferth inhaled the warm welcome. Even his father had never seemed that grateful to see him.

Titus scanned him with a critical eye. "How is Rom's ear?"

"We are alive. Rom's ear will heal. Your leg?"

"It's fine."

The healer looked up sharply. "It's broken. He won't be

getting up for a week and then we'll see how he does with crutches."

Titus ignored the comment. "Full battle reports are still forthcoming." The chatter died as the tent focused on the captain's words. "But we already know it was a massacre. The calls and the rain saved us." He let out a heartbroken sigh. "Let us hope the rain continues until more troops arrive. Between the river's sudden strength and Pelussa's work we should have a bit of time before the next attack."

Pelussa's work?

Several heads, Ferth's included, jerked toward the woman.

As if on cue, the hawk shuddered to life in Pelussa's hands.

Shale cried out in joyful relief as her hawk flopped into her open arms.

Pelussa dusted off her shirt and pants as if she could see the feathers that dotted them. "Ipsum and I have been busy these last few weeks." The raven cawed in agreement. "While you all banged your swords together, we've been flying messages to a brave human in the Draco camp who knows the power of bacaroot and had been gathering it in secret." A twisted grin split the woman's face, revealing a missing tooth beneath her milky eyes. "When Ipsum took her my store of the poison, she had enough to make the entire Draco camp quite sick."

Ferth stepped back in surprise. This could buy them much needed time, but that brave slave was doomed.

"Well done, Pelussa," Titus said.

"Who?" Shale's voice came out high and pitched. "Who was it?" Fear brightened her eyes as she looked at Pelussa.

Pelussa curled in on herself. "I didn't get her name, to protect her."

Shale shook her head and dropped her face in her hand.

"You cannot protect her," Ferth whispered.

The tent went quiet as a tomb.

"Pearl." The name pinched out of Shale. Uriah put his hand on her back as she hunched over and let out a sob that echoed through Ferth's hollow chest.

Pearl. Her face came to mind: sad eyes, pale hair, willowy frame. She'd cut his hair and treated him with kindness. He'd protected her when he could, but he should have done more. He remembered seeing her in that clearing with Kenji, finding love despite the cruelty around her. Ferth's heart cracked, and he swallowed back nausea. The Dracos would find out who'd poisoned them.

And Pearl would die.

Titus's face cinched in pain as a woman adjusted the braces on his leg. "I think it's time we all get some rest. Sleep. Eat. Report here tomorrow after breakfast. We'll send a delegation to Mitera tomorrow afternoon."

"Father," Imanna said. "Let me tend to the wounded. I won't leave the healers' hall. I can help."

"Tomark?"

The soldier straightened. "Yes, sir."

"Guard her well. She doesn't leave your sight."

"Of course, sir."

Imanna stood, her veil rippling.

"Don't uncover your face," Titus said.

"I know, Father." Her voice was annoyed. She paused at Ferth's side. "Glad you made it." She swished past and was out the door before anyone had moved.

Ferth felt Shale's eyes. Her gaze held him with questions. If he hadn't known better, he would have thought that she wished him to stay, to come to her. He wanted to hold her, cry together for Pearl and for Cal and for Keal and for all the rest. He wanted her to comfort his loneliness and kiss away his regret. He wanted to promise her a brighter future.

Uriah's hand remained on Shale's shoulder. Zemira joined them, blocking his view. Ferth slipped out into the rain. His wolves didn't stir when he entered. He shoveled down bread and chicken, stripped naked, washed his hands and face, and climbed under the blankets.

Thirro groaned when Dara came into their tent. She looked as bad as he felt. "I'm not in the mood." His laughter sounded like rocks scraping a grate. His skin burned and snakes swam in his guts.

She sneered. "Shut up."

She fell on his bed next to him, knocking him into another round of pain. If he had more energy, he would have retaliated. As it was, he didn't move.

"What's wrong with your own bed?"

"Mine's next to Keal's, and I can't stand to see his empty."

Thirro didn't have an answer for that except to put an arrow through Ferth's filthy heart.

"He killed him. Keal loved Ferth, and that traitorous swine killed him without a thought." Dara let out a bark of joyless laughter. "And to think, I'd actually felt bad for Ferth. Not anymore. He killed his own unit."

"Not his unit anymore." Unfortunately, Jade was his unit commander now. She was worse than Ferth.

"No. We're not." She growled. "And we take care of our own."

Thirro smiled at the promise of death on her words. It stirred desire in his belly, despite the fevers.

A slave slipped into the tent.

How was he not ill? The Dracos could barely move and the slaves seemed perkier. Humans were the ones prone to disease. Dracos never got sick.

"Chief Laconius invites you to his tent for breakfast tomorrow," the slave said.

Such a polite, chipper slave.

"Can I get you something to eat? More mead?"

"Get out."

With a breath, the slave was gone.

Thirro ignored the burning in his guts as he rolled on his side, curling against Dara's warm body. "We'll end him, slow and painful," he said in a husky whisper.

The scene in Titus's tent at breakfast was an improvement from the night before. The grief and shock of survival still hung heavy in the air, but with clean faces and bloodless clothes, a ray of hope pierced the gloom. The blessed rain continued to fall in protective sheets. The Draco Sang remained north of the border, repelled. *For now.*

Again, Ferth felt late to the party. The Elysium leaders and Draco-blooded soldiers sat in a large circle, conversation buzzing in the air. Being in Titus's tent instead of at command lent a friendlier tone to the gathering.

The collapsible leather stools on either side of Imanna were vacant. Between the veiled face, Titus's deference, and the large soldier standing bodyguard at her back, she had a moat of space around her. Ferth had noticed the empty seat by Shale the moment he'd arrived, but he slipped to Imanna's side, his wolves following.

"Good morning, your highness."

She jerked in her seat with a sudden intake of breath. Her gloved hand flew up to her veil.

"Excuse me," he said. "It was meant as a joke. You sitting here alone, with your guard."

"Of course." She let out a false laugh. "Good morning, soldier."

He held out a hand to try out the human greeting. "Ferth."

Her grip was surprisingly strong for a hand so small. "Titus has told me about you." He noted that she'd called Titus by his name, not father. "I look forward to knowing more about a Draco Sang captain who overcame his beast after an almost complete transformation. *Very* impressive."

Ferth stumbled over his surprise, failing to think of something to say. Unbidden and unwelcome heat rushed to his checks. His fingers twitched to rip away her covering, see the face that matched the strong sweet voice. See whom it was that Titus confided in. Instead, Ferth stared at the rippling black veil like a blushing idiot.

Rom stuck his nose up.

"This is Rom," Ferth said. "And this is Lyko." The wolves looked at her and Kira placidly. At least they weren't trying to be extra intimidating this morning.

"Two hewans. It must be incredible."

"Lyko is—"

"Callidon's. Yes. I heard. Fascinating how your twin's bond connected with you."

Ferth didn't like all his secrets handed out to strangers like holiday treats. "I see you already know all there is to know about me."

"I assure you that isn't true. And don't worry. Titus tells me things, but he doesn't blabber to the whole world. He and I have a special bond."

"But it isn't father-daughter, is it?" His boldness surprised him. Maybe it helped that he couldn't see her, almost as if she weren't real.

"Of course Titus is my father." No hesitation. "My mother

died when I was very young, and he raised me virtually on his own." Her tone was cold with offense, but for some reason Ferth imagined a mocking smile beneath the covering.

"Please forgive my rudeness."

"Done."

A server handed Ferth a heaping plate of eggs, greens, and flatbread as Titus's voice blanketed the tent.

"Reinforcements are three days out. I am confident they will arrive before another attack from Skotar, but we need more soldiers. We saw yesterday how important it is to maintain this border. Raja Darius has agreed to lead the return trip to Mitera. Having seen our struggle firsthand, he can instruct and coordinate the effort for more troops."

Raja Darius sat rod-straight in his chair, the opposite form of Captain Titus reclining in his bed, but both men had an air of leadership and poise Ferth wished to emulate.

"After the aerial attack on King Andras," Raja Darius said, "I think it wise to travel, with sufficient numbers, to Mitera. The Dracos are watching."

"And Imanna will be traveling as well," Titus said. "I'd like a full guard circle. Two hewan sets and a dozen soldiers. The travel will be fast and hard."

Ferth's mother was in Mitera. "Captain Titus, sir." He cringed inwardly at his interruption. He was needed here to fight, but he needed to see her before he died. He still had Cal's last words to Mira burning a hole in his pocket. "I'd like to volunteer."

He felt Shale's eyes on him. Did she think he was a coward who wished to run from battle? Hide from his past? Did she remember Cal's words about their mother?

Titus studied Ferth, as if he could see the hidden desires.

"Granted."

Tears pressed behind Ferth's eyes, but he forced them

back and kept his face blank. He would see her. He was going to his human mother.

"I'd like to volunteer as well," Shale said.

Ferth jerked his gaze to her, hope swelling. She threw him a brief glance before turning her focus on Titus.

"I promised you freedom, Suza, but I beg you to stay," Titus said.

Suza? That name again. Had she changed her name and not told him? The hope he'd felt at being near her on the road to Mitera dribbled away.

"You're needed here," the captain said. "You're too valuable with the calls. Even if we can't use them again as we did, you can interpret the enemy signals. When Xandra is strong enough, we need her to scout."

Ferth glanced over the few other hewans in the army that were present: a python, a monkey, a spider, a badger, a panther. Xandra and Ipsum were their only flyers. And Pelussa was more often off on her own missions instead of following orders.

Shale. Or Suza. Or whoever she was now, nodded. "I will stay."

"Thank you, Suza."

Zemira straightened in her seat, her fighting leathers scratched and worn. "I volunteer to go."

Ferth thought of the baby Zemira had sent south.

Titus looked twenty years older as he closed his eyes and sank against his pillow. He exhaled and focused his saddest, sorriest blue eyes on the warrior. "We *need* you here, Zemira."

She'd been a striking snake on the battlefield. Ferth only had eyes on her for a few minutes, but he'd never forget the fluid grace of her reaping. He wondered if she fought with such efficiency because of the power of her love for Callie. Get the job done and get home to her daughter.

But she could not go home.

She hugged her ribs and tilted her face down, but not before Ferth caught the mist of tears flooding her eyes. "Yes, sir."

Ferth's heart broke for the mother.

Titus looked gutted. "Ferth and his wolves will be enough. I'll work with Darius and Tomark on the guards. You'll leave an hour after sunset."

Captain Titus shifted the conversation to funeral arrangements for the thousands dead and plans to strengthen the camp and prepare for the next attack. Then all were dismissed to return to their personal preparations.

Anxious giddiness prickled through Ferth as he entered his tent. He was going to meet his mother. He'd dreamed about her forever, but now that she was a reality, he felt small and scared. What would she think of him and his monstrosities? Did she think of him at all? Would he be only a painful reminder of Cal, the son he'd helped kill?

Ferth went back out into the rain. He needed some answers from Titus before he left. He pulled open the door, strode into Titus's tent, and froze.

"Whoa," Tomark yelled, throwing his shield up, but it was too late. Ferth had seen her.

Titus sighed. "It's alright, Tomark. Come here, son."

He sure collected a lot of sons and daughters.

Tomark lowered his shield, revealing Imanna again. She smiled mischievously.

Thick dark hair curled down her thin shoulders. Her face was tan and freckled. Above ruby lips, eyes as pale and sharp as icebergs froze the air between them. Her beauty struck him, but not as hard as the brand on her forehead. He stared at the familiarly shaped scar—the top of a dragon's head and a sword melded together. The royal Regium family crest of Skotar shone stark against her skin. Unworthily bearing that symbol in any form was grounds for immediate execution.

The brand seemed to fly across the room and punch him in the stomach.

Imanna stood up and curtsied. Her eyes danced with delight.

Ferth's mouth hung limp, and his thoughts whirled in confusion. Jade popped into his mind, and he stepped back in surprise. She did remind him of the vicious underling. They were both petite, but their eyes belied depth and cunning.

"Who are you?"

She opened her mouth, but Titus cut her off. "Sit down, Imanna." He was not taking the pleasure from this that she clearly was.

"She is my ward." He ran a hand through graying hair. "As I told you."

"You said she was your daughter."

"In all but blood."

Ferth turned to Imanna. The first Draco king, Attor, had branded his son's forehead, but he was the last who bore the brand on their brow. What sick person did that to Imanna? Her scar was faded. Old, but done well. It was clearly the royal brand, but hers was white, lacking the purple dye the Regiums mixed into the mark over their hearts. Who was she? How had this Draco-blooded orphan come to wear an executioner's stamp? "How do you have the Regium brand on your face?"

She flinched at the name, *Regium*. Queen Mavras was the only Regium alive—she'd killed all the rest, every one of her bloodline, cousins and all. No one else bore the royal brand —except a girl who'd grown up in Elysium.

In the silence, Ferth's voice rang like a clanging bell. "How do you have the royal brand?"

Imanna's lips stayed sealed.

"It does *not* matter." Titus's blue eyes hardened. "You will forget what you saw."

Not any time soon. He couldn't blame them for not trusting him, but he didn't like it. "The Dracos will kill you." Mavras's stinger might pop off at the mere sight of this offensive girl.

"I know that," she snapped.

Titus's voice was calm. "You understand our need for secrecy and the need to get her away from Skotar."

"Yes, sir." His voice was emphatic. If nothing else had been, that much was true.

"I'm not going back." Her nostrils flared as she put her fists on narrow hips. "I may or may not be safe in this camp full of soldiers, but I'm miserable in Mitera. Darius cannot be too kind or his wife gets upset. You will not let me join the ladies at court. All day I practice my blade and bow in secret. I am being driven mad. *Please*, Father."

Ferth couldn't fathom anyone having the will to resist those pleading pale purple eyes.

Titus sighed. "Tomark, call Uriah here."

Tomark left at a brisk pace.

While they waited, a thousand questions crossed Ferth's tongue. He swallowed them all away, hoping for the day when he wasn't running from death, when these good people would trust him enough to tell him the truth.

The tent door rippled as Tomark returned and ushered Uriah inside. The wind whipped the fire. The brightness lit up Imanna's face. Uriah's countenance changed the moment he saw her, as if she'd speared him, but not with death, with life. The grief and anger Ferth had thought were a permanent part of Uriah seemed to shrink to nothing under Imanna's vibrant gaze.

"Uriah," Titus said, bringing the love-struck soldier back to reality.

"Yes, sir." His gaze flickered over to Titus for only a moment before returning to the young woman.

Anger flared in Ferth. *What about Shale?*

"Imanna is staying here."

Her squeal cut off whatever else Titus was going to say. She jumped up and clapped her hands, then rushed to the captain's bed and kissed his cheek. A smile split his scarred face as he put a hand on her shoulder, but his eyes revealed his worry.

"Uriah, you are charged with her protection. Tomark, you are the second in this."

"Yes, sir," Uriah and Tomark said in unison.

"The veil." Titus pointed to the floor at Ferth's feet.

Ferth scooped up the black silk.

Imanna slumped in her chair and held her hand out.

"You can't remain veiled," Titus said, his tone disappointed. "But you must keep your forehead banded. At. All. Times."

"I promise." She brightened. After days of talking to a veil, the massive sweeps of emotions over her face were a shock. She folded the cloth and tied it around her forehead at the top of her head in a practiced motion. Only a corner of the brand peeked out on her brow, a small crescent scar.

"And it doesn't hurt that the camp thinks Kira is a pet," Titus said.

Imanna stroked her dog's neck. "Foolish mistake."

Ferth snorted at her deadly tone.

"You will train with Uriah in private." Titus looked tired. "No one else will know of your skills."

"That shall be fun," Imanna said, her tone mocking and seductive as she eyed the man who stood a head and shoulders taller and twice as broad.

Uriah's face reddened, and his dark eyes widened.

Titus rolled his eyes, exasperated. "You will work in the healers' building."

"Yes, sir."

"Uriah," Titus said. "I can think of no safer place than your tent. The crew can install the double partition, and I'd ask that she not have a door to the outside. She'll have to go past you to leave and so would, presumably, an attacker. This is up to you."

"It's too big for me anyway without Poe." His voice faltered on his hewan's name.

Imanna focused more closely on the soldier.

"Thank you, son." Titus looked at Imanna, and with a voice soft as fleece said, "It'll be nice to have you near me again."

She smiled, and the freckles on her cheeks and nose crinkled up. "I missed you." She kissed his scarred brow. "Now you get some rest. Healer's orders."

"We'll have dinner together tonight after we send Darius and Ferth off. I want to hear about everything."

She grinned. "Yes, Father." She stood and danced out into the rain, her face free and joyful despite the destruction and the war. Tomark and Kira followed her out.

"This blasted leg." Titus grimaced as he tried to shift to a more seated position in bed.

"You should really rest," Uriah said.

"I know I should." Titus scowled. "But there is too much to do."

"I'll fetch a healer." Uriah ducked out.

"I can come back later," Ferth said.

"There isn't a later."

Ferth shifted back and forth on his feet. He had so many questions for Titus. Cal's bone knife hung heavy on his hip.

"Her name is Mira Closdaut. She should be living at her sister Elssa's house in the flower streets. She works for Darius, so he should be able to connect you quickly as you'll be staying at his azure estate." Titus pointed to the desk. "Take her that letter for me."

Ferth turned, glad for the excuse to hide his beaming face. Invisible wings fluttered against his ribs as he searched through the parchments for the one with Mira's name on it. Schooling his features into submission, he carefully tucked the note next to the wrinkled one from Cal.

"Thank you, sir."

"There's not been a heartbeat in her chest when she didn't think of you." His blue eyes misted. "I wish I could see her face when she realizes her lost son is found."

Ferth's pulse hammered in his ears. Joy and hope sang through his soul before the painful reality settled over. "But Cal is …"

"She's grieving for Callidon. But, what greater gift could we give to a woman having lost one son, than to have found the other?"

Ferth nodded, not trusting himself to speak. He'd hidden these desires in deep secret all his life. He felt naked and exposed as they surfaced.

"You were never sworn into my army properly. You have fought with valor and saved many lives already. You will be viewed with honor if you choose to remain in Mitera or anywhere else in this country."

"I will return and finish this fight with you." He would do it for Cal.

Titus nodded, his smile grim. "Safe travels, my son."

Ferth bowed, and Titus laid a hand on his head as if in blessing.

"Give your grandpapi, Closford, my regards as well."

"Yes, sir." His voice betrayed a thread of his overwhelming excitement. Eager as a newborn magu, he strode out into the rain. His smile faltered when he ran into Uriah returning with a healer. Carrying a steaming mug, the healer continued past and into the tent. Uriah turned to leave and hesitated, rotating back slightly.

"Ferth, wait."

Ferth stopped, his muscles tensing.

"I judged you too harshly. Anyone with the heart to over-come their beast has honor and deserves my respect." Uriah faced Ferth squarely, only an arm's length away. "It must not have been easy for you to kill Dracos, your old comrades. You fought well and saved many Elysium lives yesterday." He stuck out a hand.

Ferth surrendered his fighting hand as he gripped Uriah's meaty palm. Warmth spread up his arm. "You saved my life."

"It was war." His dark eyes bore into Ferth. "But, I would do it again."

Ferth smiled as the words sank in, warming his chest. "I am truly sorry for any pain I caused Shale. Er. Suza? She deserves a good man like you." He meant every word, but also hoped it came out as a reminder to Uriah that he was not free to court Imanna.

Uriah's brow knit in confusion, and then he laughed. Mirth transformed his face, softening the edges and taking years off. Rain flew from his shaking shoulders as the laughter bubbled over.

Ferth frowned. What was so funny?

Uriah finally sucked in a ragged breath and laid a heavy palm on Ferth's shoulder. Ferth tensed.

"Suza is my sister."

The blood drained from Ferth's face. His fingers went numb. *His sister.*

His laughter renewed when he saw Ferth's stunned features.

"How?"

"How did we both escape Gristlecove to find each other here all these years later? That I cannot answer."

"Your father cannot be *the* Lord Gristlecove. Even among the Dracos he has a reputation for cruelty."

Uriah's face darkened as he nodded. "And he was worse to those he professed to care about." A dangerous glint passed over his eyes. "He killed our mother. He whipped Suza."

The fury that steamed off Uriah was reflected in Ferth. Ferth had been whipped by his father too. He wouldn't wish such an experience on his worst enemy. And sweet brave Suza had endured her father's crop. Blood boiled through his veins.

"I will kill him." Uriah's voice was like far-off thunder.

"Not if I get there first."

He looked at Ferth and a bond of shared understanding passed between them. "Fathered by hate," Uriah said. "Mothered by love."

Ferth nodded. He could relate to that.

"Something Titus always says about us Dracos."

Ferth had so many questions, but one overwhelming realization usurped every other thought. "Suza is your *sister*. She's not ..."

"Go." Brown eyes danced with warmth. "Go find her. She has missed you."

Uriah pumped Ferth on the back, sending him stumbling forward. His legs barely caught his fall before they started churning beneath him. Within seconds he arrived outside her tent, his heart a racing wolf, Rom and Lyko at his sides. He stood there, panting, his emotions too strong to think. He stared at the canvas, listening to his pulse pound along with the rain.

The flap flew open. Rom barked as Ferth blocked her familiar Dracosteel knife inches from his chest. Suza's eyes widened, and he let go of her forearm as she jerked her blade back.

"What are you doing creeping out here like an attacker? You scared me. I could have killed you."

"Not a chance, lady," Lyko said.

Ferth didn't bother correcting Suza. "He's ... he's your ... brother."

"Uriah? Of course he's my brother."

He could see it now. The wide mouth, thick eyebrows, and rich dark hair. The strong legs and back.

"And your real name is Suza." It all clicked into place.

She nodded, her chin dropping. "Suzaena."

"It's beautiful. It suits you."

A coy lip curled up. "I should have told you. I wanted to, but you've been avoiding me." Her voice betrayed hurt.

Frustration welled. All this time he'd tortured himself to give her space, never once considering she could have wanted otherwise. How could she? "I was trying to let you be free from me, from your painful past."

She smiled, and his heart tripled. She stepped out of the protection of her tent and into the rain. "I don't want to forget. I can't forget. You are important to me, Ferth. You are the bright spots in my past."

A wave of heat rolled over him, fueled by hope and desire. And uncertainty—how could she say that? He had been her Draco master.

Her thick eyelashes blinked raindrops away as she turned those big green eyes up. She licked water off her lips. This was what he'd dreamed of. She stood before him, not as his slave, but as a woman. Her strength had never been more beautiful.

"I'm in love with you." He hadn't meant to release those words from their cage, but now that he had, his heart soared with wild freedom. He had no secrets left to poison him. Joy split his face into a smile.

Suza swallowed. "I think I might have been in love with you since the morning I was sent to your barrack."

Ferth laughed, a combination of shock and pure pleasure

blooming through him. "You couldn't resist me hung over and stinking?"

She chuckled. "That's not the part I was referring to."

He arched one eyebrow. "Ah. The nakedness."

Red painted her cheeks above the laugh she quickly forced into a scowl. She looked down at his chest, speaking to his shirt instead of his face. She played with a button on his sternum. "You let me think I had some power."

"You still have all the power." He wrapped her hand with his, holding it to his chest. Her eyes lifted to meet his gaze.

"You protected me," she whispered.

His blood heated. Could she truly think of him with such generosity? "And you stole my heart and my sanity."

"You're blaming your crazy on me?" Thick lips curved into a crescent.

He inched closer. His arm went around her waist. At the feel of her under his fingers, he drew her against his body. She opened her mouth to speak again, but he was done with words. His lips met hers, starting a new conversation. Rain turned to steam as it struck hot skin.

He drank her in, intoxicated by her familiar scent.

She rolled onto her tiptoes, sliding her arms around his neck and drawing him tighter against her eager mouth.

Vaguely he sensed his wolves wander off. Lyko's mocking laughter echoed behind him. A touch of pride and approval floated away from Rom.

He'd wanted to hold her and kiss her for so long. When she had been his slave, he'd allowed her to live in fear, enjoying his power. He had taunted her, touched her, and toyed with her. He'd barely held back from forcing himself on her.

As her mouth softened under his and his hands melted against her warm curves, Ferth jerked back, suddenly fearful of the memories, and overcome with guilt.

She looked at him in surprise, her eyes wide and dark.

The rain did little to dampen the fire kindling in his gut. He loosened his grip on her ribs, creating space between her softness and his chest. "I can't do this. This isn't fair to you." He was still a monster, his desire clouding his thoughts and urging him, even now, to take what he wanted. "I don't deserve you."

She laid a hand over his pounding heart. "I know you, Ferth."

"Then you know what I have done."

"I do."

He held his breath.

"And I forgive you. I trust you."

He shook his head. "It can't be that easy."

She snorted. "You think this was easy? You think these weeks of watching you torture yourself with guilt have been easy? You think it was easy to watch you turn on your own Draco unit to protect me and Cal and then again in battle as you fought and killed your friends to defend Elysium?"

He shuddered beneath her words. Could she mean it? He ran a hand over her dark wet mane. He pressed his brow to hers. Their breath intermingled. Her lips called to him. "Thank you."

He pulled away as she nodded. Her lip trembled. His thumb came up and touched her quivering mouth. His palm engulfed her cheek. His blood was a rage of wanting. He dropped his hand. She caught it before it fell. "I'll be here when you return."

Her words and her shining face filled his body with such longing it frightened him. "I will not blame you if you aren't. I expect nothing, deserve nothing, but I will hope for the chance to earn your trust and forgiveness. And maybe, if the stars are very good to me … one day… your love. If you'll let me try."

"I'd like that." Her smile warmed him more than the summer sun.

He grinned. "Maybe I'll get some tips on courting from the fancy humans in Mitera."

"Their ideas have to be better than the Draco Sang's methods."

Their laughter danced with the rain.

She sobered first. "Your mother will be so proud. I'm grateful that you will get to know her." Something like pain marred Suza's tone.

What had happened to her mother? How had she overcome her beast with a father like Gristlecove? He wanted to know everything. He hoped for the time to find out. He hoped for a lifetime.

"We will tell each other all about our mothers when we are together again." He smiled at the look of hope on her face.

She lifted a determined chin.

"Until then."

"Stay safe." He kissed her, a soft brush against her lips before letting go.

She stood in the rain and watched him walk away.

Ferth's heart was a pulpy mass of hope and pain as he made his travel preparations.

Departure was a quiet affair, a select few gathered in Captain Titus's tent with good-byes and final instructions. Heavily cloaked and under cover of darkness, Ferth, Lyko, Rom, Raja Darius, and six soldiers slipped southward. With the darkness and the rain, they had high hopes of escaping unnoticed by the Draco Sang.

"Ferth and his wolves, guarded by seven soldiers, left camp a quarter of an hour ago. They took the southern road on horseback," said a grey and tan owl flyer with long ears. He knelt before Laconius. His wings quivered as he tucked them against his back. "Although Ferth looks like he's barely hanging onto the reins." The scout laughed, but when Laconius didn't echo the humor, the Draco clamped his mouth shut.

Thirro shifted uncomfortably in his seat. The feast on the tables mocked his screaming guts. His battle wounds seemed to harmonize with his cacophony of pain. Had war been too much for Ferth? The coward was fleeing after a little blood? Did the traitor think he could escape?

No matter where you go, I will find you, and I will kill you.

Rain drummed against the tent, reminding Thirro of his injured, grounded condition. He reached out, and a slave quickly handed him a mug of mead. At least as Skotar's Arrow he was still granted access to the command tent instead of being told to eat with the common soldiers in the crowded dining tent like Dara.

"How far out are the human's reinforcements?" Laconius asked.

"The army made camp south of Kiptos when the rain hit, and they didn't travel yesterday. If they march in the morning, two thousand troops should reach the Lion's camp by nightfall tomorrow." The flyer remained kneeling; he looked too sick and tired to stand. "Ferth's small group looks set to reach this army in a few hours."

"Let's hit Ferth before he reaches the troops," Captain Mina said.

Bold words for someone who couldn't fly and looked like she could barely walk.

Laconius scanned the ashy faces of his commanders, his black eyes landing on Thirro.

Don't ask me. Thirro rolled to the side and vomited all the mead in his stomach onto a slave's lap. She gasped. Her eyes watered as she stood. She whimpered and bolted from the command station.

Laconius's lip curled in disgust. "Captain Mina, how do you plan to take him? Few of our flyers are capable of flying in these weather condition even at their peak and in their current state ..."

Mina squirmed in her seat, and red blotched her furry cheeks.

The chief continued. "The traitor escapes tonight, but he will not live much longer. Bring me a plan by morning for the head of the new baby king and the traitor. The humans didn't learn the first time. We'll strike the heart again."

"Yes, chief," Mina said.

Thirro followed Mina out when she left command.

She turned to face him when she'd reached the door of her tent. Her gaze raked over him. "Are you thinking of joining me?"

His tongue slipped over the scar on his lip from her

canine. Definitely not. He forced a confident smile. "I've got a plan to bring down Ferth."

he rain stopped after the third day. It helped
Ferth's riding tremendously, but he still sat on the
horse stiffly. He'd been given the most docile animal in camp,
but he couldn't stop worrying the large horse would buck
her stupid rider off at any moment. At least Darius wasn't
holding the lead rope anymore. Ferth had spent the first
night just trying to stay on, while his horse had followed
Darius's, nose to tail for miles.

He kept expecting Darius to lose patience and lash out as
Laconius surely would have, but three days in, even when
one of the guards had left a cooking pot behind, Darius
remained steady and respectful. Even Keturah would have
been impressed, and that woman was unflappable.

The troops they'd met up with the first night had seemed
duly roused and willing to march north in the rain. They
should have arrived at Titus's camp yesterday. Thoughts of
Suza flittered against Ferth's eyes and his skin.

Keep her safe, he willed the human troops. *Protect her.* He
wondered again if he was doing the wrong thing by leaving

her at the border. He'd be back soon. And with many more soldiers.

"We'll stop there." Darius pointed.

Ferth looked up in surprise. Pale yellow lights flickered on the horizon. They'd previously avoided the small settlements they'd passed.

"It's Zepha. We'll sleep well at the inn and travel by daylight tomorrow."

It was not far past midnight. They'd only been traveling for four hours, but Ferth nearly swooned at the thought of a warm, dry bed and hot food. His clothes were still damp in places, and his feet were wet raisins.

"It's good road now to Mitera. We've done what we can to slip the Draco scouts, and I'd like to pick up the pace."

He thought of his saddle-sore thighs and cringed. "Yes, sir."

"Make sure Rom and Lyko don't come within a mile of the village," Darius said.

Ferth smiled at the use of their names. He'd noticed that few called them anything more than *the wolves*, as if they were nothing more than wolves.

He'd sent them into the woods immediately upon departing Titus's camp. They'd paralleled Ferth's southern route. He tracked them in his mind, but he missed them by his side. Two days ago, they'd snuck into camp and slept at his back, slipping away again before the sunset.

Lyko had traversed this area once before with Cal, and he'd adopted an air of arrogant teacher as he'd led Rom around.

"This is where a stray dog thought it would be a good idea to try and attack me. This is where Cal got his boot caught in a gopher hole. This is where Eio had diarrhea from eating too much washee straw. Titus made him sleep a mile downwind of us. Nastiest tang ..." And just to prove it, Lyko drew up a

memory of the scent and blasted it across their connection.

Rom whined and sat back on his haunches as if slapped.

Ferth gagged as his brain bristled against the onslaught of stink. He pitched forward over his horse, trying to cough out the smell of acid, sulfur, and fermented seeds.

"Are you alright?" The soldier riding next to Ferth asked.

"Yes." He pulled himself together and waved a dismissive hand. "I'm fine. Excuse me."

Lyko's laughter echoed through their connection.

Ferth could almost imagine Cal here sharing his jokes with them too. *If only he had lived.* The wanting was a stone wedged in his ribs.

"How did you share a smell?" Rom asked, recovering enough to stand and sulk past Lyko. The wolves were crossing a field a half-mile to the east of Ferth.

"Never do it again," Ferth said.

"Cal and I figured it out once when we had a disagreement on whether Grandpapi's breath smelled worse than Aunt Elssa's hasii broth."

Ferth laughed, drawing more curious gazes from the soldiers around him. No wonder they kept their distance. He must look like a lunatic.

"And what did you decide?" Rom asked.

"I decided I have an excellent nose." Lyko sniffed. *"And I can share certain smells if they are strong enough in my memory."*

"Not what I meant," Rom said. *"Which smelled worse?"*

"Want me to test them both out on you and let you decide?"

Ferth and Rom both said, *"No,"* at the same time.

"Don't you have any good *scents to share?"* Ferth asked. *"This horse doesn't smell too pleasant ... and neither do I."*

"Let me try," Rom said.

The connection went quiet for a long moment. Ferth realized that the soldiers around him were talking together about their favorite meals and they'd asked him about his. And he hadn't answered. Did they think he was deaf or just exceptionally rude?

He'd opened his mouth to join in the human chatter when the familiar smell of jasmine, salt, and female blood hit him like a knockout punch. He went utterly still at the sudden wave of love and desire. His horse's ears twisted back in worry. It was like Suza was the very air around him, a tormenting breeze. He wanted back in her arms. Ferth's blood warmed at the same time a giant fist smashed his heart.

"That was meaner than lion dung," Lyko said.

"I might not have thought that entirely through." Rom sounded more like a sheep than a wolf.

"She does smell very *good, though,"* Lyko said. *"On the nose. Well done, my young pupil."*

Ferth didn't say a word, drinking in the scent of home and heart as the painful memories slowly dissolved.

Another uncomfortable half-hour atop the rolling mare's back brought the small party to the village. Massive farms spread over the land surrounding a center nucleus of buildings protected by a stone wall.

The wooden gate was closed and locked. Ferth gratefully and not at all gracefully dismounted and clutched the reins tightly. The horse gave him a long-suffering glance.

Darius slammed the iron knocker three times. When no one came, he banged it again.

Visions of wine, meat, and pillows began to fade when finally, a small window slid open.

"Who's it?" A grating voice asked. No face appeared in the hole.

Darius tugged his hood back. "Raja Darius."

"What are you doing here?"

"That business is my own. You must open the gate." He spoke as if it were the law. It probably was.

A round face appeared in the window, the blue eyes roving wildly over the soldiers. A fearful face. The face of a man who lived close to an enemy border at wartime. "I've not seen the Raja Darius before."

Darius put his fist up near the window. The man flinched back, but then laughed awkwardly when he realized Darius was only showing his insignia ring.

"Please lord, forgive my impertinence."

"On the contrary. I would have thought you a fool not to ask. Keep vigilant, my friend. Especially in times like these."

The man paled.

"Open up!" Darius's voice turned sharp and impatient.

So he could harden when he needed to, and every leader needed to turn into a blade sometimes.

The man banged what sounded like his knee against the gate and cursed as he fumbled on the other side of the wood.

Darius clamped his lips, fighting a grin.

When the door swung open, he'd schooled his sharp features into regal seriousness again.

The man stepped out from behind the door, and it was Ferth's turn to bite his lip. The man was nearly as wide as he was tall. His head stopped at Darius's elbow. Ferth eyed a stepping stool behind the gate as the man led them inside.

The door clanged behind them, and Ferth flinched. His wolves were out there in the night, separated. At least they had each other. They were not truly alone.

"Stay hidden," he said to the two sleek forms prowling in the thin woods to the east.

"I smell fawn," Rom said.

"Be ready to walk in the morning."

They ignored the comment.

"Where would your lordship and his party wish to stay?"

The man rubbed his beard nervously. "The miller's home is the nicest, and it's just up this street here."

"The inn will do fine," Darius said.

"Yes, my lord. Excuse me, my lord. All's asleep but me this hour."

He had clearly been sleeping too.

"Don't trouble yourself." Darius adopted a softer tone. "We both know I've arrived unannounced past midnight with seven soldiers."

The man's gaze flickered to bits of weaponry peeking out of cloaks and strapped to saddles. He shuddered. He stopped at a low timber house, indistinguishable from any other building. "Please lord, wait here a moment?"

Darius nodded. He pulled his cloak back slightly and laid a casual palm on his sword hilt, a silent warning.

The short man's eyes bulged. He turned and let himself into the inn.

A moment later, a woman appeared with rags tied in her graying hair and an apron hastily thrown over what looked like a slave's shift, a large breast caught up in one of the apron straps.

"An honor." Her voice was squeaky and high. She managed a graceless curtsy. "Lord Raja."

"Thank you for your hospitality ..." Darius held out the last word, waiting.

"Loama."

"Lady Loama," Darius said with a charming smile.

The woman's cheeks pinked, and she grinned, showing crooked teeth.

Darius didn't blink, but Ferth did.

"I'll head back to the gate," the guard said, eagerly retreating.

"Watch well tonight," Darius said, his voice grave.

"Aye, my lord." The guard did an X around his head—the

sign Ferth had learned humans sometimes used to ward off the evil Draco Sang.

Totally pointless.

When Darius looked back at the innkeeper, her words came out in a rush. "I've got wine and can toast up today's bread. We have a bit of squash pie and pig leg, my lord."

"That would be wonderful. Might we stable our horses?"

"Dearie me." The woman looked at the mounts. She whistled high and loud, and all eight travelers leaned back involuntarily.

A lad not old enough for facial hair appeared, followed by an even younger girl.

"Stable their horses," Loama ordered the boy. "Prepare them rooms," she said to the girl.

"But we've only got the two open." The girl pouted.

The woman turned the girl around, and Ferth pretended not to hear their loud whispers.

"They'll have our rooms and be quick about it."

"I hate the barn."

"Hush your mouth and hurry," Loama hissed.

When she turned back around, a smile plastered her face. "Please come in."

"I thank you, mistress." A small flash of gold went from Darius's hand to hers.

She stared dumbly at her palm for a heartbeat and then tried to put the treasure in a bodice that wasn't there. After jiggling around her chest for a moment, she fisted the coin and darted toward the kitchen.

Darius chuckled good-naturedly when she'd disappeared. "Nothing quite like traveling unannounced in the rurals."

Ferth imagined how different the scene would have gone if he'd been traveling with his father or Queen Mavras—fortunately, he was not. He decided right there in that dimly lit, cramped sitting room that people like Darius and Titus were meant to rule.

Darius, Ferth, and two other soldiers had had to duck as they entered the inn. Ferth's head rubbed against the ceiling. Darius hunched over his shoulders, losing inches. The scent of unwashed bodies, damp clothing, and horse clogged the small room as much as their mass did.

Loama ambled back in, holding a tray of mugs. She set them on the long wooden table against the right side and discreetly opened the window before disappearing.

Ferth had to give the woman credit for producing a warm and delicious midnight meal, although nearly anything would have tasted divine after three wet days of travel.

"If you leave your clothes out, we'll have them laundered by morning," Loama said after they had given liberal compliments on her cooking.

Darius hesitated, then said. "My thanks."

They ended up with four rooms and four beds. The soldiers divided up, and Ferth went with Darius.

The room was small but had a pleasant feel. Ferth sat on the floor, leaving the chair for Darius. While Ferth worked off his boots, the boy brought in a fresh basin of warm water, two towels, and an extra blanket.

"Thank you, young sir," Darius said.

The boy beamed before leaving, closing the door behind him.

Darius strode to the bath and stood with his back to Ferth as he undressed. The man was lean. But it wasn't the wiry muscles that had Ferth staring in shock. It was the raja's skin. Smooth, even, and *scarless*. Unbelievable. How could a grown man look as fresh and pure as a newborn—before their branding? Ferth's fingers hesitated on his shirt. His first reaction was to hide his skin and the story of violence and foreignness it told. But he was so dirty he was starting to itch. And Darius called his wolves by name. He treated Ferth with respect. Ferth didn't want to ruin that. He knew it was a risk, but when Darius stepped away from the basin, Ferth lifted his shirt over his head.

"Sorry I've dirtied the water." Darius dried off with one of the towels.

"I'm going to make it worse." Ferth tucked the letters for Mira safely in his boot before he picked up Darius's pile of clothes and added his own, then dropped the stinking mass outside the door.

Ferth scrubbed at grit and grime with a soapy cloth, trying to ignore the raja in the room. He washed over the Draco brand on his chest, the healing pink scars on his arms and ribs, the old gashes on his feet and calves from the water Draco in Azure Lake. Most of the nicks and callouses he couldn't identify, but he'd never forget that day last year when his father threw him into the cold lake after he'd failed to transform.

"I was going to see if I could talk to you about the possibility of peace negotiations with Skotar, but after looking at your back, it appears that avenue might be a dead end."

Ferth glanced at where Darius sat across the room, towel around his waist, arms folded and face grim. Ferth didn't need to reply.

Darius's tone turned warm and friendly. "And I can see that I don't ever want to face you in a fight."

Ferth's worry eased. The man was not going to reject him. "I don't know. I'd say you're the one to fear. It appears no one's been able to lay so much as a scratch on you. You're invincible."

Darius laughed, all the lean muscles in his torso ripping and shifting. He ran a hand through his ear-length hair, sweeping it back. "I don't mind leaving it at that."

Ferth held out the soapy cloth. "Some of those marks on

my back are still healing, and I can't reach. I've been ordered to keep them clean, but I don't want to ask our hostess and give her nightmares."

Darius stood and took the cloth.

Ferth turned away, exposing his punishment entirely. Stripes were a symbol of shame in Skotar, but here, somehow, they'd lost their power of humiliation.

Darius pressed the warm rag into Ferth's tired back. "You don't have to tell me." His tone was soft. "But I can't help but ask."

"My father whipped me after I let my slave escape to Elysium."

"Your fa …" His voice dissolved.

Ferth braced himself against the sting and the flare of pain as the scrubbing intensified. Darius definitely did a thorough job.

"Raoul is right. The Dragon must be killed," Darius said. "End his poisonous influence on the Draco Sang."

Ferth frowned at dirty water. *Not another person who thought Nogard might be alive.* Where did these notions come from? Apparently the idiot, Raoul.

"People like you and Titus and the others have proven that another path can be taken," Darius said. "We must teach the rest of your people to—"

"The problem is not Nogard. The problem is from birth Dracos are taught to surrender to their blood, not conquer it. How could you possibly change the attitude of an entire stubborn race?"

"By hunting down Nogard. The royal scholar Raoul has studied the histories and the winds. He has made it clear to me. We must kill Nogard, the source."

Ferth was too tired to argue irrationalities. He grit his teeth as Darius ground the rag into his wounds.

Darius didn't speak again until he dropped the cloth into the murky water. "I think they're clean."

Ferth reached for the dry towel and sent a twisted smile over his stinging shoulder. "I should think so."

"Sorry. My wife says I lack the healer's touch."

"Trust me, the healers are worse."

Darius let out a low chuckle. He turned and picked up the thin quilt the boy had brought, eying it with a frown before spreading it out on the wood floor.

Ferth dried quickly and wrapped the towel around his waist. "Thank you for making my bed."

"No, you take the—"

Ferth snorted and dropped onto the floor. "Good night, highness." With his weapons laid out at his side, he was asleep within seconds despite the cold hard surface. He was used to it from his time sleeping on the floor as a hatchling in Skotar.

Come sunrise, their clothes were indeed washed and dried and folded outside their door. The garments smelled of wood smoke and lavender.

When they shuffled into the main room, they found eight cloaks hanging by a roaring hearth fire. Loama bustled out of the kitchen. She wore the same nightgown, apron, and hair rags. The flour dusting her hands and stomach was new and so were the dark circles under her eyes. She'd worked all night. Queen Mavras or Laconius would have demanded such behavior by fear and force. Darius had done no such thing, but still he received the same worshipful treatment. Better service, really. People responded to respect.

Rested, dry, and well-fed, and Darius out another gold coin, they mounted and left through the southern gate.

As soon as they were outside of the fields and farms, Ferth turned his horse toward a small patch of trees. The horse refused, shying closer to the pack instead, ears twitching.

"At least stop," Ferth said, annoyed. He pulled back on the reins. The horse danced, but kept walking next to Darius's gelding.

Darius stopped his mount, bringing Ferth's to a halt as well.

"Many thanks, lordship." Ferth's voice dripped sarcasm. He leaped from his saddle, landing hard before rushing toward the thicket. Two wolves lunged out of the greenery to greet him. He dropped to his knees, throwing his arms out. Twin beasts struck his chest. He pushed back, barely maintaining his balance, his heart leaping. He dug his hands into thick fur, heedless of their stink getting into his clean clothes. He massaged their narrow heads and sinewy necks. Being human, he realized, meant his soul walked outside his body. The thought wasn't entirely unpleasant.

*E*very slave in the camp, nearly a hundred, except the
healers and the cooks—they left them to work—
knelt in the cold dirt. The first signs of impending autumn
frosted the ground. Dawn painted the slaves' fearful faces in
orange and silver.

Thirro and a dozen Dracos paced the lines of slaves. They
snapped whips in the air and across the ground. Thirro's
healing wounds were a constant throbbing itch. The
poisoned mead had nearly worked its way out of his guts.
His strength was returning with angry vengeance.

Jade had figured it out. The slaves would have gotten
away with their sedition and murder—two Dracos had died
from the poison—if it hadn't been for that bootlicker. Thirro
thought Laconius should have been more concerned with
how Jade knew enough about the poison Lussa—named for
the rebellious slave who first created it years ago from bacaroot—to recognize the touch of it that laced their mead and
less eager to congratulation the upstart. Jade was clearly
suspect. But no, she was currently enjoying a private meeting
with the chief so he could praise her cunning. Thirro

snapped his whip against the nearest slave's shoulder with a satisfying crack.

Captain Mina marched in front of the rows of kneeling slaves. Her spotted fur stuck up at odd angles on her head. Red framed her dark eyes and pursed mouth. She wore a coat, further display of the toll her body had taken, in battle and then from the mead.

"I'm too tired to play this game." Captain Mina flipped a long dagger in her palm. "Where did the poison come from? Which of you snakes thought it would be a good idea to bite the hand that feeds you?"

Every slave knelt as if stone, looking down, except one. A girl on the front row flinched, and Mina pounced. She grabbed the girl by her pale braid and jerked her forward. The slave screamed, and the man kneeling next to her leaped to his feet. His muscular arms reached for the girl. He froze when Mina held the dagger tip to the girl's throat, drawing blood.

"Stop," he said. "Let Pearl go. She didn't do anything. She doesn't know anything. Please."

Mina studied the man. Then she ripped Pearl's sleeve back, revealing a faded slave brand. Mina sliced an *X* through it. Marking Pearl as the worst kind of slave. *Rebellious.*

The man's eyes hardened, and his jaw flickered. He looked about ten years older than Pearl. Where his coloring was warm bronze, she was cold silver.

Mina tossed the girl back, and the man caught her. He cradled her against his broad chest. They were dirty and ragged, but standing together. It was beautiful the way he held her, shielded her—and it infuriated Thirro.

He stepped forward and let his whip fly. Pearl arched her back as the tip struck her side. "Kneel, slave."

Thirro ignored the woman as she dropped to the dirt, her hand wrapped around her bleeding forearm. Instead, he focused on the flaming rage in the dark eyes of the man. The cords in his unbowed neck stuck out.

Thirro lashed the whip across his chest. The man's arm jumped up with shocking speed, as if to catch the leather, but he stopped midair, slowly lowering his hand instead.

Adrenaline flared in Thirro, lighting his limbs with warm fire. "Careful, slave." He kept his voice velvety, taunting.

"What's your name?" Mina asked.

He didn't hesitate. "Kenji." His deep round voice grated on Thirro.

"Bind him," Mina said.

Kenji straightened his spine and put his hands behind his back. He lifted his chin and looked down his nose at Thirro. Anger ripened in Thirro. The pride in the slave's eyes were like arrows pricking Thirro's ego. Kenji's wrists bled as Thirro cinched the rope tight. Kenji made no protest. Thirro finished his knot and then kicked the slave in the side of the knee. His legs gave out, and Kenji hit the dirt.

Much better.

Thirro gripped the back of Kenji's shirt and dragged him forward. The knit tunic tore under the strain, revealing dark skin already peppered with scars. The fabric hung around his bound hands. Thirro panted with exertion as he pulled the heavy man to a kneeling position beside Mina.

Mina ran her fingers, like a lover's caress, along Kenji's scars, over his chest, across his neck. The goosebumps raising across his skin was Kenji's only response.

"Tell me about the poison, Kenji," Mina purred. "Where did you get it? Who made it?"

Kenji stared off into the gray sky, his lips a hard line.

Mina circled the kneeling man, his lifted head coming to her ribs. The captain's face lowered. Kenji turned to stone as she kissed the base of his neck. Her tongue trailed up taut muscles. Clawed hands curved over his shoulders. Mina's head jerked back suddenly, and Kenji bellowed like a volcano erupting. His raw cry of pain shook birds from the trees and rattled down Thirro's bones.

Mina straightened her spine, eyes flashing. Thirro blinked as heat surged through his veins. The tip of Kenji's right ear was wedged between Mina's canines. Blood coursed down the slave's neck and over his trembling shoulders. With a flick of her long tongue, she spit the chunk of flesh into the dirt.

Pearl fainted. She hit the ground with a *thud*. The other slaves didn't move. Mina wiped the gore from her lips with her sleeve. Thirro cringed in disgust as she eyed the rest of his ear. Kenji's face turned to ash, but he kept his mouth shut with impressive determination. No human should be that strong.

From the back row, a slave yelled out. Thirro jerked his neck to see a slave with a hunched back and white hair stand up. The man shuffled forward.

"He can't say anything because he doesn't know anything," the old slave said. "Kenji's just a brick of muscles. Not much in his brain. Don't waste your time damaging such a valuable workhorse." The man picked his way forward.

Kenji's stony expression melted into horror. He mutely shook his head. The old man smiled at Kenji. A moment seemed to pass between them that Thirro could not understand, and then the older slave walked up to Mina and stopped two feet from her. His wrinkly face stared at her with pure spite and hatred.

"I poisoned the mead, and I'd do it again." He spit. A wet glob landed in Mina's eye.

With trembling fingers, she wiped off the mucus. Her voice was icy, promising a painful death. "You must have had help."

"Why? Because you couldn't have done it on your own?

These people didn't even know about it." He motioned to the slaves. "Just because you're too stupid to operate doesn't mean I am."

"Where did you get it?" Mina voice quivered with rage.

"You make us pick up your poop. It's about time you ate it."

Thirro almost snorted at the lie. It was *almost* funny. Such foolish bravery. This slave didn't look any more likely to talk than Kenji, even if Mina bit his whole ear off.

With a flash of steel, Mina's knife slashed the slave's throat. The man crumpled, dead before he hit the ground.

Kenji's head fell to his chest, and his shoulders caved inward.

Fury rose like steam in Thirro's chest. He wanted to hit Mina and whip sense into her. A dead slave could not talk. His hand came up of its own accord. He couldn't lash out at his foolish captain, so instead he brought his whip down on Kenji's stooped back. The slave slipped forward onto the ground, resting his unbitten ear on the frozen dirt. Tears slid down his brown cheeks. Not so tough after all. Kenji's eyes were fixed on the dead man.

"Back to work, slaves," Mina said. "Your rations are cut in half."

Good. The Dracos were nearly out of food.

Time to replenish in Elysium.

Mina wobbled a bit as she strode away, still not completely recovered.

As one, the ashen-faced slaves surged to their feet. Pearl had revived. She darted forward, her fingers working furiously at the knots turning Kenji's palms purple.

Finally freed, Kenji rubbed at his hands and wrists. Keeping his head down like a proper slave, he wrapped his torn tunic around the dead man like a blanket. He scooped him up. Without looking at Thirro, he carried the old slave away. Pearl followed.

The morning sun burned across camp, defeating the frost and the chill. Summer was short in Skotar, and the north wind seemed to whisper that winter was coming early this year. It would not be long before the snow returned, and the sun could no longer conquer the cold.

Thirro would leave tomorrow to kill the king and the traitor. This season, he would winter in warm Elysium. Jade sauntered up, interrupting his pleasant thoughts.

"We're meeting now," she said.

"You've been demoted to messenger," Thirro said. "Suits you."

"If you don't want to come, fine with me. I will happily find another flyer for the mission."

He was one of nine warriors striking Mitera. Three groups of three, each with a flyer able to take to the air, a striker for fighting and sneaking about, and a carrier to haul equipment. He didn't know if he wanted to be grouped with Jade or not. He'd enjoy holding her as he flew, if she would shut her dumb mouth.

Thirro scowled.

"Pretty." She whirled and sauntered to the command tent.

He might *accidentally* drop her in the river.

He and Commander Jade were not grouped together.

Jade was the striker paired with a raven flyer and an ape carrier. As the strongest flyer, Thirro was assigned Mordick as his carrier. Thirro scowled at the heavyset ram he'd have to heft over rivers and gorges. He resented being used as a pack animal. He almost protested, but managed to bite his tongue, lest he appear weak.

"We will assume the traitor will be in Mitera." Laconius clenched his fist over the map spread on the table. "Skotar's Arrow is the commander of this mission."

Thirro kept his face serious, but inside, he exploded with pride. They didn't use that name nearly enough. And finally, *finally* he was the leader, and he'd prove that flyers were anything but soft. Even his unit commander, the upstart, had to bow to him on this mission. Jade did not look happy about it. Her hand went to her waist where he'd sliced her. He winked.

"Lead well, Commander Thirro," Laconius said.

Those words on the chief's lips were sweet music to his soul. "Yes, chief."

"The Lammas holiday is in nine days." Laconius had taken to wearing only a baldric with knives over his leathery chest, showing the puckered red scar where he'd been struck by a fallen Draco Sang abomination. The bullish chief displayed the wound like a badge and a promise of retribution. "You will strike at the royal ball. The traitor will likely be there, the king most certainly, and several rajas, at least. The king is your top target, then the traitor, then the rajas, then as many others as you can take out. When those humans come out to celebrate, I want them to find blood flowing instead of wine."

Thirro's pulse accelerated with the bull's words. He salivated. "It shall be my pleasure, chief."

"You will bring great honor to our Queen Mavras."

Thirro wondered if he imagined the mocking emphasis the chief put on the words *our queen*. Mavras was the only one in the world with more power than Laconius. How much longer would the bull be content as second?

"You will fly at dusk." Laconius brought his fist to his head, circling his crown. Then with a wave of his hand, he spread the blessing out over the travelers. Thirro and the others responded in kind.

After a nap and a meal, Thirro gathered with his crew in the darkness outside of camp. Five additional flyers joined them to assist in the flight over the Rugit. They walked southeast in silence. Near the river, but still in the cover of trees, Thirro made the motion to fly. Jade rose with her assigned raven flyer, Gavriel. The other flyers set to work hefting the strikers and carriers. No sense for Thirro and his pelican companion to wear themselves out when they had fresh wings to do the dirty work.

With a terse nod to the others, Thirro gracefully flapped into the sky. Up and up he soared until the river was a thin line. The heavy-laden flyers slackened behind as Thirro led them into Elysium.

A mile south, Thirro dropped down, landing where previous flyers had deposited their gear. At intervals, the other flyers landed around him.

Jade and Gavriel landed first. Gavriel had carried her easily in his arms, and he set the petite fighter down gently. Thirro balked at the raven treating the dangerous jackal with anything resembling tenderness. Fool.

"Thank you, Gavriel. I love doing that." Jade said it as if she'd had plenty of experience.

"My pleasure." Gavriel said it with a hint of seduction.

Thirro scowled at them.

After a bone-crushing thud, Mordick scrambled away from the panting osprey Draco who'd carried him over the river. "Bleeding skies!" Mordick said. "Do you mean to kill me?"

"I told you to hold still," the flyer said. "You nearly killed yourself. And you've strained my wing with all your thrashing."

"Good." Mordick's ram horns trembled, and his round face scrunched up like a petulant child.

"Good luck with that one, Commander Thirro. And good riddance." The Draco didn't wait for the others before he took off to the north, back to Skotar.

This was going to be a long journey.

TWENTY-FIVE - SOLITUDE
SUZA

*S*uza's legs dangled off the edge of the wooden platform. From the height of the watchtower, she could see the smoke from the Draco Sang camp across the river rise into the cerulean sky. Xandra scouted from the trees west of the Draco Camp. The hawk sent Suza chilling reports of rapid battle preparations.

All the storm clouds had fled, and the Rugit River lost strength every hour as the rain swells diminished. The sun was well in the sky. Uriah had completely missed the sunrise. Apparently, he was not coming.

She got to her feet and dusted off her leggings as if she could brush away her mounting irritation. She hadn't put on a dress since that first day in her fighting pants. She might never again. When she made for the ladder, a watchman stepped up and held out a hand. She ignored it as her foot found the first rung. She went down the ladder and marched along the neat rows until she came to Uriah's tent. And Imanna's—the mysterious girl who'd wormed her way not just into his tent, but into his heart.

Suza pulled back the door. She paused as her eyes

adjusted to the shade. Uriah and Imanna didn't so much as shift their focus off each other. Uriah shuffled forward, shirt-less—that seemed unnecessary. His broad shoulders and thick muscles glistened with sweat. He held his practice sword poised for a strike. Imanna brought her wooden short swords forward defensively. Although she carried two blades, they were only a third of the length and width of Uriah's massive weapon. Suza wished she had known Uriah's hewan, Poe. At the moment, he greatly resembled a bear compared to the petite woman.

Imanna looked even smaller without her usual vests and cloak. She wore only tight-fitting leggings and a cotton blouse that looked like they might have fit Suza when she was eleven. As always, Imanna wore a scarf over her head. It was an odd fashion.

Suza opened her mouth to interrupt, but held her breath when Imanna darted forward. Uriah's sword greeted her first, but with all her momentum, she knocked it aside, whirling closer. His hand came up as if to punch her in the side of the face, but he stopped his strike, letting her break his defense.

He huffed as her blunt blade slapped his side. A large palm wrapped her ribs. He pushed her back outside of her sword range, and then withdrew his hand from her belly. Panting and shuffling feet echoed.

As far as Suza could tell, Uriah let the woman have her way. However, Imanna still struck with surprising speed and skill. She held the blades with confidence.

Suza frowned. Since abandoning her Draco Sang training and becoming a slave over three years ago, she'd only had access to knives and daggers. She envied Imanna's prowess with the battle weapons. Suza scowled. She was going to have to ask Imanna to teach her.

Uriah's sword struck Imanna's arm, but it had little power behind it.

She snarled and darted forward. "You're going too easy!"

Her wooden blade hit his hand, and he dropped his sword. "Ouch."

Before she could strike again, his hands flew forward. He gripped her wrists, and her swords clattered to the ground. She twisted her arms. When Uriah let go, red and white blotches covered her tan hands. The sprinkling of freckles stood out. Imanna struck, punching Uriah in the chest with considerable force. He grunted and wrapped his arms around her, pinning her arms to her sides. In an embrace he would have never used against a foe, he lifted her completely off the ground.

Chests pressed together, their eyes locked. Uriah's gaze drifted to Imanna's pouting red lips with an emotion decidedly not for an enemy.

"Hello," Suza said, her voice too high.

Two heads jerked toward the sound. Imanna's mouth carved into a cocky smile.

Uriah set the woman down and strode forward. His eyes burned with a living fire Suza had never seen in her brother. The spark illuminated his whole face and shined out as if he could light the world. He'd never looked so handsome.

Suza's anger dissolved. She was happy for him, even if she didn't see what was so great about the tiny stranger, and even if the man she dreamed about was probably to Mitera by now. She would be happy for her brother. She would.

"Hello, little sister." His goofy grin fell. "Oh. I'm sorry. The sunrise."

"It's fine." She waved a hand. "You were busy."

"It's my fault," Imanna said.

Yes, it was.

"I've never trained with anyone so skilled. I have much to learn from him." She flicked her long lashes up at him.

Ugh.

Suza couldn't deny the woman's beauty. For one fickle heartbeat, she was glad Ferth wasn't here, and that Imanna had trained those impossibly pale eyes on Uriah and not Ferth. How could a man resist?

She'd be even more beautiful if she got rid of that head rag.

Uriah picked up his tunic and started to put it on. "I lost track of time."

"I see," Suza said.

A touch of pink dusted his cheeks. "Come with us to breakfast?"

Us? No thanks. She was in no mood to play third fiddle to their love-addled conversation. "I have a meeting with Captain Titus and Commander Oscar. Xandra completed the morning scouting." She wasn't looking forward to telling them the bad news.

"Dinner then?"

She paused, and as if Uriah could sense her thoughts, he said, "Imanna is working with the healers this evening. Tomark will be with her. I can bring food to you?"

Yes, she desperately wanted to spend time with him. "Fine."

His mouth carved up in a crescent, and some of her childish resentments melted away.

Suza excused herself and darted to the dining hall. She shoveled down breakfast as quickly as she could and sprinted out before Uriah and Imanna appeared. In her rush, she bumped into a broad soldier outside the door.

"Excuse me." She rebounded off his solid chest.

A strong hand snaked around her waist, steadying her. "My fault, my lady." Warmth penetrated her side as he let his fingers linger on her abdomen. "Have you got your feet?"

She stepped back, ruffled by the contact, and looked the man in the face.

He was handsome, with russet eyes and a wide mouth. "Guap, is it?" she asked, recognizing one of the highly celebrated swordsmen in camp.

He smiled, clearly pleased. "At your service ..." He held out the ending, waiting for her name.

"Excuse me again. I was rushing to my meeting. I must go."

He opened his mouth, but she didn't wait to hear what he had to say.

She wasn't sure what it was, maybe the trousers, maybe the influx of thousands of soldiers increasing the ratio of men to women, maybe it was the look she got on her face when she thought of Ferth—which was often—but suddenly men charmed her at every corner. It was a strange experience after being a slave. Here she could hold her head high, but the old fear of being taken by force still lay dormant in her belly. Surprisingly, the thought of Ferth, her old master, was her biggest comfort. Ferth, a powerful and cunning Draco Sang, had been her savior, her escape, her protection. His goodness, despite growing up surrounded by greed and lust, gave her hope.

He'd only been gone four days. She chided herself as images of Ferth crept into her thoughts—again. She knew the war effort needed her here, but her heart gave her grief about it at nearly every moment. Her fingers touched the soft smile on her lips, remembering the feel of his hungry kiss. She pictured his return. He would run to her, his beautiful wolves following close behind. He would gather her in his arms and kiss her. He wouldn't be afraid to love her anymore. He would never let her go.

Suza stopped at the front of the command tent. Xandra landed on the thick leather band Titus had given her to protect her forearm. She ran a hand over her hewan's downy head. She thrust thoughts of Ferth from her mind as she prepared to tell Captain Titus that Skotar had begun preparations for their next attack.

TWENTY-SIX - WALKING
THIRRO

*I*rritation and pain rippled across Thirro's wing as it caught on a branch he hadn't seen in the darkness. He hated walking. He tucked his wings in tighter on his back as he plowed through the trees. Progress was slow marching on the ground. After three days of travel, they were not halfway to Mitera. Keeping this group secret was only going to become harder and slower. He could be sending an arrow through the king's neck tomorrow night if he took to the skies. He pushed the thought away before it took root. He wanted a hot meal and a bed. Dara, the only one in the group he cared to talk to, walked silently in his wake.

"I'm going to scout," he said over his shoulder. Finding a break in the trees, he shot into the sky.

They traveled south on a westernly route, hugging the sparsely populated foothills of the Seraf Mountains. With an hour until first light, he glided lazily over the terrain. A raccoon caught his eye, but he let it go. He had bigger game to hunt tonight.

He widened his range, flying east over the flatlands. A farmhouse came into view, a black silhouette against the gray. Lovely. He flew closer. The lonely home stood at least a half-mile from the nearest neighbor. Two-story, but not so large as to be difficult to overtake. Perfect. He calculated two or three humans to deal with. He glanced at the large fields and added a few slaves to the count. Not much of a fight. He imagined it took at least two strong women to run the estate. He licked his chapped lips. He wasn't quite so tired as he flew back to his soldiers. He dropped out of the sky, landing a foot in front of Dara. She reeled back at his sudden appearance. Amusement pulsed in his belly.

"You forgot to look up," he said.

The darkness blurred the edges of her scowl. "Where will we make camp?"

"I've got the perfect place."

"I hope it's close."

They reached the edge of the fields minutes before the sun.

Jade slipped up next to Thirro as they surveyed the scene. "The humans are up. Look at the smoke."

"I know that."

"I can slip in and get food without them seeing me."

"Good for you."

He glanced down at her when she didn't respond. Her purple eyes iced over.

Thirro faced the group. "Mordick, you and Gavriel go around back. Jade, you can scout the fields and make sure we don't miss anyone."

Jade darted away before he finished his orders.

"The rest of us will knock at the front door. Kill the men. Bind the women."

"Yes, sir."

No gate or wall barred their way to the house as he led them forward. With a whine, weapons slipped free of their restraints.

Sword in hand, Thirro pounded on the wooden door. Feet shuffled inside and then a low voice said, "Who's there?"

"Travelers, sir. We're headed north to join the armies." He tried to adopt the sharp accent of the humans. "We've got an injured lad and would beg some broth."

The door swung open. Light flooded out, illuminating six bloodthirsty Dracos. Thirro smiled.

The man's jaw dropped, and his face blanched.

"Hello, papi," Dara said.

His eyes bulged. Her dagger flashed, and he dropped to the ground with a stunned thud. He hadn't even moved.

Too easy.

Thirro stepped over the body and into the room. A woman stood frozen at the hearth. Alluring scents of cinnamon porridge wafted from the kettle near her fingers.

Thirro jerked toward a flash of movement and brought his sword up just in time to block an axe aimed at his head. His next move ended the young man's life.

Jade appeared in the open door. She held a bloody dagger lightly between her fingers. "There were two in the field and one in the barn."

And she was already back here? "Well done," Thirro forced himself to say.

"It was menial, trivial, and pathetic. They didn't even see me before I took their lives." She spoke with callous pride, but Thirro detected a hint of disgust—*weakness*.

The woman's eyes rolled back as she fainted. She hit the floor. Thirro strode over. He grabbed a handful of fabric and heaved her up. Dara approached and slapped the woman across the cheek with the back of her paw.

She gained consciousness with a jerk and a grimace. "What do you want?"

"That porridge is a good place to start." He set her on her feet.

"Three empty bedrooms upstairs," Gasson, an ape Draco, said as he came down the stairs.

Six mismatched chairs surrounded a worn table. Jade sat first, her gaze unfocused. She twirled her stained Dracosteel blade in her hand. Flip. Catch. Flip. Catch. Flip. Thirro's hand came down, slamming her wrist to the table. The knife clattered against a glass, breaking it. Jade jerked to her feet, drawing another blade with her free hand. She pressed it against Thirro's groin.

Gavriel, a foot behind Jade, drew his sword, but did nothing else with it. Unclear whose aid he would come to. Unhelpful. The others watched as statues.

Thirro's insides had turned to brittle ice at the threat of Dracosteel to his tender parts, but he forced a nonchalant *tsk*. "So touchy." He lifted his hand off her wrist and stepped back. "No bloody blades at breakfast. Clean your steel and put it away."

Spit flecked Jade's lips as she snarled at him, but she obeyed.

Pulse pounding, he inhaled a steadying breath as he padded to the head of the table and perched on a stool. He motioned the human forward. Silent tears streamed down the woman's ashen face as she served the nine Dracos crowded into her home. Thirro felt a handful of soft flesh when she poured his drink. He pulled her into his lap, checking the size of her hips after she refilled his bowl. With his hunger satisfied, other needs pressed.

Dara scowled at him from across the table. Maybe he should have left another human alive for her to play with.

Jade and the others focused intently on their food. She rubbed at her wrist.

Hand firmly on the woman's waist, Thirro shifted, preparing to stand.

"Woman," Jade said. "I noticed whiskey in the kitchen. Do

you mean to keep it from us?"

"I didn't. I don't have any liquors. All I have is yours." The woman's voice rang clear, but Thirro could feel her racing heart beneath his palm.

"Show me." The jackal rose from her seat, her face hard.

"Yes, ma'am." The woman wormed her way out of Thirro's grasp.

He let her go. His lust could wait for whiskey. Jade disappeared behind the human. Thirro ripped off a chunk of cheese from the table. A smile formed on his lips as he popped it in his mouth. *Sweet Elysium is ours.*

A moment later Jade appeared with a tray of honey cakes. "I knew she was holding out on us." She wedged one in her canines before dropping the rest on the table.

The cakes disappeared before the tray stopped wobbling.

"Where is she now?" Thirro asked. "You left her alone?"

Jade shrugged. "She promised to bring out sweet wine."

Thirro held up a fist and the group silenced, as did the house. He knocked over his stool when he jerked to his feet. He stormed into the kitchen and howled.

The dead woman lay pitched forward over the table. The tip of a kitchen knife stuck out of her back. Blood coated her dress and soaked into the wooden countertop. Lifeless eyes stared at Thirro.

"Jade!" His booming call reverberated through the house.

The jackal padded into the kitchen and stopped short when she saw the corpse. "I didn't think she had it in her."

His eyes narrowed. "That would have taken a lot to drive a dull knife so deep. And silently. And in exactly the right spot. Seems unlikely, doesn't it?"

"Since the alternative was your bed, it isn't that surprising."

Thirro's hand twitched to strike, betraying his anger. He itched to smash the innocent look off Jade's annoyingly pretty face. She glanced down at his fists, and her hands dropped to her swords.

"You need me on this mission."

"For now." He took a deep steadying breath and marched back into the main room.

"The woman's dead," Thirro said to the group. "Saved us the trouble. Let's get some rest. We'll move again a half-hour before sunset. Take what you want, but leave the biggest bed for me."

Jade headed for the door.

"Where are you going?"

"I'll sleep outside, keep an eye and an ear out for visitors."

Thirro should have thought of that. His frustration made him foolish. He looked at Mordick, planning to stick Jade with the irritating ram for the day.

"I'll join her," said Gavriel, the sleek raven Draco. As he glided toward the door, Jade's face softened, betraying her youth.

They were outside with the door shut behind them before Thirro could protest.

Mordick and Gasson jockeyed on the stairs, eager to claim the remaining beds. The other three Dracos stretched out on the floor. Exhaustion rolled over Thirro.

Dara hadn't moved from the table. She picked at what little remained of the food.

Thirro reached out a hand to her. "Come on. It's been a long night. Let's get you to bed."

She glowered at him, flicking her eyes toward the kitchen.

He smiled as warmly and seductively as he could muster. "I'll sleep on the floor."

Dara snorted at the obvious lie, but she accepted his hand, and he pulled her to her feet. His arm went around her hips as he led her upstairs.

TWENTY-SEVEN - PROMISED
SUZA

*T*omark stood guard out front of the tent Uriah and Imanna shared. He smiled good-naturedly at Suza as she approached.

"Uriah still here?"

"Yes, but he's—"

She brushed past him and strode into the tent. A partition divided the tent, but two forms slept on Uriah's bed this morning. Uriah's body carved around the girl, cradling her.

"Good morning." Suza's voice rang out like a bell, louder than the jealousy and irritation clanging around her skull.

Two heads jerked up.

She even slept with that head wrap?

"Tomark has one job," Uriah said.

"I'm not a threat."

"You look plenty threatening right now."

She relaxed her face, trying to hide her annoyance. She was happy for them, but she felt isolated and missed Ferth. And she had to ask Imanna a favor. She was not particularly happy this morning.

"Are you going to get up?" Staying all snuggled together like kittens was just rude.

"I'm not dressed," Uriah said.

Imanna giggled, an inch of her bare shoulder visible.

Heat rushed Suza's face. She whirled around and strode outside. Tomark gave her a mildly amused glance as she waited at his side.

A moment later Uriah threw open the door, shirtless and still buttoning his pants. The Draco brand on his pectoral had faded to a dull white: *GU02281*. "I haven't missed a meeting, have I?"

"No. I came to speak to Imanna."

"Do I need to be worried?"

Suza rolled her eyes and ducked into the tent. Uriah followed.

Imanna sat lacing fine leather boots. Her dark hair rolled over her shoulder in a curly mass. Perky pale eyes met Suza. In the light they cast a violet tint. Enchanting.

"Hello, Imanna."

"Good morning, Suza." The words were formal.

Uriah folded his arms and settled into a seat. He watched with increasing interest and a hint of anxiety.

Imanna looked on impassively, her face blank.

Suza hadn't been particularly warm to Imanna over the past days. She could ask—would rather ask—Zemira for extra training, but Suza was doing this for her brother. She took a deep breath. "You've impressed me with your skill with the short sword, and your knowledge is greater than mine. I am learning, but this army doesn't have many who are experts with the twin short swords." They were much more popular in Skotar than Elysium and a particular favorite among the female Dracos. "I was wondering, hoping, that you would be willing to teach me. If you have the time, of course."

Uriah's mouth fell open.

Surprise flickered over Imanna's pretty face, and then her expression opened. Her welcoming smile relaxed Suza's tension.

"Of course. I'd love to."

She checked Imanna's face for signs of mockery.

"I'd like a partner to practice with. Uriah's no good with a short sword anyway."

He snorted in disagreement.

"Really, dear. You won't even fight back. You've turned all soft."

Muscles ripped under his shirt as he flexed.

Suza snorted out a laugh.

"This one will fight me." Imanna flicked her gaze at Suza.

True.

"Bring us breakfast, my big bear?" Imanna asked in a trilling voice.

Suza recoiled at the bear reference, but Uriah didn't even flinch.

"Yes, my lady." He stood and kissed Imanna. "Don't kill each other while I'm gone."

She smacked his butt. "You'd better hurry."

Suza was glad to see him go. He could take his time. She'd come here to work, not watch them flirt.

"Let's see your weapons." The playfulness was gone from Imanna's voice. Good.

Suza handed over the twin swords she'd stolen from Skotar when she'd escaped. Imanna checked the Dracosteel blades and twisted them experimentally before handing them back with a satisfied nod.

"First thing every morning we'll do the routine sets. Once you've memorized them, we'll pick up speed. Follow me." Imanna's body shifted, and she bent her legs. Her wrist and arm rolled as she drew her blade around.

Suza grinned as she mirrored the motions.

An hour later, she left Uriah's tent, sweaty, smiling, and sore. She'd picked up the routines quickly. They reminded her of lessons years ago as an underling. Every morning, Imanna increased the speed and complexity. For three days, Suza lunged and struck and sliced at nothing but air. On the fourth day, Imanna broke routine.

"Switch me," Imanna said. She held out one practice sword.

Suza gripped the blunt wood.

"Engagement."

Uriah laid aside his papers and turned his full attention on the women. At his feet, Kira lifted her head.

Imanna set their four real blades on the table. She took off her weapons belt and laid that down. She stood in front of Suza in leggings, a loose blouse, and her headscarf. She held up empty hands in defense. "Kill me."

Suza, inches taller and stones heavier, took a tentative step forward. With half strength, she threw the blade up at Imanna's hands. Imanna gripped her wrist and twisted. Painfully. Suza struck with her free hand, but Imanna's knee connected with her elbow. Painfully.

Uriah chuckled.

Suza jumped back and shook out her sore limbs. This time when she attacked, it was with a furrowed brow and full strength. She jabbed, but couldn't make contact. Imanna danced out of reach.

"Cut me," Imanna said. "I'm weaponless. Cut me."

When Suza attacked again, Imanna kicked the sword out of her hand. Imanna picked up the practice blade. "Defend yourself." She spoke as she moved. "Distract with the blade, attack with your other hand." A fist punched Suza's belly. "Fast strike when the enemy reacts." The wood scratched Suza's neck. "Dead." Imanna's voice held no gloat.

She was good. "Again," Suza said.

Suza blocked Imanna's kick to her ribs.

"Good." Imanna closed the gap. "Short sword fighting is close, personal. Contact can help you, especially if your attacker is bigger." Imanna held the blunt tip against Suza's stomach.

Suza panted.

Imanna stepped back and tossed Suza another practice sword. As they engaged, Imanna often stopped the attack and shifted Suza's hands or feet, or to demonstrate a move in slow motion.

"How do you know all this?"

"I've spent countless hours playing with blades."

"Where? When? Who taught you?" Suza hadn't been able to piece this girl's past together. The answers were not forthcoming this morning either.

"Ready?" Imanna didn't wait. She attacked.

Suza blocked the first strike. Imanna's hand clamped around her neck. Suza twisted, groping for breath and freedom. Her sword fell. Imanna's blade came toward her face. Her palm wrapped around Imanna's. Brute strength was one advantage she had on Imanna. She forced the smaller woman's weapon away from her face. Imanna's practice sword inched toward her own neck. Imanna shoved up. The tip caught on her headband and the silk slid off.

Imanna's scarred forehead was inches from Suza's eyes. She blinked, bringing the brand into focus. *The royal brand.*

Imanna disengaged with a shove. She whirled around and grabbed her scarf.

"What? What is that? Why is that on your face?" Suza's voice was as sharp as their short swords.

Imanna sighed as if she were suddenly weary to her very bones. She stopped rushing for her scarf and turned her mottled forehead back to face Suza.

Uriah had leapt to Imanna's side. He stood angled in front, as if protecting her.

From me? Suza stood in frozen confusion. "That's treason."

"Not in this country." Uriah's voice was hard and defensive.

Imanna put a hand on his forearm. "It puts me in danger everywhere. You see why I must cover my head all the time."

Suza nodded dumbly. Without the scarf, Imanna looked older. The brand was faded and old, although clearly recognizable. The symbol decorated Shi Castle. "How did you get that?"

Imanna looked to Uriah. Suza bristled as they excluded her from their silent conversation. He nodded almost imperceptibly. Imanna exhaled. "My mother branded me."

Suza could not wipe the look of horror off her face. Who would write a death sentence over their daughter's face? "Why?"

"Because she was dying, and she was only thinking about how much she wanted the world to know who her daughter was." She smiled, and her pale eyes sparkled.

Uriah took Imanna's hand in his. He spoke with pride. "The rightful heir of Skotar. The only Regium to survive Mavras's murders."

That claim was too much. "Mavras killed King Icor and Queen Sacor and *every one* of the royal bloodline fifteen years ago. Princess Sacora died—"

"Princess Sacora Imanna Regium—"

Suza interrupted Uriah, "She died!"

"That report was false." Imanna's quiet voice was in stark contrast to Suza's shout. "Aunt Mavras will be so disappointed."

Aunt Mavras. Suza's focus snapped to Imanna's lighthearted face. "Is this a joke?"

Imanna's mouth dropped to a frown. "No. There is

nothing funny about having your aunt kill your entire family, being forced to flee your home and country, and having death burned onto your face." Her chin lifted. "You wouldn't understand."

Heat roared through Suza's chest. "Oh really? I wouldn't? How dare you. You mock what you don't understand. I thought I'd lost my brother forever." She motioned to the ashen-faced man standing between them. "My mother died beneath me as my father whipped me to pieces. I spent years as a slave to your precious *aunt* while you lived in luxury in Mitera." She pointed a shaking finger. "You have no right to judge. You have no right to lay claim to sorrow that isn't yours." She inhaled, her emotions a violent storm. "You think you're a Draco queen back from the dead? What proof do you have besides a crazed mother's mutilation?"

"Suzaena." Uriah's voice was a low warning.

The light left Imanna's face as Suza's cruel words slammed home. She pulled the neckline of her shirt down, revealing a purple, perfectly executed, royal insignia above her heart, where every Draco was branded at birth. Only the Regiums were inked with violet dye, trapping the color permanently within the scars.

Suza staggered back a step, staring.

"I think you'd better report at the healers, Imanna." Uriah's face was grim.

Imanna retied her scarf. "What happened to you isn't right. It breaks my heart to see Skotar so poisoned. You don't have to believe me, but it doesn't make it less true. And it doesn't matter. I have a new family and a new home now." Pale eyes turned away.

Suza heaved in deep breaths as Imanna slipped out of the tent. She narrowed her eyes at Uriah. "It's true?"

Sad brown eyes locked on her as he slowly nodded.

Suza's head dizzied, and her heart tightened. "You knew?"

"Of course, I knew."

"You lied to me." Her voice was low and lethal.

"It wasn't my secret to tell." He held big hands up. "And I followed Titus's orders."

"I'm your sister. You didn't think you should tell me she's the heir of Skotar?"

"You are my blood. You are my family. But you've also been free less than a season. You didn't need to know."

Betrayal cut deep and cold. "You don't trust me?"

"I do. With my life. And now I'm literally trusting you with Imanna's life. You must never utter a word of this."

She let out a pent-up breath, trying to release some of her frustration. She would be careful, but she was not ready to make any such promise. This was too huge. What if … What if! "I don't want her harmed." The truth of that statement struck her. And now she'd hurt Imanna. She vaguely noted that she'd have to apologize as her thoughts raced ahead. "I can't believe it. The proper queen of Skotar is hiding in my brother's tent. Think of what we could do if she ruled."

"Forget it, Suzaena." His voice was hard as granite. "Her only hope to stay alive is to remain in hiding."

"If we could get enough support and overthrow Mavras …" Excitement built as she imagined a different Skotar. One she would want to live in.

Her brother did not mirror her emotions. "We could never succeed in marching through Skotar and taking the crown."

She thought of those years as a slave. Her back itched in memory of Draco brutality. "Mavras represents all that is wrong with Skotar. She's vain, greedy, cruel, selfish, manipulative … She murdered her family."

"You want Mavras to finish the job?" Uriah's voice deepened.

She shook her head. "No, Imanna will free the slaves and

enforce just laws. She will deliver Skotar from the Dracos. We'll save our home."

"*Elysium* is our home." His jaw rippled.

A chasm seemed to open between them, and Suza stepped back lest she fall into the divide. They shared blood and birth, but their last many years had been diametrically different.

"This is why I didn't want you to know." His brown eyes softened, but the words stung like a slap across her face.

"How can you not dream of saving all those people and underlings? Are you so selfish?"

Uriah flinched.

She sighed, seeing she would never convince him to risk his love. Skotar was not their home to fight for. "I'm sorry."

He didn't look at her. "I would give her up. I would walk into death if I thought there was even a thread of hope that we could restore her to power and change Skotar." He glanced up, eyes blazing. "There. Is. No. Chance. Don't pretend there is and don't fill her head with hopeless dreams."

Suza deflated. He was right. Skotar could never come back from the brink of destruction. It was hell up there. But still she thought of the beautiful forests and mountains. She thought of Kenji and Pearl and Ferth—shining people. Brilliant stars reflecting off fresh snow. She'd fled Skotar, but that wild place remained ensconced in her heart.

They sat for a moment in silence. Uriah's brow pinched as he watched her.

"You really love her?"

He nodded. "With my whole soul. In Elysium, it's tradition to officially commit yourself to the one you love in a marriage and promise to be with and love only that one person for the rest of your life."

Her shoulders tensed against his condescending tone,

even if she was ignorant of civilized ways. And besides, lots of Dracos—well, some—paired off for life. She thought of Ferth.

Her brother's grin lit the room. "Imanna and I made our promises to each other. I am hers now. And I will follow her anywhere."

Suza was stunned silent. He did what?

"Did you think otherwise?"

She hadn't thought at all. She didn't know her brother. Hadn't for over a decade. Self-pity welled at the constricting feeling of loneliness. "Congratulations?" What was she supposed to say? She wished it didn't feel like she were losing her brother before fully getting him back.

Happiness painted his face in handsome strokes. "I know I have only known her," he laughed, "a very short time."

She raised her brow. "Very short indeed."

"It doesn't matter. I love her like Poe."

"Then I am happy for you. And I must admit, I think she might even be worthy of you."

A trickle of Uriah's joy wormed through to Suza. She stepped forward and embraced his broad shoulders. "I will do what I can to protect her secret and her life. I want nothing more than for you to have a good life together after this."

He didn't answer, his gaze heavy.

"And I know it's my turn to make it right and apologize."

He kissed her brow.

"Up." Darius unfolded from his seat on the grass and stretched his lean legs. "I want to be in my own bed tonight."

"But not alone in your bed," one of the soldiers said with a guffaw.

"As you shall certainly be," Darius responded without a moment's hesitation.

Good-natured chuckles filtered through the small group. With each southern mile, the tension had decreased.

Ferth shook cornmeal crumbs and bits of earth off his pants as he stood. After six days of riding, his thighs no longer chafed, and his back no longer sparked, but after endless hours on horseback, a deep fatigue had wedged its way into his body. Thoughts of his mother lightened his feet as he stepped over to his horse. He was finally going to put a face to his dreams.

"You're first," Ferth said to Lyko.

"There must be a better way." Lyko stayed hidden in the bushes with Rom.

"You had days to think of one."

"We will sneak into the city after dark."

"No."

Lyko growled, and the soldiers with Ferth jerked in surprise. Hands flew to sword handles.

"Out. Now. Both of you." Ferth's tone had turned hard.

Two sets of golden eyes glared at Ferth as Rom and Lyko sulked out of the bushes. With stilted steps, one of the soldiers led her horse over to Ferth.

He sent her a reassuring smile, but her eyes remained fearful. "Once you mount, I'll help Lyko up."

"Yes, sir."

He held out a hand to help, but she ignored it, leaping into her saddle with ease.

"I'd rather ride with you," Lyko said as a last effort.

"Then you shouldn't have eaten that badger."

No one was happy about the arrangement. The two women soldiers had traded with the males for the largest mounts so the horses could more easily carry the weight of wolf and woman. Ferth had suggested it before realizing how attached the humans were to their particular horses. He eyed the large animal he'd sat on for over a week. He didn't feel any connection with the creature.

With the woman mounted, he checked the security of the saddle basket.

"I'll help you up," Ferth said.

Tail between his legs, Lyko allowed Ferth to spot his awkward climb into the low cradle. The horse grunted and shifted with the increase in burden. Ferth guessed the wolf weighed more than the woman.

"My legs hurt, and I feel like I'm going to fall out," Lyko said.

"Welcome to the last week of my life."

Lyko laughed, and it came out as a howl. The woman nearly toppled out of her saddle as she and the horse both bucked.

"Whoa." She patted the horse's neck with a nervous hand. When the beast settled, she speared Ferth with angry eyes.

"Sorry about that." He draped a blanket over Lyko. The hidden wolf looked like a lumpy saddlebag. "Take a nap, Lyko," he said aloud.

"Take a hike."

He chuckled as he rounded on Rom.

The gray wolf refrained from scaring his hosts with menacing noises, but since there was only one saddle cradle and Lyko was heavier, Rom had to lie across the second horse's shoulders.

The woman's hands shook as she helped Ferth fit straps over Rom's torso. The wolf couldn't help turning a toothy grin and bright golden eyes on the woman as he settled against her warm thighs. She swallowed, her fingers trembling.

"Don't worry." Ferth handed the woman her reins and tucked a blanket around Rom. "He's like a big puppy."

Darius chuckled.

"And the Draco Sang are snuggly bunnies," Rom said.

With one hand on the saddle, Darius threw his leg over his horse, mounting with enviable grace.

Ferth stepped up to his horse. *Okay, beastie. We're going to get it this time.* He imitated the raja, gripping the saddle and throwing his weight up and over. The horse whinnied as Ferth's considerable bulk landed on its back with a thud.

"I did it."

"If you mean you nearly broke the horse," Darius said, "then yes." But the royal's thin lip curved up before he pulled his cowl over his head, hiding his features. Darius gestured forward, leading the soldiers back to the road. Ferth's horse dutifully followed before he had a chance to turn the reins. Useless, he let the leather straps rest across his thigh.

With each mile, traffic thickened. They shared the wide

road with merchants, farmers, and peddlers. Posters and placards along the road advertising a need for soldiers increased. To Ferth's satisfaction, many young men and women appeared to be accepting the summons, traveling in groups to rendezvous points. When people saw Ferth and the other soldiers' uniforms, many respectfully saluted, but with Darius cloaked, they drew no other interest.

Ferth soaked up the new vistas with interest. Temperate compared to Skotar, the climate and weather allowed for sprawling estates and outdoor markets. Homes and small farms appeared alongside the road. Mitera, the glistening black dot on the horizon, grew larger.

"Hello, soldiers," a child yelled out. "You're going the wrong way!" He ran alongside their horses, two dogs chasing his heels.

"Got to get more weapons," one of the soldiers in Ferth's group replied with an easy smile.

"They won't let me join the army," the boy said. "Say I'm too young. Say I don't know how to kill a beast. But I do. I've killed plenty of beasts. Just ask my mamma. How else would she get all that meat for her stew?"

"Sounds like you're needed more here. We don't want your mamma to go hungry."

"Have you ever seen a real Draco Sang?"

Ferth bit his tongue.

"I have." The soldier lost some of his frivolity.

"Did you kill one?"

Ferth had ended many more than that.

More children had joined the boy as they raced along the side of the trotting horses. The soldier shifted uncomfortably in his saddle.

One of the girls who now paralleled their group saved the soldier from having to reply. "My brother joined the army.

He's going to kill them. He's going to keep them from eating me."

Ferth's hand clenched on the reins. Dracos didn't eat children. At least, most wouldn't.

"Don't you worry. They'll be no match for your brother," the soldier said.

She beamed.

The soldier spurred his mount faster, and the gaggle of children fell back. The black dot grew into a ribbon of rock. The walls of the city rose. Turrets and roofs appeared over the top.

"The castle." Darius indicated the green towers jetting over the eastern side of the city.

Mitera. Ferth's head spun. He'd never expected to be entering the city as anything other than an enemy invader, certainly not as one of the raja's guards. And yet, he knew he would fight harder for this raja than he would have for his own father. He had no father.

Ferth gaped at the sprawl of humanity outside the gates. What was the point of the wall?

The Vasil River flowed along the left side of the road and split near the black wall. Massive twin bridges spanned the river on either side. Ferth's group joined the unregulated flow of traffic over the bridge. A gaping hole in the wall allowed entry into the inner city. An ornamental gate, secured permanently open, welcomed them into the heart of Elysium.

They weaved through the crowded streets. Roasted meat, baking bread, and steaming spices hit Ferth like a tidal wave as they passed shops preparing for the evening meal. Vendors displayed mounds of jewelry, fruit, and pottery. Glass gleamed in nearly every window. The women wore silk and velvet and their hair up in intricate patterns out walking in the streets. The men dressed for beauty, not battle. As they circled closer to the looming green castle, the opulence and luxury increased. No wonder Skotar had salivated over this lush city for centuries.

Ferth couldn't help salivating now, but it was more from the tempting smell of a hot meal than the desire to dominate everything he saw. He found his eyes darting from face to face, as if his mother or grandfather would appear at any moment, as if his heart would know them instantly.

Darius stopped at a crossroads and motioned his traveling companions close. "Ferth and I will go directly to report at the castle. Pinton, lead on to Azure. Before you reach the stables, drop the wolves off in the gardens. Ferth, can we trust them to stay put and hidden in your absence?"

"Yes, sir," Ferth said after acquiescence from the two sullen animals.

"I'll come get you the moment I return," he promised Rom and Lyko.

Ferth considered disobeying the raja's order and instead going with his wolves and search Darius's estate, this entire city, for his mother, but he squashed the thought away.

The six soldiers split off down the road to the south. The women carting Rom and Lyko turned pleading eyes on Ferth, as if he had abandoned them to a mysterious doom. They should consider themselves honored he let them near his wolves at all.

Ferth followed Darius east. Instead of going through the front gate of the castle—that entrance at least had guards— he led Ferth around the castle wall to a southern door, barely distinguishable. He dismounted and pulled a key out from one of the green stones and unlocked the gate.

Ferth dropped off the side of his horse and followed Darius into the heart of Elysium. They entered at the stables, although the smell of animal and manure was shockingly faint.

"Raja." A young man bowed at the waist. "Please leave your horses with me. They will be attended to with care."

"Thank you." Darius handed over the reins.

Ferth gladly did as well. If he saw the horse again, it would be too soon. Draco Sang traveled on the strength of their own legs. *You're human now.* As if the more he told himself that, the more he'd believe it.

Darius strode through the raked dirt path. A manicured garden rolled out on the right and the castle towered up ahead. The sunset painted the glistening green stones in gold. Ferth's breath caught at the splendor of the mighty fortress.

The guard at the door saluted. "Welcome, raja." She held open the wooden door.

Ferth stepped into a small entry behind Darius. Cream tiles covered the floors and ceiling.

"You there," Darius called.

The maid nearly dropped her basket in surprise, but she quickly caught herself and curtseyed.

"Send Cora to Raja Darius's chambers immediately."

She nodded and ran.

After a short walk through the southern wing, Darius pulled out a key and unlocked a door. The suite was nicer than anything Ferth had ever seen, intricate furniture, heavy curtains. The bed called to him. Darius quickly opened closets and checked behind curtains.

"Expecting someone?"

"Always. Last time I was here, the king took an arrow through the throat."

By Thirro. "Yes, of course." Ferth stood awkwardly near a desk, wondering whether he should help rummage through the man's things.

A round-faced woman appeared carrying a tray with delicious-smelling steam wafting off. "Welcome home, raja."

Ferth guessed she was about Darius's age; maybe a little older if time had been kind.

Darius smiled, and the short woman stood a little straighter. For a maid, her dress was of surprising quality. "Hello, Cora. I'm glad to see you are well. You've anticipated me, one of your many talents."

The woman beamed, her cheeks like ripe apples. "Shall I draw your bath, raja?"

"Cora, this is Ferth."

Only then did the woman seem to realize that Darius was not alone. She curtseyed politely.

"Ferth will bathe first. Set out a suit of mine for him to wear."

"Yes, raja." Cora set the platter on Darius's desk.

He turned his attention to a stack of parchments and waved a hand at the food. "Help yourself," he said to Ferth, not looking up. When Darius grabbed a handful of olives and started popping them in his mouth as he read, Ferth followed suit.

The sound of rushing water drew Ferth through the doorway into a room covered in glass and shining tiles. Cora bent over a massive copper tub, but what stopped Ferth in shock was the spigot of steaming water pouring into the basin.

"How do you do that?"

"First time seeing piped water, huh? Most of the city has it."

"And it's hot!"

She ignored his exclaims as she dropped flower petals and powder into the water.

Ferth removed his boots and set his weapons on the pile. He had his shirt off and his pants halfway down his thighs by the time she looked back at him.

"My lord!" Her face turned crimson. "Wait just a moment." She twisted the spigot closed with a jerk.

"What's the matter?" Ferth's question died on his lips as she darted from the room, face turned away.

Humans were the strangest creatures. He stopped worrying about the skittish slave—no, *maid*—the moment his skin touched the hot, fragrant water.

He rubbed his limbs with a soapy sponge. How was he going to wash his own back? For a fickle heartbeat he missed having a slave. He thought of Suza, remembering how good she was at scrubbing the grime out of his fur. He'd forced her to be good at it. Shame replaced his greed. He ached for her. And not because he couldn't reach his back. Reluctantly leaving the warmth, he dried off with a fluffy towel and then stood in the middle of the gleaming room, naked and confused.

"Excuse me," he called, feeling stupid, but not wanting to offend the sensitive woman by walking out. "What should I wear?"

"My lord, your clothes are laid out in the room to your right," Cora called, her voice too high.

"I'm not a lord," he yelled before turning into a plush closet that had a luxurious suit laid out on a bench. The silky undertunic kissed his warm skin. He and Darius stood head-to-head, but Ferth's shoulders and thighs were inches wider. He made a mental note not to make any hasty movements. He tied his sword to his waist and stuck his daggers into his boots and rejoined Darius.

"Maybe Abner will name you a raja when he sees how well you wear my suit," Darius said.

"Thank you for loaning it to me." He barely breathed for fear of popping a button.

"Eat." Darius disappeared into the bathing room.

Cora returned and pointedly ignored Ferth.

"Excuse me," he said. "My lady."

"I'm not a lady." Her pink face remained turned away.

He sighed. "Do you have a brush?"

She allowed a quick glance at his wild mane. Wet hair hung down past his shoulders.

"Oh, skies." She threw her hands up and disappeared out the door.

He groaned. What had he done wrong now? He sat down to eat.

A moment later, Cora returned. She held up a brush and bottle of oil.

What would it take for him to convince her to please do this one thing for him?

"I'm good with hair."

Relief flushed through him. "I'm not."

She smiled, her face relaxing. She stood behind Ferth as he ate flatbreads, pickled vegetables, and sliced fruit. Her hands worked through a week's worth of knots.

Darius emerged, tall and regal, his short hair neatly combed. He wore a navy-blue suit with silver embroidery. Cora dropped Ferth's hair for a moment as she drank up the raja. Reining her focus back on her work, she hastily tied his wavy hair at the base of his neck with a ribbon. Clean and fed, he eyed the fluffy bed longingly before he stood and followed Darius out. The raja strode through the maze of cream hallways with confidence and poise. Ferth matched his long pace.

They ascended three flights of stairs. The few sentries they passed saluted as they recognized the raja. Music and voices echoed off the walls. The scent of feasting grew stronger. Darius turned a corner and a vast room opened up. Pink marble columns outlined the space. The ceiling seemed to spiral into the heavens. Long tables laden with food and well-dressed people ran along three lengths of the room, leaving the polished floor in the center open. Musicians played from an alcove. At the head table, the fourteen-year-old king sat at the center, distinguishable by his ornate chair and gold crown. Massive windows behind the king looked out over the wall and across the sprawling valley.

As Ferth followed Darius forward, he couldn't help comparing this to when he'd feasted in the halls of Shi Castle. King Abner was a far cry from the fearsome Queen Mavras. The patrons dining here looked small, weak, and clean. Even the loudest laugh didn't compare with a howling Draco ruckus. This music was *pretty*, as were the garments and decorations. Mavras liked music that boiled her blood, and it mattered little what was worn. Ferth had seen Dracos wearing nothing more than a baldric of knives welcomed at Mavras' tables. The absence of slaves felt weird too. Painted faces watched the two newcomers' progress through the center of the room.

It's not that Ferth didn't like the feel of the human court, but compared to the grit and power of Shi Castle, this almost wasn't real. He felt as if he were playing pretend.

"Your Majesty." Darius bowed at the waist.

"Raja Darius," Abner said in a tenor voice. "Welcome home."

Darius glanced sideline at Ferth, and his eyes widened, a silent warning.

Ferth wiped the frown off his face, replacing it with a forced smile. Not sure whether he should kneel, he bowed slightly deeper than Darius had before straightening up and looking the boy-king in the eyes. The sandy-haired king stared back, his eyes betraying insecurity and open curiosity.

"Your Majesty." Darius motioned. "Allow me to introduce Commander Ferth. He joins me from Captain Titus's unit as an expert on the Draco Sang."

"Welcome," Abner said and turned his attention to Darius.

"I did not expect you so quickly. I am glad to see that you've returned and are well."

"Thank you, Your Majesty." He put a hand on his chest. "I have much to report and have traveled with speed to bring word from the northern border."

"We look forward to your report. Come and eat. We shall meet first thing in the morning." The king lifted his smooth chin in dismissal.

"I wish to request that we convene immediately." Darius's lips thinned when Abner glanced to the woman sitting on his right before responding. "Raja Forsyth," Darius said in stark greeting.

"Darius." Raja Forsyth omitted his title. Forsyth stood and then the king scrambled to his feet. Unfortunately, Abner had not hit his growing. His hairless face came only to Ferth's shoulder.

"Let's convene," King Abner said. As if this were his idea.

Raja Forsyth nodded to several gray-haired men sitting in proximity. They stood as well.

Where Darius was willowy and angular, Forsyth was squat and round. She had gray hair pulled back in a tight bun. A heavy belly pressed against her gilded belt. She wore men's clothing. It would not have been of note among the Draco Sang, but she stood out here. Forsyth and the five other rajas followed the king out of the hall. Darius exhaled a pent-up breath before striding after the royals.

"You'll have to stand behind my chair," he whispered to Ferth.

They conferenced in a room not far from the great hall. Four guards who looked like they knew how to use their weapons stood at the doors. Only the king, his rajas, and Ferth went in. When the heavy door closed, the king sat at the head of a round table with twelve ornate chairs around it. Darius and Forsyth both reached for the chair on the king's right at the same time. Forsyth retracted her hand with a sour expression and took the next one down.

"My thanks for warming my seat in my absence." Darius's voice was cold.

King Abner's voice sang across the tension. "Raja Darius. Your report."

Although there were five empty seats, Ferth stood behind Darius as the raja painted a brutally accurate picture of their impending doom.

The king said little and the discussion quickly whittled down to an argument between the youngest raja, Darius, and the oldest, Forsyth.

"I'd like to see Ferth leading ten thousand troops north within the week," Darius said.

"Do you have any idea how much that will cost? We can't afford that," Forsyth said.

"We can't afford not to."

"Coming from the man who sits on hordes of gold." Her plump fingers tapped the table.

Darius clenched his sharp jaw.

"And all this country has left is little boys like Tobin. Weak and totally inadequate for anything."

"You are wrong about Tobin," Darius said. When Forsyth opened her mouth, he continued, "We can discuss your blind spot when it comes to your son another time. The point is that we have many people here who are qualified to defend Elysium solely because they are strong and love this country."

Her lips thinned.

"I was lucky to get through their first attack with my life. Chance and trickery are the only things holding back the wave of destruction that hangs above us. We have lived in ignorance for centuries. This is no fairy tale. This is your worst nightmare." Darius's voice shook a bit, as if he were seeing the Dracos in his mind. "We will not be able to stop them once they get their claws into Elysium. We *must* hold the river border."

"You say Skotar attacks with an army less than four thousand str—"

"Less than three thousand currently."

"You already outnumber them three to one. Are our soldiers so inadequate?"

"Yes."

"Then I propose we train our troops a little better." She chuckled as she glanced at the others at the table.

Darius twisted in his seat to look at Ferth, and the other faces followed his gaze.

"That's good in theory and should certainly be a goal." Ferth took a small step forward. "But there isn't time. The Draco Sang will attack again within days, if they haven't already. They are low on food, and they are angry. They must take Elysium before winter forces them back to their homes. With the latest reinforcements, Captain Titus's army *might* be able to hold off the Draco Sang for another attack before they lose too many numbers and cave. Of course, it's likely the Dracos have already wiped out our meager defense, and we can expect them here within weeks."

The king's face paled.

Forsyth looked at Ferth as if she'd eaten something rotten. "Who are you?"

"I'm a squad commander under Captain Titus, as Raja Darius stated, your highness."

"What makes you an expert?"

Ferth's eyes narrowed, and Forsyth's head moved back a fraction.

Darius cut in. "He has done extensive scouting and research on the enemy."

He *was the enemy.*

"I have no intention of allowing those animals anywhere near this city or my people," Raja Forsyth said. "And I don't appreciate you coming in here and trying to scare us into meeting your ridiculous demands." Her narrow gaze was trained on Ferth. He could imagine to many she was intimidating, but he had grown up with Laconius. His pulse did not so much as flicker.

"You would not appreciate it if I did not explain exactly what you are up against." Ferth's voice held steady and strong, lending him credibility. "Draco Sang are faster, stronger, and tougher than humans. You called them animals. They are not. They are monsters." His deadly tone froze the room. "Take, for example, their army chief, Laconius. He has curling horns, hooved feet, and leather for skin. He's a head taller than I and broad as this—" he held out his hands to his sides. "He's as strong as a bull, but it's not his size so much as what he does with his power that's dangerous. He's cunning and cruel with a heart as cold as the northern mountains. He cannot wait to ravish this country and revel in its destruction. The kind of man who would not hesitate to whip his only son as punishment." He regretted saying that part when Darius's keen gaze filled with pity. Ferth straightened. "Shall I tell you about the murderous scorpion queen or the sickly state of the slave barracks?"

The king's face had gone pale, whereas Forysth looked like she'd sucked a lemon. "No."

He could not respect a leader who chose ignorance over unpleasant truth. "The Draco Sang do not fight in orderly lines or by your—our rules of war. They have been preparing for this invasion for seventeen years. They want this land with a frenzied passion. And, they are *very* difficult to kill."

Forsyth spoke over the purse in her lips. "You are like Darius here. Young and inexperienced and easily scared. You lack the wisdom of age."

"I am honored to be compared to Darius." He fought back the desire to shake the pompous raja. "He counsels with wisdom. He fought with courage. And I would argue that anyone present at that battle would have the experience to agree with me about the power of the enemy."

Forsyth eyed Darius with contempt and then turned back to Ferth. "I met a Draco Sang once. She was, as you say, fast and tough. But she was brainless. It was not so hard to kill her."

Anger flared in Ferth at the woman's callousness. The jacket tightened against his shoulders. "Then perhaps you should lend your exceptional skills to defend your country."

"You forget yourself, boy." Spit glistened on her mouth. "I am a raja. My life is service to this country."

"Raja Forsyth," Darius said. "We here at the table are the leaders of Elysium. We love this land. We must unite to defend it. I have seen posters gathering troops. That is a good start. I pledge a thousand from my lands."

He had that many people?

"They will be ready to march north in five days, the day after the Lammas. I plead with you all to assemble what you can."

"Does the king make an order?" a man with a long beard asked.

All eyes turned to the young king. He shifted in his over-sized seat. Abner glanced at the scowling Forsyth and seemed to wither further.

"The crown will match Darius's thousand troops and orders each raja to contribute five hundred. Each soldier is to be equipped with at least one weapon and boots."

Forsyth's eyes bulged. "That leaves you with only the guard. That leaves us all practically defenseless and without workers. That sends our naïve youth to die."

"Have more faith in Tobin," Darius said.

She glared at him.

"War is sacrifice." His words seared the heart like a brand. "Or worse will come."

King Abner straightened his spine, and Ferth was forced to reconsider the boy when he said, "I believe it's worth the risk."

"Abner," Forsyth said, her tone disappointed.

"Forsyth." The king's tone mimicked hers exactly. "You are always welcome to continue staying in your suite here within the safe walls of the castle and near the guard."

Darius tilted his head so Ferth could see him bite down hard on his lips, conquering the urge to grin.

"Unless we have these *untrained* soldiers there and back within the month, it will cripple our economy." Forsyth scowled. "And our future."

King Abner looked to Darius.

"The outcome will be decided before then. For better or worse."

"*If* we manage to push the Draco Sang back," Ferth said. "Be warned, they will return next spring." After a heavy pause he added. "The irrigation canals need to be destroyed or you will never live in peace." *We.* He should have said *we.*

"Impossible," Forsyth said. Several others echoed her outrage. "We are gathering your troops—an unprecedented force. Kill the enemy and be done with it."

Darius lifted a hand. "Instead of the canals, we must target Nogard, the Dragon."

Ferth barely held back a groan.

Abner turned to his right. "I listened to Raoul, as you requested, but I am not convinced."

Forsyth nodded. "I pondered the *theories* too, and a mission to the northern reaches of the world to hunt a ghost is ridiculous and suicidal. Who would ever agree to such a foolish quest?"

Ferth didn't like to admit that he agreed with the pompous woman.

"A matter for later." Darius stood. He smiled, but his jaw twitched. "We've got work to do, friends."

King Abner scrambled to his feet. "We'll convene again at noon tomorrow. Bring your officers."

TWENTY-NINE - JEALOUSY
THIRRO

*I*t had been a long miserable day. Thirro hadn't slept well crammed into that too-small cave with his eight traveling companions. With Gasson's primate stench clogging Thirro's lungs, he made them continue their journey before the sun set.

As they skirted a farming village, the smell of dinner fires wafted through the air. He was hungry. To pass the time, he planned out a raid of the village. One that he would never get to lead. They couldn't risk being seen. He motioned Mordick over and dug through the carrier's pack for an apple and some jerky.

They'd followed shallow western foothills and long trailing fingers of the Seraf mountains. Civilization thickened as wilderness and its hiding places diminished. It was full night when they reached a gorge blocking their path.

"I'll scout." Thirro leaned over the cliff without fear. "Wait for me behind that thicket." He pointed behind the group, then gratefully spread his dark wings and soared into the air. A town lay at the end of the canyon to the east. To the west, there was no end in sight. He dove into the narrow canyon.

Gleaming ebony walls reflected his shadowy form. Deeper he went, until he alighted near a clear river. He drank. He sighed with pleasure at the privacy, the peace. He stripped off his travel-worn pants and tunic. He scrubbed them and himself in the cool water. He sat naked, staring at the strip of stars far above. His body was heavy. It would be so easy to sleep. Regretfully he stood and put on his damp uniform.

His clothes were nearly dry by the time he scouted the southern bank and returned to his comrades.

"Run into a bit of trouble?" Jade asked. "Because I can almost scout the other side of the gorge from here and you've been gone a long time."

"Better to be safe." He didn't look at her. "We'll take the carriers across first."

Gavriel went to work checking Gasson's packs. Thirro watched while Mordick fixed his. He'd take Mordick over first and then come back for the packs. When Mordick stood ready, Thirro inhaled and stepped behind the stocky ram Draco. He wrapped his arms around Mordick's chest. Blunt horns pressed at Thirro's neck when they took off with a grunt.

His wings strained and throbbed. Mordick's hands clamped on Thirro's forearms.

"Don't look down," Thirro said with a taunting tone.

Mordick held tighter, his nails digging in.

"Let go of me or I'll drop you." The threat hissed between tight teeth.

Mordick's head shook, the horns banging into Thirro's throat. Anger lit through him as he dove toward the southern rim of the gorge. Five feet from the ground, he let go. The ram slammed into the ground with a bleating *thud*. Thirro hovered above him in the air. His restraint wavered. That little drop wasn't enough; he wanted to shred Mordick, claw his eyes out. Panting, Thirro checked the deep grooves in his arms from Mordick's nails. His neck ached with bruises, and his head throbbed. They'd only gone two hundred yards. Never again would he fly with that big dumb animal.

Gavriel landed and released Gasson. The gangly ape shook out his arms and let out an anxious laugh. Gasson was bigger and heavier than Mordick, but Gavriel had managed him with annoying ease.

"Mordick is yours now," Thirro said to Gavriel. "I'll take Gasson on the next run."

Gavriel cocked an eyebrow at the whimpering lump on the ground. "Needled our fearless leader, have you?"

Thirro hated how Gavriel always said the right words, calling him fearless and such, but the raven's tone suggested he didn't quite mean it. Jaw tight, Thirro flapped his wings, heading back to the northern ridge of the canyon. Muffled laughter filtered over from where the three strikers, Jade, Dara, and Dan, sprawled out on the grass. Thirro glared at them as he jerked up Mordick's heavy pack and took off without a word.

Mordick hadn't moved. Thirro landed at his side and dropped the pack.

"My ankle is not right," Mordick said.

"Get up and see if you can walk." Thirro's brows lowered in anxiety.

Mordick obeyed, but when he put weigh on his left ankle, it wobbled and gave out. "I can't walk."

"Wrap it and give it a bit of time." Thirro didn't have time for this.

Mordick turned beady red eyes on Thirro. "I don't know how to wrap it."

Thirro scowled. It was the least he could do. Mordick sat and propped his ankle up on a boulder. Thirro pulled a bandage from the pack and wrapped the rapidly swelling ankle tight. When Mordick tried walking again, his ankle held, but the fat carrier would need a crutch. Thirro hacked at the tree with more vigor than necessary.

The four Dracos on this side of the gorge wordlessly joined Mordick near the trees. Thirro left the ram resting, crutch in hand, glower on his face. He turned north to continue his debasing courier duties. In the air above the gap, Gavriel cradled Jade in his arms. The raven's low laugh rumbled on the wind as Jade unbuttoned his vest and pressed her face against his feathery chest. With silky black wings, Gavriel carried them unnecessarily high. Moonlight gilded them in silver. He shifted her petite frame around so she faced outward. He held a firm hand on her taut belly and another across her chest. Thirro's insides stirred. Gavriel dove. Wind whipped at the wide smile on her face and fluffed her furry scalp.

Thirro stood near the southern edge of the gorge, watching. He scowled as Gavriel and Jade sailed into the gorge. Gavriel's raven wings flung out, halting their descent. Inky rocks surrounded them. Gavriel landed on a shallow ledge. The sheer cliff continued down into darkness. He backed her against the rock wall. He tilted his face so he didn't hit her with his beaked nose, and then they were kissing.

Thirro nudged a loose rock with his taloned toe. It dropped into the gorge and sailed at Gavriel's head. *Nice shot.*

The flyer jerked with a startled cry. He leapt back from the wall, Jade tight in his arms. Thirro kicked another rock. It bounced off their tiny ledge.

Jade was already storming out of his arms by the time Gavriel had landed on the grass next to Thirro.

"What do you think you're doing?" Her dagger appeared in her palm.

"I'm waiting for my flyer and my striker to land." He folded long arms. "Took them long enough. Can I be blamed if they get injured disobeying orders?"

Gavriel touched his downy head. His hand glistened with blood when he pulled it away. Jade's eyes sang a murderous tune.

Thirro smirked as he rose out of her reach. "I'm off to get Dara."

Gavriel grabbed Jade's wrist. Would she have dared throw her knife? The upstart was a little too arrogant.

He'd have to put her in her place again. Soon.

Thirro flew quickly. They'd already wasted too much time crossing the gorge. Dara was a pleasant passenger, easy to grope while airborne, didn't talk or flail, lightweight. He released her on the southern side and picked up Mordick's heavy pack.

"I'll help you get this on."

The ram stood and hobbled over, leaning heavily on his crutch.

"He can't carry that," Jade said. "He can barely walk."

"What good is a carrier who can't carry?" Thirro's voice rose in exasperation. He thrust the pack at Gavriel. Red tinged the thin bandage now wrapped around his head. "You'll have to help him."

"As the strongest flyer, I suppose it is my duty." His black eyes gleamed.

Thirro opened his mouth to dispute, and then closed it again. He didn't want to carry that pack. It was heavy.

Gavriel grinned.

"Lammas is in four nights," Thirro said. "Let's move."

erth followed Darius out of the castle and into
the lamplit streets of Mitera. It was late, but he
wanted to ask if Darius knew Mira. If he knew where his
Aunt Elssa lived and could he take him right now. He wanted
to meet his mother, but fear clutched him. What if … What if
… His throat dried up, and the questions withered away.
"How did you become a raja?"

"Our current king's grandfather, King Jacque, appointed
me a raja on the day I was born. That's how I'm the most
senior member at my young age of thirty-four."

"Is that typical?"

"No. Usually the seat is inherited."

"So, what happened?"

"After her husband died, my mother spent a lot of time
here at the castle. She fell in love with the king. I'm Jacque's
youngest son."

"Oh."

Darius led Ferth to the neighboring mansion.

"This is your home?"

"When I'm in Mitera. But I prefer to stay on my land to the east of the city." He opened a heavy gate.

Ferth's awe-filled gaze racked over a manicured garden and focused on the imposing house. It butted up against the wall as the castle did, but instead of green glass, it was built from gray rock and blue tiled roofing. *Azure Estate.* A carpet of slate paved the way to the front door. Darius led Ferth around to the side and flinched as twin wolves shot out of the hedge.

"It's about time," Lyko said.

"We were ready to eat one of his chickens," Rom said.

"Wait here." Darius unlocked a side door to the house and disappeared. His head popped back out. "All clear."

Claws clicked on the polished marble floors, the only sound as they followed the raja through the empty entry. Darius opened the first door on the right and motioned them inside.

Ferth blinked at the grandeur, a shocking difference from his stark barrack room back at Shi Castle. Wood columns framed the wide bed. A desk stood in front of tall windows. Darius crossed the room and drew the drapes, blocking out the stars, and any unwelcome eyes. Lyko rolled in the plush carpet. An open door led to a private bathing room.

"This is far too nice for us." He let out an awkward chuckle. "Can you point us to the barn?"

"I wouldn't trust those two with a night near my pigs."

"Probably wise."

"Probably wise," Rom's words echoed in Ferth's head at the same time and in the same tone.

"Ugh," Lyko said. *"And I'm stuck with two of you."*

"I'll have breakfast brought up first thing." Darius strode back to the door. "I'm sorry Rom and Lyko can't walk freely here. I hope the mentality changes soon, but with our efforts to gather an army now, I think it is best if we save that battle for after this one." Thin lips turned up in an apologetic grimace.

"I understand."

"But please make yourself at home."

"Thank you."

When the door clicked closed behind Darius, Ferth let out a contented sigh. He took off the tight coat and unbuttoned the pinching waist of the pants. He flopped onto the cloudy bed. *"This is the life."* The Regiums didn't even live like this at Shi Castle.

"Yes. I love hiding in gilded cages," Lyko said.

"You'll get used to it," Ferth said.

"Did you find out anything?" Rom asked.

"Not yet. I have to be back at the castle at noon, but I'll find her in the morning."

There was a soft knock at the door. Ferth jumped from the bed. *"Hide in the bathroom."*

Lyko and Rom slunk away with matching scowls.

Ferth opened the door to a man in a suit holding a tray piled high with food. "My lord."

Lord? Ferth stood and stared. Should he do the handshake thing?

The man cleared his throat. "Might I come in, my lord?"

Ferth leaped aside. "Yes, of course. My apologies, sir."

Despite the hour, the man brought a small feast. He laid out tea, bread, fruit, and a bowl of what looked like red marbles.

He gave Ferth a questioning look as he set out two entire roasted chickens. Ferth shrugged, patted his flat belly, and tried to keep his smile innocent.

The man stepped toward the bathing room. "I'll just prepare your bath."

Ferth headed him off. "That won't be necessary." How many baths did a man need in a day?

The man wrinkled his nose slightly in disapproval.

"He thinks you stink," Ferth said to the wolves.

"Actually, he thinks you *stink,"* Rom said.

"You could tell him it's not you, it's the wolves hiding in the tub," Lyko said.

"Tell him he needs a bath," Rom said, *"I can smell his perfume from here."*

"Essence of old man with a side of anise," Lyko said.

Ferth grinned, and the man's brows drew together, literally together in one gray caterpillar.

"As you wish, my lord," he said.

"Thank you, sir."

The man strode to the door. "Good night, my lord."

"Yes, good night. Thank you." So much posturing.

Before the door even closed, four bright amber eyes were staring at the chickens.

"Cal loved those cherry candies," Lyko said.

Ferth picked up a red ball and set it in his mouth. His eyes popped at the shock of sweetness. He rolled it over his tongue, not sure about the stickiness but wanting to surrender to the riot of flavor.

Lyko's narrow jaw clamped on a chicken.

"Do not make a mess, and do not even think about eating that over the carpet," Ferth said.

"And you were worried you wouldn't be able to sound like the prissy humans," Rom said.

"Prissy." Lyko bumped Rom. *"Nice one."*

Rom flashed canines. Ferth thought it wasn't such a good idea to leave his wolves on their own for so long. Rom wedged the second chicken between his jaws, and the duo padded back to the tiled bathroom.

Ferth crunched down, sugar shards splintering over his taste buds. *"This is the life."*

"It's not bad," Rom said.

The three savored their meal and their surroundings. Ferth chuckled as he stacked the wolves' leftovers back on the plate. What would the servant think of the pile of clean bones?

Exhausted, Ferth stripped and spread out over the silk sheets. From the floor, Lyko and Rom were a symphony of heavy breathing. Sleep didn't come easily. The bed was too soft, the air too floral, the space too quiet, his mind too active, his heart too hopeful.

Mother.

Mira.

He recalled the images Lyko had shared. Golden hair, kind eyes, smooth skin, thin hands.

After a night of uneven dozing, he got up with the sun. He snuck Lyko and Rom outside to the garden. He shaved. He brushed and braided his hair. In the hutch, he found black pants that fit well and a white shirt with buttons up the front and on the sleeves.

"I'm off to find her."

"We're coming," Rom said.

"I'm the only one who's actually been to her house," Lyko said.

"I wish you could sniff her out for me." Ferth called them inside, and the wolves resentfully trotted back into the first room on the right.

"We want to see her too." Lyko's voice was demanding.

Rom slumped in sadness, and that hurt worse than Lyko's whining.

"I'll bring her here as soon as I can. I'm sorry. Stay hidden." Ferth stepped into the hall and firmly closed the door, trapping his annoyed wolves in the plush suite.

He hesitated. Excitement welled. He was going to find his mother today. But how? Walk the city? Search Darius's kitchens?

Ferth turned toward footsteps. A woman came around the corner and started his way down the hall.

She looked up and jerked to a halt. Her hand flew to her mouth with a sharp intake of breath. Her tray of food clattered to the ground, broken glass tinkling against the stone floor. Fire spread through his veins as he recognized her.

"Cal?"

Ferth froze, horror icing through his chest. She blinked rapidly, her face white. She fell back and slammed against the wall. Her legs shook. "You're alive?" Tears obscured her golden eyes. "You're alive."

She regained her balance and rushed toward him, arms outstretched, picking up speed. Fifteen feet. Ten feet.

Watching her hope swell was an exquisite type of pain. He shook off his paralysis. "No. He's still...I'm not Cal."

Confusion cracked her brow. She slowed.

"A vision?"

He swallowed, shaking his head. His eyes burned. "I'm Ferth." He forced his voice to lay claim to what he most wanted. "I'm your firstborn."

She stopped, and the remaining color drained from her pretty face. Her eyes widened as she studied him, now certainly noticing the differences. He sensed it before it happened. He dashed forward as her eyes rolled back and her knees crumpled. He caught her head in his outstretched hand. His left arm wrapped her waist, twisting her on top of him as he slid. His elbow and hip barked in pain as he hit the tile. He huffed out a breath as she landed with her thin shoulder pressing into his ribs, her hip spearing his side. He inhaled the smell of sage and orange blossoms. Silky blonde hair slipped through his fingers. He had her. He held her. His *ma*. She was real.

He laid like that for a moment, silent and still except for the thrashing of his pulse and the pressure behind his eyes.

Gathering his emotions, he carefully shifted up. He cradled the thin woman in his lap and sat, legs folded. Her skin was lighter than his, like crushed pearls. Thick eyelashes brushed her cheeks.

A memory that Lyko had shared came to mind. The wolf wouldn't be coerced into sharing, but he'd opened up on his own a precious few times when the feeling struck. Ferth relished the memories.

Cal was seven-years-old. He'd climbed up the gate of their desert home and sat on the wall, pretending it was a ship. As captain, he'd looked out over Siccum. He'd faced north—always north. Mira sat in a rocking chair in the sand, sewing larger pants for him.

"Storm coming from the north," Cal said. "We'll hit it head on. Treasure lies beyond."

"Will you take me with you?" Mira asked.

"How you talk, mother. I wouldn't leave you. Don't you know you're in the belly of the ship now? You're cooking dinner."

She laughed. "Guess I best get to work on it."

"The sea captain needs a hearty meal." Cal shifted atop the nine-foot wall.

"The sea captain needs to be careful."

"Sea monsters!" Cal scrambled to his feet; he'd done it before, but this time he slipped. His right side scraped against the rough mud bricks as he slid to the ground. Fabric ripped.

Mira was there when he opened his eyes. She'd scooped him onto her lap. His elbow and side bled onto her dress.

"The demons defeat the captain. They take his ship." His lip quivered as he fought off tears.

"Never." Mira kissed his brow. "The brave captain was wounded in his valiant fight, but he killed the monsters and threw their corpses to the depths of the sea."

"That's very grim, ma." Cal grinned, revealing the gap where he'd lost his baby tooth. "And wasteful. I'm keeping the meat."

Ferth cradled Mira now just as she'd held her young son. He felt her neck, relieved at her strong pulse. He brushed an errant strand of hair off her brow. "Mira." He swallowed and whispered the word, "Mother."

She didn't move.

Anxiety sprouted. He opened his hand, hesitated, then slapped a palm across her cheek.

Her eyes flew open. Honeyed gold, like Cal's, like his wolves, like his.

She opened her mouth to speak, but tears came before the words. She sobbed. Thin hands clutched at his arms as she pulled herself up and out of his lap. She knelt before him on the marble floor, rivers coursing down her cheeks. She leaned in, eyes like stars. Heat bloomed in his heart at the depth of hunger and hope in her devouring gaze. When rough hands touched his face, his own tears escaped. She didn't move to wipe them away. He didn't either.

"My son." Her voice a whispered plea. "My baby."

Yes. A million times. Yes.

He held his joy in his heart as she studied him. He took in the worry lines on her brow and the smile lines on her cheeks. His square teeth and thick mouth matched hers. A pink outline of his hand marred her cheek where he'd struck her. He cringed. Should he have waited longer before *helping* her wake?

Confusion and disbelief spread over her face. "But *he* took you. He took you away from me. He took you to Skotar to become a mighty Draco Sang."

"And he almost succeeded." He shuddered at how close Laconius had come to turning Ferth into a powerful, vicious Draco. Her enemy. "But Cal found me. He saved me."

Surprise blanched Mira's face again. Her hands shook, and her shoulders trembled. He stood and helped her to her feet. He needed to address her shock before any more startling revelations. He put his arm around her shoulders and steered her toward his room. She tripped on the smooth floors, and her eyes glazed in and out of focus.

When Ferth opened his door, and the wolves sprang forward, she barely had time to whisper, "Lyko," before she fainted again. This time, Ferth caught her easily in his arms.

Rom whimpered.

"Bleeding skies," Ferth said. *"She's in shock."*

"I did not know my own power." Lyko pressed his nose to her arm and inhaled. Pleasure rolled over their mental connection as he drank in the scent of Mother.

Ferth carried her to the bed. He piled four blankets on her while Lyko licked her cheeks. Ferth fetched a glass of water and a piece of the candy.

Mira opened her eyes and jerked away from the looming wolf face.

"Back up," Ferth ordered Lyko. The wolf sat on his haunches, but didn't retreat. He thumped the carpet with his tail in excitement.

"I'm sorry." She ran a trembling hand over her slobbery face.

"Drink this." He brought the glass to her lips.

She took a few gulps, and then he set the candy between her teeth. Ferth moved to sit on the end of the bed, giving her space and trying to make himself look smaller and less imposing. Rom set his head on Ferth's lap as they waited. Slowly Mira sucked on the sugar. Her gaze drifted in circles around Ferth and the wolves. The lost look on her face gradually dissolved.

"Come, Lyko," she said, her voice raw.

The white wolf eagerly leapt onto the bed, his tail

wagging. Mira stroked Lyko's head as he lay on top of the blankets at her side.

"I miss him," she said.

Lyko nodded and nuzzled closer.

"I am glad to see you. I see him in you."

"*I see him in you,*" Lyko said.

Ferth spoke. "Lyko says he sees him in you too."

"You are connected with Lyko? How is that possible?"

He shrugged. "We are womb brothers." He determined to be honest with this woman so he said, "I was there when Cal … died. He was injured after a brave attack in Skotar. I tried to save him, gave up my beast after turning traitor to the Draco Sang." Mira's chin tilted. Maybe that wasn't the best way to say that, but he plowed on. "I don't know how to describe it except that it felt as if we were in transition together. One sweet taste of connection before I was reborn, and he passed on." He sighed. "I don't know how it happened."

Mira looked at Rom, and the gray wolf padded forward.

"This is Rom, my hewan."

He touched his nose to her palm.

"Nice to meet you, Rom."

"He says we've been waiting our whole life to meet you." Ferth's chest tightened.

Mira's smile relaxed Ferth's nerves. "I know exactly how long you've been waiting." Her eyes stayed on her son. She held out a hand. Hot tears threatened as he gripped it. "You cannot imagine how it feels to be a mother who had lost her son to a monster only to find him eighteen years later grown into a strong and handsome man. Gloriously human, with eyes deep and clear and full of goodness, exceeding all her dreams."

A tear escaped Ferth's walls. He had some idea. He knew what it felt like to ache for her in secret, because his wanting her was considered a weakness. He knew what it felt like to live not knowing what he'd lost. He knew now. And it was overwhelming. "I'll get us some breakfast," he said.

"Oh!" Beautiful eyes widened. "Your breakfast is now a mess in the hall." She sat up. "Raja Darius gave me the order to tend to the guest in the cream suite. He had such a strange smile on his face when he said it. Sneaky man. But I see why he told everyone else to stay away." She waved a hand over the furry predators.

Ferth stood and motioned her to lie back down. "I'll take care of it." He needed a moment to collect himself anyway.

He left his mother on his bed with his wolves. Rom had followed Lyko's example and he now lay on her other side, enjoying a head massage. Ferth halted at the door and took two wrinkled letters out of his breast pocket—one from Cal and one from Titus. He handed them to her before striding out.

Azure Estate was a picture of wealth. At Shi Castle, everything was brash and blunt and bold. Here, sophistication reigned. Every corner gleamed. The forest painting on the wall would never grace Mavras's castle. He stepped over the mess in the hall and followed his nose to a massive kitchen at the back of the house. The room wasn't smoky or oppressive, as he'd expected. Open windows welcomed in sunlight and a floral breeze. He felt like pulling up a chair and staying. Three faces turned up at his arrival.

A middle-aged woman set down her knife and wiped her hands on a stark white apron. "Good morning, my lord."

"It's just Ferth."

"Lord Ferth. What can I do for you this morning?"

"Just Ferth." These people weren't slaves to order around. They weren't even his servants. "Where could I find a broom?"

She blinked. A girl not much younger than Ferth came and stood at the woman's side. They both looked him over.

He bristled. "I've got something that just needs a bit of cleaning up."

"Where's Mira?"

"She's fine. It's my fault completely. I made the tray fall, so I've come to find a broom."

"Ash."

The girl at the cook's elbow squeaked.

"Help the handsome master."

The girl darted to the corner and returned with the broom. He held out his hand for it.

"I'll take care of it, my lord." Her words were high and rushed.

Ferth followed her out. She danced down the hall, peeking over her shoulder every few steps. Red bloomed over her round face when he crouched at her side and started piling up crumbled biscuits and glass shards. With the mess cleaned, he picked up the tray and followed the wispy girl back to the kitchens.

"Sorry about this," he said.

The cook whisked the wreckage from his hands. She replaced it with a new tray, heavy-laden with eggs, pie, bread, potatoes, and sausage—a much better and larger meal than had previously been prepared for him.

"I can't feel too bad about the spill when this is the replacement. Thank you."

The cook winked. "It's from Ash."

Ash bent over a row of carrots. She didn't look up, but her knife stalled for a heartbeat.

"Then please tell Ash she has my thanks."

"You can tell her yourself later."

Ash squeaked and bent lower over her work.

Ferth's pleasant smile wilted in discomfort. "Good day,

ladies." He strode out of the kitchen before they had a chance to say more. He missed Shale—Suza. He wanted her eager lips on his again. She had said she loved him. Could she really have meant it? She felt like a world away.

He opened the door to find his mother talking to Lyko and Rom. She stroked their fur as she spoke. He didn't know her yet, but if she could sit with his wolves without fear, they were going to get along fine. His face split into a wide smile.

She looked up and mirrored his joy. It was not long ago when his heart was his own, locked in an isolated cage—safe and cold. How quickly his heart had expanded. It now encompassed so many. How did he even have the capacity? How could he protect his heart when it walked around in so many other bodies?

"Breakfast?"

THIRTY-ONE - MISERY
THIRRO

ordick was slowing them down and dragging Thirro into a gulf of misery in the process. Jade, Dara, and Gavriel looked at Thirro as if Mordick's broken ankle was his fault. They'd barely made it half the distance they needed to cover last night as Mordick hobbled along at a worm's pace. Thirro wouldn't need a supply carrier on the way home. They would be running for their lives after they killed the king and the traitor.

Thirro perched high in the tree, keeping first watch over his sleeping company below. The sun illuminated Elysium and his thoughts.

He had to kill Mordick.

THIRTY-TWO - HEALING
SUZA

*I*manna wasn't at her tent the next morning for knife practice.

Suza wanted to slip away, sure the girl was never going to forgive her, but instead she went searching. She stopped at the entrance of the healers' building. No one seemed to notice her over the commotion. Imanna and four others surrounded a bed near the right wall. The injured soldier sobbed.

Imanna lifted his head and forced him to drink. "We must set your legs if you ever want to walk again." Her tender voice was unyielding.

"Please, my lady." His voice was a blubbering whimper.

Two attendants held his arms. Imanna and a thick man stood at his legs. "Count to five for me," she said.

"One, two." The word three turned into a gut-piercing scream as Imanna and the man straightened the broken thigh. They fitted a splint.

"This time count to four for me," Imanna said as they moved to the next break.

No reply came. The soldier had fainted. Imanna nodded

to the other healer, and they snapped the calf into place. Suza held her breath, her body tight as a bowstring until the work was done and the man opened his eyes again.

"You did great," Imanna said, her voice chipper and kind. "Very brave." She kissed his sweaty brow. A touch of color returned to his face. "Get comfortable and rest. I'll check on you later."

Suza hovered in the shadows as Imanna checked in with each bedridden body.

Imanna washed her hands. "Do you need a healer this morning, Suza?" Her voice was warm and friendly.

"How long have you known I was here?"

"I've spent my entire life looking over my shoulder, watching the shadows." Her gaze flickered to where her dog hewan watched from the far corner.

Of course. "Want to get breakfast with me?"

Imanna smiled as if pleasantly surprised and nodded.

Suza's belly remained tight with guilt and memories of her earlier rudeness. She glanced at the soldier with the broken legs. "What happened to him?"

"He fell."

"He fell?"

"From the sky—returned from Skotar to deliver a message."

Oh. "What message?"

"We're coming for you."

They walked to breakfast in silence. Along the way, Imanna brightened faces with her smiles and greetings.

After a quick meal, they stood for a moment absorbing the sunshine. "Thanks for the visit." Imanna hesitated for a breath before striding away.

"Imanna, wait."

She stopped and turned her head.

"Do you have a minute?" Suza cringed inwardly. They'd

just spent several minutes together eating, during which time she had hardly said a word and probably made things worse.

Imanna shrugged. "For what?"

Suza motioned her to follow. Thankfully she did, Kira on her heels.

The moment Suza's tent door closed behind them, affording privacy, Suza spoke. "I'm sorry, Imanna."

"I forgive you."

She held out a forestalling palm. "Wait. Let me apologize properly first."

One side of Imanna's red lips teased up.

"I should never have said your mother was crazed—"

"She was. At least when the end was near, fear and desperation had replaced much of her rational thought."

"Stop letting me off easy."

"It's okay, Suza. It's a lot to absorb. I didn't mean to shock you with it. Or burden you."

"Thank you." Suza looked around, unsure. This was not how she had planned this to go. "Come sit." Imanna settled in Suza's one chair, and Suza sat on the edge of her bed. The women sat for several heartbeats in heavy silence. She wanted to ask Imanna how she'd survived Mavras's massacre and escaped, but that seemed callous. Instead, a more personal question popped out. "Do you love him?"

Imanna relaxed. "Who wouldn't?" Her laugh was tinkling glass.

"Be serious."

She bit her lip to stifle her giggles.

"He said you pledged to love him and only him for your whole life." The more Suza thought about the idea of such a powerful commitment, the more romantic it seemed. "Did you mean the promises you made or are you going to break his heart?" She didn't mean for her voice to be quite so forceful.

"Definitely the first, hopefully not the second."

Suza didn't return Imanna's playful countenance. "Then I am happy for you both, and I'm glad to see my brother so alive again."

Without a hint of teasing, Imanna said, "I hope we can be true sisters. I've always wanted a sister, and I feel really lucky to think it could be you."

Flattery calmed Suza's ruffled feathers. "Me too." She stood and took two steps to her trunk. "I have a little something for you." She shifted through her army-issued belongings and wrapped her fingers around cold metal. She held her fist out in front of Imanna. She closed her eyes. She took a deep breath. This was the right thing to do. It wasn't supposed to be this hard to give it up, though. She opened her eyes and found curious blue eyes watching. "I've kept this since my mother died. I kept it for luck, and it reminded me of her." Suza peeled her fingers back, revealing a gold coin the size of a thumbnail with the royal insignia of Skotar impressed on the top. A token from life before slavery. She'd hidden it at times in loose mortar on the back wall of Shi Castle, and then in the lining of Ferth's trunk at the Draco camp. It had spent plenty of hours against the blade of the knife she used to strap to her thigh under her slave shift. She thrust the gold forward. Imanna didn't move. "I want you to have it. I thought with the Regium stamp … You should have it."

To Suza's shock, the young queen had tears in her eyes. "I've never had anything but weapons from Skotar."

She dropped the coin into Imanna's palm. It wasn't so hard to say goodbye to her treasure after all. After years of icy isolation, the joy of sisterhood blazed like warm fire.

Imanna hugged the coin to her breast. "Thank you."

"Thank you for forgiving me for my petty jealousy and cold words."

Imanna paused and a sneaky smirk that Suza was learning to distrust spread across her face, breaking the somber moment. "There is just one more thing to prove you're really sorry."

She couldn't help but grin back. "I don't even want to know."

"Kira needs a little bit of practice."

"With what?" She didn't love where this seemed to be headed.

Kira padded forward, pointy ears up.

"This will do for a practice weapon." Imanna picked up a stick from a pile of kindling and handed it to Suza. "Get ready for her to disarm you."

This sounded like something Queen Mavras would think of. "You definitely have Regium blood."

Imanna cackled. The dog leaped at Suza.

*F*erth hadn't stopped smiling. He smiled through the long meeting with the king and the rajas as they discussed details of gathering an army for war. His smile wavered slightly while he sparred with Darius—his respect increased for the young raja. He smiled as he soaked in the salted bath. He had a mother, a wonderful woman who accepted him. He'd believed her when she said she loved him —she'd always loved him.

Back in his room at the Azure Estate, Ferth opened the door at the knock.

"Please come with me," Mira said. "You've been summoned." She got down on her knees and rubbed Lyko's head.

"Summoned?"

She giggled. She looked so young and bright today—like Ferth felt. "Darius's suite."

He waited.

"You'll see." She stood and brushed a palm along Rom's neck. "I'll bring treats later, you two."

The wolves nodded and jostled against her legs. He hated

shutting the door on them, leaving them locked up. It wasn't right.

As he walked through the halls next to his mother, he kept thinking of things to say and coming up short. He had a long way to go to know her. Hopefully he'd live through this war and get the chance.

Mira passed a seated guard. He jumped to his feet when she reached for the double doors.

"Allow me," he said.

"Thank you, Galan." Mira sent a pleasant smile his direction.

Ferth cocked an eyebrow at the man's hopeful expression, and then the doors opened up to a bright room. Raja Darius stood in the middle, hands on hips. Three women danced around him, bearing sewing tools.

Oh no.

"Ferth. You can't leave me to suffer this alone." Darius's voice was airy and welcoming. "Thank you, Mira. Please stay and help, if you wish."

She bowed slightly. "Thank you, raja."

A tall, elegantly dressed woman strode in from a back room. She was beautiful, with angular lines and deep-set eyes. Her silks flowed over her straight spine like water.

"Angeline, meet Ferth, a commander in Captain Titus's army. Ferth, this is my wife, Angeline."

What was he supposed to do? The handshake thing? That seemed impertinent. Ferth folded at the waist. It seemed acceptable as she dipped her head in return.

"It's a pleasure to meet you, Commander Ferth." Her voice was formal, as was the set of her lips.

"Thank you for welcoming me into your lovely mansion."

A lip tweaked up—just a touch. "I understand this is your first Lammas."

By the shrewdness of her eyes, it was clear she understood why he'd never celebrated the Elysium holiday before. She knew he was a barbarian from Skotar.

He exhaled in relief. Pretending—lying—was onerous.

"Cas, Trissha, help our guest. Let's make sure he's dressed for it."

Two young women rushed to his sides. He glanced at Mira. She had a far-off look in her eyes as she watched them take his measurements.

"Darius is wearing navy." Angeline looked Ferth over as if he were a floral display slated for her grand hall. "You shall wear black. With gold trim, to match those incredible eyes." She said it without a hint of flattery.

"Yes, my lady. I will find a way to repay." Although he'd much rather skip the entire charade.

"Hush." She waved thin fingers. "It is our gift and our pleasure."

"Thank you, my lady."

"You will eat dinner at my table tonight. I will teach you manners."

That sounded terrible. His gut tightened. "Thank you, my lady."

"First lesson, you must think of more to say besides, yes, my lady and thank you, my lady."

No other words came.

Darius laughed. "And I'll serve roast veal. So you'll at least get some enjoyment out of the evening."

Ferth wasn't sure it was going to be worth it.

THIRTY-FOUR - DEADLY
THIRRO

Thirro adjusted his cloak—the hateful thing. They all wore them now as they traveled down the human roads. They didn't have time for cutting through woods anymore. They had to get to Mitera—before it was too late.

He stopped. He'd let himself outpace the others again. Dara, Dan, Gasson, Jade, Gavriel, Kor, and Tai—*his* unit—approached in a clump of strangely shaped shadows. No human walked the warm summer night with a hooded full-length cloak. Mordick lagged. The ram was getting slower.

"I'll help Mordick. Stay vigilant. Remember, leave no witnesses." Thirro jogged back the way he had come, his cloak chafing against his folded wings.

He'd loosened his sword and was almost within striking range of Mordick when he heard wagon wheels. Thirro stepped into a tree's shadow. Mordick continued his bent-over, hobbled walk. He looked almost human—an old man with a cane. The wagon pulled by twin horses stopped at Mordick's side. Mordick froze when a man hopped down in front of him.

"Hello there," the human said. "Can I give you a ride this evening? You've a long way to go before town."

Mordick shook his head under his hood.

"Come on. I'll help you up. I can't leave you here like this." The man blocked the Draco's path.

Mordick hobbled faster, trying to get around the farmer.

"Come on, old man. I'll take you wherever you want to go." The man put a hand on Mordick's shoulder.

With a flash of steel, the ram Draco thrust a blade into the human's chest. Mordick's hood fell back, revealing leathery skin and brown horns. The man's eyes widened and his face paled. He dropped.

Thirro had let go of his sword and finished stringing his bow. He cocked an arrow.

Mordick bent down and wiped his blade clean on the man's pants. When he stood, an arrow protruded from his chest. He glanced down at Thirro's signature dark-brown fletching. Mordick knew that Thirro added feathers from his own wings to each of his arrows—marking his kills. He roared. Thirro cut off the offensive howl with a second arrow through his windpipe. The Draco slumped over the human. The horses shied away. They pranced. Thirro sprinted. He gripped the lead ropes. The horses neighed and jerked, but he held tight. Nostrils flared and eyes bugged, but the animals stilled.

Hands vibrating with adrenaline, Thirro pulled his arrows out of the dead Draco Sang. He unstrung his bow and tucked his weapon away, putting the wiped-clean arrows back in his quiver. Mordick's knife went into Thirro's baldric. He heaved the two bodies onto the wagon bed. Wood panels creaked in protest as they slammed home. He climbed into the driver's seat. He'd seen horse-drawn wagons before. How hard could it be?

"Go."

Nothing. He shook the reins. Nothing.

He picked up the whip that lay coiled at his feet. With all his might, he brought it down on the horses' backs. They jerked forward with a mighty charge. He barely kept the straps in his hands as his wings slammed into the seat. The wagon shook and rattled as they nearly flew down the road.

Now they were in business. This would get them to Mitera with time to spare.

Within minutes he spotted his unit. But no Jade—she'd have her arrow trained on his heart by now. He yanked on the reins and the horses shuddered to a walk, neighing and whining and tossing their tethered heads. He whistled—one high note followed by two short low ones. Jade emerged from the trees, bowstring slackened. The horses stopped, eyes spinning as the Dracos crowded around.

"We've got a ride to town." Thirro's chest puffed.

"Where's Mordick?" Jade asked.

"He's dead."

Her eyes narrowed.

"The driver found him. He killed Mordick before I got there to help."

"Mordick wouldn't let a human get him."

"Took him by surprise, I guess."

Jade didn't look convinced. He could practically feel the unit's judgmental stares, like sticky fingers poking at him.

Thirro didn't care. "Bodies are in the back. We'll dump them when we find a good place. Hop in."

"You want us to sit on corpses?" Dara asked.

"You can sit in the driver's seat with me." He extended a hand and pulled her to his side.

Jade huffed. With jackal grace, she leaped into the wagon's flat bed.

Thirro fit his arm around Dara's waist. He whipped the

horses, though not as hard this time. They lunged forward, straining under the new weight. Hisses issued from behind him as his soldiers jostled and banged into each other.

He exhaled with a grin as the star-lit road to Mitera rose to meet him.

THIRTY-FIVE - DREADING
SUZA

"*They will attack at dawn,*" Xandra said to Suza as she flew off the roof of Laconius's command tent. She glided low through the trees outside of the Draco Sang camp. The red-tailed hawk knew the forest well, having hidden there for months while Suza was a slave.

"*How many?*" Suza asked. She was across the river in Titus's tent along with the Elysium commanders. Captain Titus sat on a low couch with his broken leg resting on a stool. Eio, Titus's golden-maned lion, slept on the floor next to him.

"*Nearly eight full units.*"

Suza sucked in a sharp breath.

Titus cut off mid-sentence; she hadn't been listening to his instructions anyway. His focus snapped to her face. The other commanders followed his gaze.

"Four thousand Dracos will attack at dawn." Her words rippled over the room like poisonous gas.

Pelussa cleared her raspy throat. It was easy to forget the old woman was here. She melded into the shadows and rarely spoke. "Ipsum counted three thousand eight hundred and ninety-one warriors in tomorrow's attack."

Bit of a show-off. "They're going to try and spread us out along the border," Suza said. "They'll cross in tight units and then fan quickly."

"We're expecting this," Titus said, his voice a calm that seemed forced. "We'll be ready. Commanders, let's walk through your assignments and then go prepare your units."

A bit of color returned to the blanched faces as they got to work. Suza was glad to be assigned to Uriah's unit.

Twenty minutes later she trudged out of Titus's tent with instructions to eat and sleep. Xandra glided silently through the darkness and landed on her armband. Xandra's claws hooked into the leather, no longer worried about piercing Suza's thin skin.

"It's going to be a slaughter tomorrow," Suza said.

"The humans number nearly ten thousand."

"We can hope, Xandra. We must have some hope." Although she didn't feel much now.

A wolf Draco with half a human face and bright golden eyes filled her mind before the vision shifted to his fully human form. Was Ferth safe in Mitera with his mother? Did he find her? Suza ached for him. After so much pain, they had come together for one torturously brief moment— shared a kiss that still burned on her skin. She rolled her bottom lip between her teeth. Would she live to hold him again? At least he was safe. She was willing to die to keep it that way. And soon she would have the chance to prove that.

Zemira crossed the path twenty yards ahead, and Suza darted to catch her. She wasn't ready to face the night alone yet. She wasn't ready to close her eyes and see the familiar faces of her enemy getting closer. Zemira's panther noticed her first, training glossy black eyes on Suza.

"Hello, Opal."

Zemira looked over her shoulder.

"Are you busy right now?"

"Not really. Shem's at the smith. He'll be working late into the night."

Zemira didn't mention her baby. Suza missed Callie so much her stomach hurt. How much worse it must be for the mother.

"Come in," Zemira motioned to her tent.

Suza followed the lithe fighter inside. She sat in silence as Zemira checked her armor and sharpened her already-sharp blades.

"Tell me something about Cal," Suza said.

Zemira's hands stilled. She set down her belt but didn't look up. "He would do anything for the people he cared about. Anything." She rubbed her polishing cloth over a gleaming short sword. "I had been training for years when he joined our unit. Titus brought him in, as he did me and Uriah, and so many of us Draco-blooded. Cal was cocky and aggressive." The rag stopped moving over the Dracosteel. "He had talent but was raw as fresh meat. Unskilled. He worked hard, though. We all knew he would be a great warrior. I was being petty. I didn't like that he'd only just arrived and thought so much of himself." She grimaced. "I played a mean prank on him." Dark eyes got a far-off look. "Cal knew it was me, and he never said a word. He got in a wad of trouble. Titus punished him for it."

Suza thought of Ferth's striped back and shuddered.

"Cleaning the dungbuckets and extra training sessions. He never said a word. I felt terrible."

Xandra shifted in her lap. Suza traced a finger down soft feathers. She wanted to ask what Zemira had done, but the sour look of regret on Zemira's face had her voicing a different question. "He loved you, didn't he?"

She laughed. "He might have had a bit of a crush at first.

But after everything that happened, with Poe's death, and his saving both Callie's and my life, he became family. I miss him. Shem misses him. We all do." She sighed. "It is hard for me to see his face on another man."

What could Suza say to that? Would Zemira ever see Ferth as anything other than a kidnapper and killer?

The hard-jawed warrior's eyes glistened as Zemira turned away. "I think of Cal during battle. I live for Shem. I fight for my baby. But when I kill, I kill for Cal." Her voice was quiet, almost as if she didn't want to be heard.

Suza wore the same tight-fitting black uniform, but Zemira looked like a fighter, all angles and sinew—hair cropped short above her ears. Suza's long hair framed a curvy chest. She was going to war tomorrow, but she didn't look or feel like a warrior. She wanted Cal's bravery, Zemira's strength.

"Cut my hair?" The words popped out.

Zemira's eyebrows shot up.

"Short, like yours. I'm going to war tomorrow, not a party."

The tension shook out of Zemira's shoulders as she chuckled in surprise. "Alright, my lady. That seems like as good a way to prepare for battle as any."

Suza smiled. She'd been forbidden to cut her hair as a slave. Now the choice was hers.

Wide-eyed, she watched the mirror as Zemira expertly cut off her hair at her shoulders. Some shorter pieces over her forehead framed her eyes. Suza's nerves gave way to a new resolve and a new freedom.

"It's not as short as mine." Zemira brushed the cuttings off Suza's shoulders. "Your hair is too beautiful to cut it all off."

Suza ran her hands through her soft weightless locks. Loose curls flew around her head in a playful mass that tickled her neck.

"I love it."

"Thank you for coming to see me. I should have done a better job welcoming you. I was selfish in my grief."

Suza stood, waking Xandra and forcing the sleepy hawk to take flight. She gave Zemira a tight hug. "Thank you. Stay safe tomorrow."

The haunting shadows hanging over camp failed to hack into Suza's composure. She was calm as she prepared for war. She slept without nightmares.

THIRTY-SIX - BARE
FERTH

*L*yko and Rom dozed on the plush carpet. Ferth sat in front of a polished mirror, but he didn't look at himself. His eyes were on the woman standing behind him. Mira bit on her lips as she fought through tangled curls. Ferth smiled—he did that when he focused too. She caught his gaze in the mirror. Her face relaxed, and she chuckled. She lifted a mass of hair.

"You know, son …"

Son. His chest warmed.

"Long hair is out of style."

"You want to cut it."

Her eyes twinkled. "Please."

How could he say no to that giddy smile? Would he appear more human? He would look more like the clean-cut Cal—although Ferth's features would always be sharper, rougher, wilder than his twin. "Whatever you want, Ma." That was fun to say. Happiness bloomed across her delicate features. She pulled scissors out of her apron. "You planned this."

She pulled a long face. "I'll admit nothing until the job is done."

"You probably knotted it up on purpose."

"It worked."

The joy on her face triggered his widest grin.

When she brought the shears down, he jumped to his feet.

"Wait. I have to wear this shirt to dinner." He pulled it off without thinking. He was too absorbed in the comfortable connection forming with his mother. He realized his mistake the moment her gaze touched his skin. His healing wounds and lashes were angry red stripes.

In a snap, horror replaced happiness. Her golden eyes darkened. Her face paled.

In a breath, the shirt was back on, but it was too late. She sat with a thud on his stool. He carefully took the scissors out of her shaking fingers.

She gripped his hands—hard. "He did this to you. He hurt you. All those years I wasn't there." Gigantic tears spilled over her cheeks. "I failed you—my baby. Can you ever forgive me? Can you ever forgive me for not being there? For not protecting you?" Her voice broke into a sob, and her body trembled.

His heart cracked. He drew her to her feet and pulled her against his chest. A lifetime apart, but he could feel that this was right. This was home. "Laconius is done taking from us. Don't give him any more. He's done hurting you. You've always had my forgiveness. Now, will you stop blaming yourself?"

She cried harder.

What had he said wrong?

"And you are so good. How?"

"Thank you, but I'm not." He pulled her out of his embrace and looked her in the eyes. "I was a captain in Mavras's army. I was harsh and demanding, cruel even. I was feared, Mother. This punishment came because I let my slave escape." He conjured up Suza's beautiful face, bright green eyes and high cheekbones. Those lips he'd tasted only briefly. "Suza is free. I'd have suffered a lot more for that."

Mira blinked, a knowing look crossing her face. "Will I get to meet her?"

Ferth couldn't stop the grin. "I hope so." If they lived through this. He handed Mira the scissors and sat down, shirt on.

Her silent working calmed his nerves. Sharing the truth with her had brought unexpected comfort. Chunks of brown hair fluttered to the ground. Her smile returned when she lifted his chin to face the mirror. Brown waves ended halfway down his forehead. His neck and ears were bare. He looked *different.* Tame.

"Very handsome," she said.

"Thank you. You did a nice job." Even if he wasn't sure what he thought of his tailored look. It felt like a lie.

She moved as if to leave, hesitated, and turned back. "I had lots of practice with Cal. I cut his hair like this."

He held his breath.

"But I know you are not Callidon. I'm not trying to turn you into him. You are my first born. My son who was lost and now is found. Do not think I wish you to replace him."

Ferth exhaled with a shiver as relief cascaded through him. "Thank you."

"I'll be back with a broom, and then I'll show you to dinner." She halted again. "After dinner, if you are not too tired, there are some people who are anxious to meet you."

"Yes. I would love to."

She smiled as she slipped out the door.

Ferth sighed and ran a hand through silky short hair. Everything here was too soft, too lovely, too breakable. *"Feelings are exhausting."* He needed to work some of them out.

"We're sleeping," Rom said.

Ferth took his shirt off and shook out the hair. He laid the linen tunic on the bed. He took off his boots and set them aside. Lyko opened one eye in his direction as he rolled up the bottoms of his pants. Ferth grinned, half-feral. Lyko shuddered to his feet as Ferth leaped. He slammed into Lyko's side, and the wolf hit the floor.

Lyko barked.

"Shh," Ferth said with a chuckle.

Lyko barked louder in his mind.

Ferth's responding laughter was cut off when Rom jumped on his back. His stripes screamed.

"Low blow." He turned and threw the gray wolf off. Lyko had escaped, and now the white wolf rammed his head into Ferth's belly. He kept his feet until Rom leaped at his chest, adding his strength to Lyko's. Ferth's back slammed into the thick carpet. He flipped, catching Lyko's legs. Lyko landed on his chest, and they rolled. Ferth came out on top, but Rom brought his open jaws down on the back of Ferth's neck. His canines caressed his spine, sending chills along his skin.

"Point, Rom," Ferth said.

Rom's teeth pressed deeper. *"Victory, Rom."*

"And Lyko."

Laughing, Ferth dropped to the floor. He rolled to his back. Rom dropped next to him.

There was a knock. The door muffled her voice. "It's Mira."

Ferth jumped to his feet and threw the shirt over his steaming skin. "Come on in."

She eyed the three panting creatures before sweeping the mess. Plenty of gray and white fur caught in her broom.

Ferth got a drink, put on his boots, and found his dinner jacket—a gray linen button-up Angeline had given him to wear.

"At least let us outside," Lyko said.

"Dinner could be hours." Ferth sure hoped not. *"What if their guests go outside?"*

"We'll scare them."

"We found a good place to hide. No one will see us out there. We're clawing at the walls in here." Rom lifted a paw, claws within an inch of the paint.

"You better not."

"Please," Rom and Lyko used in the same demanding tone.

Ferth caved. *"Darius is a gracious host. Be polite. Stay hidden."*

"We like him too," Rom said.

Ferth checked the hall before opening the outside door and sneaking them through. Two happy streaks blurred across the darkening lawn and into the trees near the wall. He would have rather joined them instead of learning human manners.

"Have fun," Lyko said, not at all jealous.

Ferth smoothed his hair, which now took only a sweep of his hand. He followed Mira down the hall, past the kitchen, and into a well-lit ballroom. He balked. There were nearly fifty people here.

"I need to go help." She squeezed his forearm. "Have fun, dear." She slipped away before he could reply and tell her she sounded too much like Lyko.

Pale marble walls gleamed in the lights. An inlaid wood floor spread out at the feet of five musicians. New and interesting smells washed up from two heavy-laden tables. Could the Lammas holiday feast be grander than this?

Ferth's attention snared on the people. The humans were beautiful. The women wore long shining dresses, some with big skirts, others with cloth that clung to their curves. The men wore jackets like his. *Thank you for the suit, Angeline.* He didn't need more reasons to stand out.

Darius saw him rooted on the threshold. "Commander

Ferth. Welcome." The booming voice drew every face his direction.

Ferth squared his shoulders and strode forward. He accepted Darius's hand. Under his breath, he said, "I didn't expect a large party."

"Just a few friends to welcome you to Mitera."

Angeline overheard as she strode up. "Best way to learn is to dive in." Laconius had said something like that before, but he had not been referring to dinner parties. Nearly Ferth's height, she rocked forward and kissed him on the cheek. "I like the hair. You don't look so feral."

"I liked that about him," Darius said.

"He still looks plenty deadly." She winked at him. Ferth was at a loss. Was she making a joke or being serious? He *was* plenty deadly. She hadn't let him bring his sword, but he had three knives on his person. All sharp and within easy reach—didn't everyone? "But he looks smarter now, I think." She lowered her voice. "Smile." She turned her shoulders, opening a path from him to the crowd pressing forward. "This is Tamaria."

Ferth forced his mouth to curve up as a woman came forward. Her lips were shockingly red, as was her dress. It clung to her body—revealing a silhouette that rolled like the Seraf foothills.

"Nice to meet you, Commander." Her brown eyes gleamed in pleasure. She flipped unbound black hair over her bare neck. She bowed just low enough to give him a peek down her dress.

What is happening? Was she a gift to him? His memory flashed back to Shi Castle and the slaves that entertained the officers. *Never* had they approached with such convincing invitations.

"Take her hand," Angeline instructed. Ferth obeyed

dumbly. The girl looked up through painted lashes. "Tell her you are enchanted and that you wish to dance later."

Ferth jerked his gaze to Angeline. Parts of him most certainly did wish to be with this stranger tonight. She was beautiful, but he was Suza's. "No," he stammered.

"She's agreed to teach you," Angeline said. "You'll have to dance at Lammas. And the whole city will be watching."

He already felt like the entire city watched. Ferth's face heated as he realized that these guests must already know he was uncivilized. They had come to participate in his culturing —or to mock it. He cleared his throat and his annoyance. So he had to do this. "Enchanted to meet you, Tamaria. It would be my pleasure if you would favor me with a dance later."

"A bit wordy," Angeline said before Tamaria could reply. "But it has a unique charm. That would work on any woman here."

"Yes, it would." Tamaria gave him another coy smile. "I'll look forward to it, sir."

In Skotar, he would have understood her intentions—and known how to reject them. Here, he was clueless. The next young woman who came forward seemed to offer her body in invitation as well, although less aggressively. His frown deepened in confusion. He relaxed slightly when introduced to the men. Darius made the presentations. He was less outspoken and more casual than Angeline.

"Your first time in Mitera," one of the men said. "Raja Darius says you are from Miston."

Miston. Miston. Remember that.

"Ferth was a blacksmith apprentice there until he joined the army two years ago with the surge," Darius said, feeding Ferth information.

The man looked like that was boring. Ferth agreed. He would have much preferred to spit out that he was a Draco

Sang traitor. Enough pretending. Enough of this strangling shirt.

"Ferth is now a commander in Captain Titus's army."

Also not exactly true. He commanded a unit in one battle. Now he had no official position in the army. Or anywhere.

"How are you enjoying Mitera? You wouldn't want to go back to Miston *now*." The man leaned forward conspiratorially.

"I think you're right," Ferth said.

The cook entered, carrying a steaming roast.

"Dear guests," Darius spoke loudly. "Thank you for joining us tonight and for your warm welcome to my dear friend, Ferth. Let's dispense with the formalities and eat."

Ferth started to relax and almost let a real smile slip, but then Angeline was at his side. He tensed, but her focus was on Darius. He held out his elbow, and she slipped her hand around it.

Angeline speared Ferth with a look as Tamaria appeared at his right. Ferth forced his elbow out like a duck. Her fingers cupped his forearm muscle. Angeline nodded. Darius led them forward.

"Pull out her chair," Angeline said. "Not that one. You'll sit by me. Yes, good. Hold her hand. Just her fingers. Now you sit."

Tamaria giggled.

Ferth sank into his seat.

"Back straight. Don't even think about touching the seatback."

Nogard forbid.

He was sweating. Mountains of appealing food lay in front of him. His mouth watered. With a force of will, he kept his hands in his lap—as did everyone. Not for the first time, he thought of the halls of Shi Castle. There, no one set food out and made him sit and stare at it—unless as punishment.

"Pass each dish clockwise. Hold the bowl. Not for me, for Tamaria."

Ferth held the rice pilaf while Tamaria took one spoonful.

"Now, I hold it for you to serve yourself," Tamaria said. She held the dish while he took one scoop of rice. "At Lammas, servants will walk the dishes down the tables."

"Okay, thanks."

After nineteen dishes had made their way around the table, Ferth was allowed to pick up his fork.

"It's not a weapon," Angeline said from his right. Steely fingers readjusted his grip.

"She loves bossing people around." Darius waved at his wife's ministrations as if they were nothing but annoying flies. Easy for him. He wasn't the one being pestered.

"It's true. So of course I married the one man who refused to be bossed."

"It's your favorite thing about me." He kissed her straight nose.

The food was delicious, but Ferth took no pleasure in eating. Between each bite, he ingested information about the Mitera elite. He ate painfully slowly. He didn't dare take one sip of the fragrant wine. He needed all his wits and a wall of restraint tonight.

Mira came into the hall. He perked up at the look of pride on her face as she gazed on him. She joined two others in clearing away dishes and bringing more wine.

"Hello, son," she said into his ear as she refilled Tamaria's glass.

"Are you eating?"

"Yes, I'll have my fill in the kitchens," Mira said.

"Take me with you."

She smiled as if he were simply paying her a compliment, not begging for relief. Then she was gone.

During flaky chocolate pudding cake, the musicians began to play. There was no deep beat, no pulsing brass. The stringed instruments sounded like song birds in spring. How could they dance to this? As if in answer to his thoughts, Darius stood.

"Dance with me, darling." He swept Angeline to her feet and onto the open floor.

They moved together in graceful swirls. Their fluid movements matched the airy music. It was strange and lovely and foreign. Ferth slouched, wanting to disappear.

"That looks fun," Tamaria said.

Ferth said nothing. It did not look fun. It looked stressful.

"Now you ask me to dance."

"I can't. I'm sorry."

"You can't dance or you can't dance with me?" Big brown eyes looked hurt.

Both. "I can't do *that*." His eyes flickered to the twirling couples.

"You've never danced—ever?"

"No." Ferth pictured the dim smoky rooms of Shi Castle. Sweaty Dracos smashed together. Bodies gyrated. Drums pounded. Laughter swelled.

"I'm an excellent teacher." She stood and smoothed out a wrinkleless dress. "Come."

Ferth sucked in a deep breath and stood. He would conquer this human dance thing. Tamaria took his hand and drew him forward. The shiny black shoes Angeline had given him pinched his toes. Couples twirled around him in synchronized duets. Tamaria stood before him. She stepped close as she put his left hand on her lower back. She curled a hand over his left shoulder. She clasped his right hand in hers.

"Step when I step. We'll make a triangle on the floor with our feet. One, two, three."

He stepped on her toe.

"Other foot. Step right."

His knee banged into her thigh. "Sorry."

She closed her eyes for a breath. "Try again. One, two, three."

One, two, three. Ferth thought of his sword training—how often he'd spent hours working on footwork. He'd mastered those dances just fine. *One, two, three.*

"Now we keep the same rhythm, but move across the floor." She moved closer, leading him to the right with her entire body. Her front pressed into him, and he lost his count. Her embrace slackened as they jarred out of step. He stepped back and rubbed sweaty palms against his pants. He was overheating.

"Think of it as art," Angeline said over her shoulder, loud enough for the entire room to hear. "You're making art with your dance."

He couldn't make art. He couldn't do this.

Ferth searched out his wolves. They were wrestling near the outer wall. *"We don't belong here."* He wasn't sure he wanted to anymore. This was not home.

"You belong with us," Rom said. *"In the wolf pack."*

Ferth was deciding whether to walk out and find his wolves or take Tamaria's hand as was his duty when Mira appeared.

"Pardon me, my lady, sir, I have an urgent message for Commander Ferth."

Ferth could have kissed her.

"Please think nothing of it." Tamaria turned away, surely eager for a suitable partner to make *art* with.

Darius was at his side in an instant, worried. "What's happened?"

"Nothing for alarm, raja," Mira said. "It's a personal matter."

He relaxed. "Yes, of course." He shook Ferth's hand and lowered his voice to a whisper. "Thank you for dinner tonight. It was a hard situation we put you in. Forgive me."

"No apology necessary," Ferth said, his voice equally quiet. "You've given refuge to a barbarian. I'm in your debt." After a night of pretense, he gladly embraced the truth.

"You're a good man. I'm glad to be your friend."

"I feel the same."

"Good evening, Ferth. Good evening, Mira."

Mira bowed as Raja Darius strode back to his waiting wife.

Mira led Ferth into an empty hall.

"What's the urgent message?"

"It's from me." She wrung her hands. "The message is that you don't have to fit in here. Not for me, at least."

He smiled. "I looked that out of place? Even with the hair cut?" He tried to jest, but inside coils of tension loosened.

"You got the same twitch in your brow Cal got when he was stressed out or unhappy."

She had watched him, noticed him, and cared about him. This wasn't home, but with her help, could it be?

"I want you to be happy."

"Thank you, Mother. I'm happy you got me out of there."

Her lips curved up. "Ready to meet your family?"

"Yes."

THIRTY-SEVEN - FAMILY
FERTH

*M*ira kept an excited half-step ahead of Ferth as she led them west, away from the castle. Warmly lit taverns and dining rooms spilled humans out into the streets. At intervals, music played—not all of it the lofty strings he'd heard that evening. A rhythmic drumbeat drew Ferth's attention and relaxed his shoulders. Wafting spices and roasted meats reminded him that he was still hungry.

"Closford is my dad, your grandpapi," Mira said. "My mother died before you were born. Elssa is my sister. We're going to her home. She and Aron have four boys and two girls."

"Will they be asleep by now?"

Mira leapt over a broken cobblestone. "Not tonight. They're excited to meet you."

"Me too." And he was nervous. Please let this not be like dinner.

The city changed. Fewer streetlamps. Less marble. Less shine. More comfortable.

She stopped on a long street where the homes were tall and narrow, butting up against each other like soldiers. The

Draco Sang would destroy this beautiful city. Heavy sadness slowed his steps. He determined to enjoy this while he could, but his heart still pinched.

Mira ran up six steps to a blue door. She opened it and stepped onto a smooth stone floor. "We're here!" Her voice betrayed her excitement.

Ferth faced an indoor staircase and a long hall.

"In the kitchen."

They followed the voice. Mira opened another door on nine staring faces. In a flash, Ferth took in the eager, apprehensive eyes. Tears ran down the oldest man's wrinkles. A feast sat on the wooden table, a cake, meatballs, salad, bread —all untouched. *All this for me?* He forced an unsure smile as his belly flip-flopped.

"Welcome," Elssa said. She looked like Mira, although heavier and her hair grayed in the front. She stepped forward and put her hands up to his shoulders. He bent down into her quick embrace. "I'm your aunt, Elssa."

"Ferth."

"Yes, we know, Ferth. We're so pleased to meet you. So pleased."

It was unbelievable. "Thank you."

Closford approached. "Please call me Grandpapi." His eyes glistened. "I can die a happy man. My lost grandson is found. And look at you."

Ferth's shoulder's tensed under the weight of their scrutiny, knowing he couldn't live up to their hopes. This man had kind eyes and a warm smile and deep wrinkles that spoke of hardship, yet Ferth did not know him. *Give it time.* This was his *family* now. But he still felt lost.

Elssa introduced her husband, Aron, and their six children. Their innocent eyes and accepting smiles lifted a portion of his fears. He wanted to know them. His cousins. He wanted to be a child again and play with them without the world feeling so heavy. He tucked a picture of them away in his mind, for when he was fighting against the Draco Sang, his lost home and childhood. He would be fighting for these children, for their home and freedom. He was willing to die for it.

THIRTY-EIGHT - WAR
SUZA

Suza's heart raced. She shifted her grip on her sword with a sweaty hand. Uriah stood at her left. Two hundred yards south of the Rugit River, they waited with the Elysium army. The Draco Sang had crossed the river and were filtering though the timber fencing.

"Archers," Captain Titus yelled.

At his command, dozens of flaming arrows whistled through the air. The dry grass and hidden piles of kindling lit up the ground at the enemy's feet. Oil-soaked timber burst into flames. Fire licked at the Dracos. Screaming rent the air as the enraged barbarians raced out of the pursuing inferno.

"Archers!"

Arrows thinned the herds of Draco, but not enough. They slammed into the waiting Elysium soldiers with deadly force.

"Archers!"

A horn blared. The Dracos had changed their calls. Suza had expected it, but it was still a blow. She tucked her useless pipes into her belt. With her twin short swords in her hands, she inched forward with Uriah.

"Stay right next to me," he said.

"You too, big brother."

A screaming Draco broke through the line of shields. Uriah's sword silenced her. Suza hadn't moved. Fear clogged her throat. She failed to swallow it away, but when the next attacker broke through, she shook off her paralysis. His sword came down hard. She blocked it, but the reverberations shook her spine. She twisted inside his arms and dug her sharp Dracosteel into his heart, a move Imanna had taught her. He reeked of animal sweat and gore. She gagged and jumped back.

Together with Uriah, she fought Draco after Draco as the enemy broke through the weakening shield wall. She could hardly move her feet with the fresh corpses piled around.

"We've pushed them back on the west side," Xandra said. *"They're retreating and gathering their forces down the middle."*

Between huffs, Suza relayed the message to Uriah.

"Shift east," he yelled to his troops. "Sprint back a hundred paces. Archers, cover us."

Suza tried not to step on dead bodies in her retreat—she failed. *I'm sorry. May the Dragon keep you.* She probably shouldn't think such a thing anymore. The phrase felt more like a curse now than a blessing. What good had the Dragon ever done?

She blocked out the world as she fought and killed and fought and killed. Numbly she followed Uriah's orders.

Ten paces to her left, a spider Draco came into view. Suza shuddered as the Draco shot silk threads out of exposed holes in her abdomen. The webbing tangled around limbs and gummed up swords and axes. Soldiers dropped before the scuttling Draco's twin swords at a heartbreaking rate. Inhaling strength, Suza forced her feet to march toward the bulging eyes and hairy arms.

The spider saw Suza and turned, her triangular mouth splitting to reveal black fangs. Hopefully she couldn't shoot venom out of those. The Draco angled her swords at Suza. Suza swallowed, bent her knees, and rolled to the balls of her feet. Sticky silk shot at her. She jumped to the side, her sword clanging against Dracosteel as the spider hacked down at her. She panted as she whirled away from another blow. Pearlescent webbing smeared over her hip. She wouldn't win hand to hand like this. She opened her mouth to call for her brother, but no words came as a figure leaped through the air and landed on the Draco's shoulders.

She'd have to ask Zemira to teach her how to jump like that.

Gore coated Zemira's black leathers. Eyes hooded and face relentless, she gripped the Draco's neck. Her knee buried into its shoulder. The enemy hissed and twisted, her fangs seeming to grow longer.

Suza struck, but her sword didn't pierce the carapace over the Draco's chest. More silk shot out, barely missing Suza's hand. The enemy held her swords like skewers and shoved toward Zemira, but Zemira flipped off, landing on her feet behind the spider.

Suza blinked, frustrated that Zemira had failed to kill the Draco. A heartbeat later, the spider shuddered and toppled to the side. Her head rolled, revealing a gaping wet throat.

Suza stared at the menacing corpse. She hadn't even seen Zemira's strike. "Whoa."

Zemira's dark eyes flashed her way, but her only response was to shove her short sword into a Draco that lunged out from behind his fallen comrade.

Opal trotted into view, her jaws dripping red.

Suza fell in next to Zemira, fighting side by side with her sister. Even with her focus on the various Dracos who tested her steel, she couldn't stop watching Zemira and Opal. They took down three Dracos to every one that Suza vanquished. Zemira was like water, flowing and uncatchable as she permeated the enemy lines and drained their blood. Suza knew that the new mother should be in Mitera, nursing her baby and singing lullabies. Instead, she was here, forced to perform her deadly dance.

"I haven't seen Thirro," Xandra said from her perch on the watchtower.

"Good."

"I don't think so. He's up to something."

"Check on camp. Check on Titus. Check on Imanna." Suza decided she'd better check on her brother. "I'm moving east."

"Watch your left side." Zemira didn't take her eyes off the lizard Draco she battled. "You're holding your sword too low."

The cursed thing was getting heavy. Suza nodded in thanks, touched that Zemira had been watching out for her. She swallowed the Draco blessing that popped to her tongue and fought her way back to Uriah's side.

"Don't get so far away from me." He grunted as his foot slipped in man-made mud. His shield dropped, and the ram Draco pressed his advantage. Suza leaped to help, but Uriah pulled a knife from his chest strap and flung it. It buried itself up to the hilt in the Draco's neck.

Uriah panted as he got to his feet and retrieved his knife.

"Nice shot."

"Stay next to me."

His love and concern spread warmth through her icy chest, fueling her as she lifted her sword against the dog Draco who sprang at her.

It was never going to end. No matter how many Dracos they killed, more would take their place. Always more.

The Draco's war horns blew a new message. Suza held her sword at her opponent's throat. "What does that mean?"

The furry face spat blood. She closed her eyes as the warm ooze hit her cheek. She blinked, and a blade flew forward. She dove, but pain sang across her shoulder. Her sword dropped in her useless grip. Hot liquid spread over her chest and arm. Lightheaded, she fought with her other sword, but she was weakening at an alarming rate.

Uriah's blade severed the Draco's head clean off. Rage and fear obscured his face. "Guap, take Suza to the healers now."

"No, I'm fine. He needs to stay here and fight with you."

"Yes, commander." The man sheathed his bloody sword and scooped her into his arms. He danced over red dirt and lifeless mounds. At a near sprint, they crossed into camp.

How did he have the energy? "I can walk from here."

He didn't slow. The building they entered sang with groans of pain. Blood and sweat clogged her nose. He set her on one of the few open cots and sagged against the side for an instant. Exhausted.

"Get something to drink." Her voice was hoarse. "Thank you for carrying me in, but please go back and help Uriah. Please help him." She couldn't bear that Uriah was out there without her or Guap.

Guap kissed her forehead and staggered out.

"Can you see Uriah?"

"Yes, Zemira has joined him. The Draco Sang haven't broken the line yet."

Suza sagged in relief and fell back against the cot. Zemira had Dracosteel in her veins. She would protect her brother. She would protect them all.

"Suza?" Imanna's worried face came into view, and then the world blurred into darkness.

THIRTY-NINE - DISGUISED
THIRRO

They made good time on the wagon. The humans didn't seem to notice that the enemy passed them on the road. Thirro briefly worried the dead man's family would come looking for him, or at least for their wagon and horses, but so far, no one had found them. After shaving off many miles, the horses stopped walking at noonday.

Thirro cracked the whip down on their backs. They pranced sideways and stopped. The horses' mouths frothed, and their heavy breaths rasped. He raised the whip.

"They need rest," Jade said. She popped up to her feet on the flatbed so her pretty face was annoyingly close at his shoulder.

He brought the whip down. One horse jumped with a whine; the other didn't move.

She turned her pale eyes on Thirro. "They're our ticket into Mitera. Don't kill them now."

"Don't tell me what to do."

Her red lips curled. "Of course, commander." She shifted on her feet and stared forward.

Dara nuzzled against his side. "I'd like a rest too. And something to eat."

A group of humans appeared on the road ahead. Pasture spread on the right, farmland on the left. Not a good place to camp. They'd recently passed a barn ...

"There's an abandoned barn a hundred yards back," Gavriel said.

He sneered at the pretentious raven. "Just what I was thinking."

Dara raised skeptical brows and quickly lowered them.

He glared at her. He *had* been thinking that. "Let's move. Jade, you bring the horses. You seem to know what they need. And with that cloak on, you actually look like a weak human." His voice dripped with disdain. But it was the truth. Her face was like a woman wearing paints and dyes, and irritatingly attractive. Too bad she was such a shrew. "The rest of us will secure the barn."

Jade sauntered over to the horses and cooed.

By the time Thirro reached the empty barn, she had them turned around and plodding back up the road. The humans on the road dipped their hats and exchanged salutations with her as they passed. She was a powerful tool on this mission. Probably any mission. He hated that he had to depend on her sneaking them into the castle.

Hidden in the abandoned barn, Jade nursed the horses back to strength. After a meal of stolen milk, parsnips, and apples, and a day of rest, the eight remaining Dracos resumed their southern journey.

The wagon jostled down the widening road in the predawn hours. The lights of Mitera brightened and grew on the horizon. The cargo in the wagon bed looked more like lumps of blankets than Draco Sang warriors. Thirro's hood pulled far over his beakish face as he sagged in the driver's seat. His wings cramped from hours folded under his cloak.

The trickle of early-morning travelers paid them no heed. He smiled. Mitera had not learned her lesson after his first visit. Foolish trusting humans. The rising sun threw golden rays over the city. The castle was a vision of green flame.

"It's beautiful," Dara said.

The others had woken and crouched, awe-faced, on the flatbed.

"This will all be ours," Gasson said, his voice greedy.

The Vasil River churned to their right, and the gates of Mitera rose before them—wide open in welcome. Houses and farms sprawled in every direction. Before reaching the bridge toward the city, Thirro steered the horses off the road at the sign for *The Speckled Fox Inn*.

"Jade," he said. "You're up."

Keeping her hood over her pointed ears and furry head, she leaped off the wagon and sprinted ahead. Thirro slowed the horses as Jade disappeared into the inn. A man approached, and Thirro's hand slid to a dagger handle.

"Will you be stabling your horses?"

He sank into his hood and bowed his head. "Yes." He hopped down, hugging his wings to his back as tightly as he could.

The man's brows creased as he took in Thirro's tall, humped frame. Under his cloak, Thirro drew a knife.

The door opened, and Jade strode out. "Come, cousins," she said. "They've room for us."

The stable slave—servant—relaxed at the sight of her bright smile.

"Thank you, sir," Thirro said as he strode by.

The man froze, reins in hand, as seven misshapen figures, mysteriously cloaked, strolled by.

He could be trouble.

Thankfully, the inn was empty, save for a slave girl sweeping. Jade rushed them through the parlor and into a bedroom—one. One large bed, a basin, a table, and two chairs were the only furniture.

"They only had the one," Jade said. "I didn't want to draw attention. The mistress is bringing food."

Thirro ripped off his cloak and shook out his wings. Jade flicked a feather off her arm. "Jade, follow the stable slave and make sure he doesn't get snoopy. Dispose of him —discreetly."

She frowned.

"I can do that," Dara said.

Thirro glanced at her eager amber eyes. Dara's ear bore the scar from Ferth's knife. She wasn't as good as Jade.

"Lammas is tonight," Jade said. "I already have little time to map out the castle."

Everyone froze at the knock. Thirro jerked on his cloak. Jade answered it.

"That looks lovely. Thank you." Her foot wedged under the door as she blocked it from opening more than the width of the tray.

"Let me bring it in." The female voice was warm and worn.

"No need," Jade said. "I've got it."

"It's too big and heavy for you, dear."

Jade jostled the tray into her hands. "Thanks again." She shut the door.

Thirro breathed out.

Jade set down the tray. She picked up the bread—the only loaf—and ripped it in half. She gave the other half to Gavriel. He winked at her.

"I'm going to scout." She stuck a thick piece of meat and some tomatoes in her roll.

"Be back three hours before sunset," Thirro said.

"With an invitation to the ball," Jade said. With her hood over her head and not a spot of her furry scalp visible, she was the image of a beautiful young human, eyes lined in kohl and lips painted deep red. Sandwich in hand, she strolled out.

Thirro's attention shifted. "Dara, remember—you can't be seen."

"I won't." She adjusted her hood, and with a giddy grin, she followed Jade out.

Thirro locked the door. Five travel-worn, stinking Draco males stared at him.

It was going to be a long day.

FORTY - SORROW
SUZA

*S*uza woke to a shoulder on fire. The air groaned with unfamiliar breathing. Firelight danced through her blurry vision. Her head swam.

"Talk to me."

"Dracos retreated," Xandra replied. *"Uriah is fine."*

Suza blinked away tears of relief. The ceiling of the healing tent came into focus.

"Captain Titus survived, but his horse was killed. Guap is fine."

Fear rose at the tremor along their mental connection. *"What is it, Xandra?"*

"Zemira."

A weight slammed into Suza's chest.

"She ..." Xandra's voice faltered. *"The Draco lines were breaking, but they weren't in full retreat. Several pockets were still pressing forward. The battle rested on a knife's edge. It could have gone either way. She was the difference. She was a tornado as she attacked their last foothold, fighting with injuries that should have rendered her immobile. When she finally died, swords still gripped in her hands, Opal went berserk. Howling and snapping, she chased the Dracos back. When the last Draco was in the river, Opal*

lay down. She didn't get back up." Xandra's voice broke. *"They saved Elysium today."*

Suza's heart collapsed. *"How long have I been out?"*

"Four hours."

Brine poured down her temples and into her short hair—the hair Zemira had cut. Suza had been in here, safe and asleep, while her friends fought—died. Guilt built a tower on her sternum.

She forced her head up. She gagged as a fresh wave of pain spiked her shoulder. She sat up on the cot. Moaning bodies clogged the low building. Her chest plate had been removed. Her sleeve was cut off, and her shoulder, wrapped in a thick bandage, pinned her right arm to her side. Her head spun. She brushed brown wisps away from her eyes and stood on wobbly legs.

Imanna appeared at her side. "Lie down, Suza. You lost a lot of blood." Dark circles ringed her pale eyes, and her usually red lips were ashen. Sweat soaked her scarf. She'd had her own battle in here.

"I have to go see."

"You need to rest."

"I can't rest."

Imanna held out a cup.

Suza shook her head. "You should drink it. You can use this cot."

Imanna smiled. It didn't reach her tired eyes. She wasn't going to rest either.

"Thank you for this." She gestured to her shoulder before turning toward the door.

"Really, Suza, be careful. The laceration is deep."

"Thank you, Imanna." She brought her left arm around her sister in a quick embrace before shuffling into the dusk.

Xandra swooped down from the roof and landed on her good arm.

"*I'm glad to see you.*"

"*It was a massacre.*" Xandra's voice quivered. "*We barely pushed them back.*"

"*Ferth is getting reinforcements.*"

The hawk shifted, and her green eyes bore into Suza. "*I think Thirro is hunting Ferth.*"

Suza stumbled; her shoulder flared. "*What? Why?*"

"*He wasn't here. He wasn't fighting today. Why would he miss battle? I haven't seen him for a few days on my routes, but I didn't realize it before. Others are missing too. Dara, Gavriel, and Jade.*"

Suza sat with a thud on a bench. "*What can we do?*" Her heart beat frantically. *Not Ferth.* Panic swelled.

"*Maybe I'm wrong. And who's to say Thirro will be successful? Ferth is a good fighter.*"

"*He can't stop an arrow he doesn't see coming.*"

"*I'm sorry I brought it up.*"

Suza gulped down smoky air. "*I love him. He can't die.*" She thought of her mother, Cal, and Zemira. "*You must go. You must warn him.*"

"*Thirro flies faster than I. It's no use. I can't catch him now.*" Xandra shifted her taloned feet. "*I wish I could. I'm sorry.*"

She brushed her cheek against Xandra's small head, then trembled as she got to her feet. *Please, not Ferth.* She was personally going to kill Thirro.

She staggered toward a golden haze at the northern edge of camp. An enormous fire blazed along the banks of the Rugit—fueled by the dead. The air smelled of burning flesh, fabric, and fur.

Chills racked her despite the waves of warmth. Ash burned her eyes. Titus hobbled forward on crutches. The flames cast sharp shadows on his sorrowing face. He put a strong arm around Suza's neck and kissed her brow. His lips were dry and papery. "It was a slaughter."

She could see that.

"We can't sustain that again."

She knew that too.

"Let's hope Ferth returns soon with reinforcements."

Ferth was a dead man. Thirro was going to kill him, just like he had King Andras. She shuddered. Titus pulled back. She was trembling.

"You're injured. You're in shock." He grimaced. "We're all in shock. You shouldn't be here. Go. Go to your tent. The Dracos won't attack tonight, and we'll keep this fire going as a barrier as long as we can."

Throat dry, she turned away from the flames, but they still burned across her eyes. *"Where is Uriah?"*

Xandra took to the sky, and seconds later, she reported, *"East of you a hundred yards."*

Suza's head spun, and her shoulder throbbed. She found Uriah and Shem kneeling next to Zemira. The body was caked in blood and peppered with wounds. *How long has she fought with her injuries?* Suza's hand flew to her mouth. Her stomach lurched. Opal's body lay motionless next to Zemira. Suza held her breath, trying to pull in her fraying edges.

It was all so terribly wrong. She kept seeing her mother's ashen face and the light fade from Cal's eyes. Ferth was soon to join them, the lost ones she loved. She looked up from Zemira's torn body. Thousands of souls piled up in the fires, their lives snuffed out like candles.

Uriah's song was low and sad.

When we fall into the pit and darkness swallows us whole,
There we find that the Great Ones descend below.
They rise up and carry us on.
Though the road is grim and bleak,
They go before our feet.
Carry her home.
Raise me up.

If they leave us on the brink, for them we will not sink.
Let us carry the sacrifice on. Carry it on.
Grant us their mantle of honor that we might carry it ever onward.
Ever forever onward.

Shem picked up his wife's body. Tears rolled down his round face. He kissed her bloody lips. "I'll take care of her." His whisper barely reached Suza. "I will make sure Callie Poe knows of your strength, goodness, and courage. She will know that you died for her freedom." His voice hitched. "I'll always love you, Zemira."

Uriah picked up Opal and followed Shem toward the fires. Head bowed, the blacksmith held his love's body for a long moment before he gave her to the flames. Uriah swung the panther over to rest next to Zemira. Time stopped as their sacrifice was engulfed in the consuming gold. Shem was a silhouetted statue. Uriah turned away. His gaze found Suza. He came to her. Char smeared his face and shirt. Flames flickered on his dark eyes. Careful of her injury, he drew her against his chest. She huddled into the shelter of his arms. Ash drifted through the air like snow.

*F*erth stifled a yawn. He'd spent most of the night at Elssa's, with his new family, and now, back at the castle, he struggled to focus on the argument between Darius and Forsyth.

"We march north at dawn," Darius said.

"I'll lead the troops." King Abner leaned forward in his oversized chair.

A feline grin spread over Raja Forsyth's soft face. Clearly she hoped the young king wouldn't return. Ferth thought she could get some tips from Laconius on how to hide her true motivations. Fortunately Darius seemed to know not to expose his back to her.

"Please re-think this, Your Majesty." Darius held up a thin hand. "It is better for you to remain in Mitera. Keep a strong presence here. It is best for the country."

"Our country needs a battle leader." The king said it as if reciting a line he'd once learned.

Ferth agreed, but unfortunately, Abner was far from a war chief. They needed a Laconius or a Mavras.

"We need you safe." Darius's voice turned soft, and Abner looked less certain.

"I will lead the army with His Majesty." Forsyth put her hand on the mountains of flesh covering her heart. "Darius, you can stay here in Mitera."

Darius frowned. "It's a little too late to be chasing battle glory."

Her lips twisted. "It sounds like it's exactly the right time."

King Abner stood. He didn't look like he'd slept either. "Raja Darius will lead the troops. He's the most qualified and experienced in battle. Raja Forsyth will remain here in Mitera." The king wilted under Forsyth's frown. "I need you here by my side."

Her scowl softened, and her gaze turned calculating.

"I'll visit the northwest camp this afternoon and send wine for Lammas." The young king put his knuckles on the table. "Maybe tonight's celebration should be pared down in light of tomorrow's departure."

Darius brightened.

"Absolutely not." Forsyth cut a swift hand through the air. "Our celebration tonight must continue as usual."

It was Darius's turn to scowl.

"We must show the people that we are not afraid of the Draco Slangs."

Slangs? Really? Ferth fought the urge to lean against the wall and close his eyes entirely.

"Elysium will celebrate Lammas as we always have." Forsyth set her jaw, ready for a fight. If only she would point some of that stubbornness toward the real enemy.

Abner wilted under her gaze. "Fine." He sighed. "I'll see you both tonight."

Ferth followed behind Darius, who gave way at the door as Forsyth barreled past. In the hall, she whirled around. Her belly nearly pressed against Darius's sword hilt. "Don't get any ideas about turning that army around and taking the crown on your way back."

Darius frowned. He looked down his straight nose at the red-faced raja. "The thought would never cross my mind. It concerns me that it has crossed yours."

She sniffed, jerked around, and waddled away.

Darius's jaw twitched and his brow furrowed.

Forsyth certainly had visions of increasing her power and prestige, but Ferth found he couldn't rise to concern over it. She wasn't scary like the Draco officers at Shi Castle. Her insubordination felt petty. Despite her assertive girth, she seemed insignificant.

He hoped he wasn't underestimating her.

He stayed respectfully quiet as he trailed the worried Darius through the castle. Flowers, streamers, and ribbons hung in blues and gold. Enticing smells of baking sugar and roasting meats tempted him to linger. He was beginning to look forward to tonight's party. Outside, they crossed the gardens to Darius's estate.

Angeline greeted them at the front door. "Come, boys."

Her voice seemed to draw Darius back to this world. She led them to the anteroom of the master suite. With a flourish, she pointed to the fabric spread over the couch. Ferth wasn't sure what he was looking at. Swaths of fuchsia, silver, and black lay in the shape of a body.

"A bit bold for our Ferth, here. Don't you think?" Darius said.

"With his body, he'll look splendid. It's the latest fashion." She sent them an encouraging smile. "Try it on." She handed Ferth the pants and shirt and shooed him into the dressing room.

He sighed as he stripped. The shiny black pants were

tight, hugging his thighs and calves. The silky shirt tickled his healing scabs. It didn't close. The silver fabric hung open in front, revealing tan skin and white scars. He held it closed, hiding his Draco brand. He forced a smile and stepped out.

Darius sat in a chair and stared out the window.

Angeline instructed the woman, Trissha, to wrap him in swaths of fuchsia. Nimble fingers grazed his skin as she opened his shirt six inches. Not quite wide enough to reveal his heritage. He exhaled. She tied purplish-red ribbon impossibly tight around his ribs and waist, leaving crisscrossing windows of skin visible on his chest and abs. Smaller fuchsia ribbons wrapped his biceps and wrists. She smiled coyly and pointed to the full-length mirror.

I hate it. I hate it. I'm not wearing this anywhere.

"Perfection." Angeline clapped her hands.

Darius turned from the window and his thoughts. He took one look at Ferth's stricken face and doubled over in laughter.

His wife's elegant face fell. "What? What is it?"

"It's just that he's a farm boy, dear."

"Not tonight. Tonight, he is a member of my household. He'll sit with us, and he'll wear the latest fashion." She turned to Ferth. "Won't you?"

His refusal caught in his throat. He glanced at the mirror. He was wrapped up like a pompous present. "I've never seen an outfit like this," he said weakly. All bright colors and exposition. Thirro would love it.

"You look wonderful. All the ladies will swoon."

"I shouldn't dress above my rank. I'll wear the suit I wore to dinner."

"To Lammas at the castle?" She looked aghast. "You will do no such thing. I'll send Trissha to help you dress *properly* in three hours."

"Yes, my lady."

Trissha unwrapped him, and he darted into the dressing room to change back into his simple, comfortable shirt and pants.

FORTY-TWO - INFILTRATING
THIRRO

*J*ade locked the door behind her. "It reeks in here." She surveyed the cramped room. Dracos lay in various states of consciousness over the bed and floor. Her gaze lingered on Gavriel, lounging against the wall. Dara drew her knife slowly over a whetstone—she'd nicked the tip of her blade while disposing of the stable boy.

"What did you find out?" Thirro asked. The hours he'd spend cooped up while she frolicked through the city had put him in a sour mood.

She dropped a bundle of emerald fabric on the floor, took off her cloak, and ran her hands across her furry brown scalp. She pulled out a scroll and unrolled it. "To the esteemed Lady Lucus. Blah blah Lammas. You are invited to dine and dance with the esteemed King Abner and his royal rajas. Blah de blah. Please present this invitation at the Lilac Ballroom. Et cetera." Jade rolled the invitation back up and grinned.

Thirro frowned.

Her frivolity died. Her next words were crisp—all business. "There are four entertainment troupes. Two are in full costume. Our best chance is the theatrical group. They have several actors dressing up as beasts for a play they will be performing during a break in the dancing."

Thirro beamed. "It's perfect."

"It's later in the evening. You will have to maintain your guise until you can come out with the troupe."

"Doesn't matter. We won't be performing." He turned away from her. "Pull out the costumes."

Gasson levered up from the floor and pulled one of the bags he'd carried from Skotar to the center of the room. Out came masks, gloves, fabrics, and paints.

"The performers are entering the castle through the south wing," Jade said. "I don't think the guards will know that you aren't part of the show, but the performers will."

"Once we are in the castle"—Thirro looked over the beaked mask in his hand—"you will meet us and lead us to where we can see and not be seen."

Jade grimaced.

"Are you not up to the task?" He took satisfaction in the thought, despite the mission.

"I am." Her brows lowered. "But it is more heavily guarded than I expected. Only four of us should go. You will be Dara's wings, and Gavriel will be mine."

Thirro nodded, happy to be leaving some of his cumbersome crew behind. "Dan, you will make sure the wagon is ready to go and that we have provisions for the return journey."

Dan looked about to protest.

"You will *take care* of this inn."

Glossy eyes sparkled at the implication. "Yes, sir."

With a piece of charcoal, Jade drew a simple map. "Let's plan on meeting here." She pointed to an area inside the south wing. "Don't go wandering around the castle."

*F*erth was back in the pink silk. Trissha left him with instructions to meet Darius and Angeline at the front door.

In his room, Ferth stood with his back to the mirror. He couldn't face his reflection. He braced himself. *"You can come out."*

Rom and Lyko padded out of the bathroom. They stopped midstride. Narrow jaws dropped. Raucous laughter echoed painfully through Ferth's skull.

"You look like a peacock," Lyko said.

"I feel like one."

"Dara would have fun unwrapping you," Rom said.

Is that what was bothering him? Draco Sang loved to stand out, flaunt their bodies. He had expected the humans to be different. He had wanted the humans to be different.

What would the old Ferth—the Draco captain—have done? He turned to his human face in the mirror. He wouldn't have worn this. He would have ripped the fuchsia ribbon to shreds with his own claws. He would have marched into that ball wearing only his scars and stripes for a shirt. And he would have been feared and respected for it.

He fingered the silky sash, considering. The temptation was almost too much, but in the end, he dropped the silk. He couldn't do it. Not when he thought of the consequences. He needed an army to protect his mother, Suza, and himself. For now, he had to play the idiot in pink.

"Have I traded one tyrant for another?"

"I wouldn't compare Angeline to Laconius," Rom said.

Ferth smiled at the thought of Angeline talking down her nose at the chief. His face fell. Laconius would destroy her. His father wouldn't grovel to humans. He would never bend his will or his pride to a weak human's whims.

And Laconius wanted his son dead. Ferth straightened. *"Tomorrow I march north at the head of an army. Who cares what I look like at tonight's ball?"*

"We're coming with you," Lyko said.

"I wish you could."

"We're coming," Rom said.

"Tomorrow the hiding will end. Tomorrow we will go north together." To Suza. They would follow the tug deep inside that called them home.

"If you leave us locked in here, we will destroy this room," Lyko said.

Ferth might have called Rom's bluff, but not Lyko's. He let them out the back door and into the gardens before he marched down the hall.

Darius wore all black under a long velvet red cloak. He looked elegant and regal. Like a falcon, not like a peacock. Angeline's red dress matched her husband's cloak. Rubies sparkled in her hair, braided into a crown. A dozen other people Ferth recognized from the previous dinner party stood with them. Three of the young gentlemen wore outfits like Ferth's, with patches of skin showing. Two wore brightly colored suits. One wore a robe-like dress that was worse than Ferth's outfit.

Tamaria stepped forward, adoration in her eyes. "Commander Ferth. Good evening."

She wore the same fuchsia swathes of silk wrapped around her curves. Slivers of ribs, breasts, and thighs peeked through gaps in the fabric. Ferth's blood warmed against his will. "A pleasure to see you again."

She lowered her chin and smiled, peering up at him through thick lashes.

Ferth looked away. He refused to be seduced, no matter how tempting. He belonged to Suza.

FORTY-FOUR - PARTY
THIRRO

*J*ade adjusted long cream gloves over her furry hands and arms. She wore an emerald gown that covered every inch up to her neck. Thirro knew she'd left her boots and pants on underneath. Cream silk wrapped her head and pointed ears. The only skin showing was her lovely, nearly human face. A black baldric disguised as a corset cinched her already tiny waist. She slipped four knives into the ribbing. Thirro tried not to stare as she applied red paint to her already dark lips and kohl to the black outlining her eyes.

I hate her.

Jade handed Dara her bow and quiver. "Don't forget these."

"Good luck in there," Dara said.

"We'll see you soon, soldier." Thirro folded his arms.

"Yes, sir." Jade's lips curved up on one side.

She wouldn't be smiling by the end of the night—Thirro would make sure of it.

Gavriel bent down. His long fingers gripped her hips as

he lifted Jade off the ground. "Be safe." Their lips met. His hands roamed.

Heat spiraled down Thirro's core. "She needs to go." His voice was hard. Angry, *not* jealous.

Gavriel pulled away. Red smeared his lips. He gently set her down. Jade's cheeks flushed as she fixed her rouge, then she slipped out.

"Are you ready to focus on the mission?" Thirro's words came out edged with venom.

"I'm ready and focused." Gavriel grinned like an idiot.

Thirro jerked his attention to his own preparations.

Dara stepped forward and pointed to his costume. "I'll help you get it on."

His temper calmed as her fingers worked open his buttons. She held out a loose tunic with feathers sewn over it. He couldn't just bare his own feathery chest. He had to wear a costume of feathers—be dressed up as a bird, not actually *be* a bird. Dan handed him a helmet with a large beaked face-mask. Gavriel put on a matching costume. Dara wore fox furs and a mask. She rolled the weapons in a leather blanket and put them in a musician's case.

Time to party.

FORTY-FIVE - EMBARRASSMENT
FERTH

*H*undreds of people clogged the halls and filled the ballroom. Ferth suffered through an endless line of introductions before he abandoned Tamaria with a group of chatting young people. He weaved over to the banquet tables and mounded food on a silvery plate.

"Excuse me, my lord." Ferth turned to face an anxious servant. "It would be our pleasure to serve you."

Ferth glanced around. The food was untouched—before he had disturbed it. No one else had a plate.

Tamaria looked at him across the room, her eyes wide in horror.

He sighed and handed his dinner over. The servant looked relieved and slightly embarrassed as he accepted the loaded plate.

Ferth picked up a strawberry from the top and popped it in his mouth. "When might I look forward to such an event?"

"The king will announce dinner. Shouldn't be too long." The servant whirled around and darted away.

But it was too long. He'd been introduced to twenty-six people before King Abner announced dinner.

On the outside, Ferth looked like he belonged. On the inside, he was far away. He was with Suza in his barracks at Shi Castle. He was with Keturah in the basement of the laundry. He even thought he saw Jade's face on one of the women. He blinked, and she was gone. What would it be like to see her teasing smile again? *She would spit on your humanness. You're not her friend anymore. You're her enemy.*

He wished he could have gone with his mother to her quiet Lammas party at Elssa's house. He wished he could go home. He wished he had a home.

"Ferth." He jerked out of his daydreams and focused on his mother's face. She wore a yellow dress, nothing fancy like Angeline's, but she was beautiful. He was so grateful to see her friendly face.

"I thought you were at Elssa's."

"Elssa will be here later. You leave tomorrow. I couldn't miss out on any precious time with you. I've just got to run something to Darius's suite for him, and then I'll be right back." She looked suddenly shy. "Then would you dance with your old lady?"

"I'm not very good." He grinned. "But I'd love to." And he meant it.

FORTY-SIX - GUILTY
JADE

*J*ade was ushered into a brilliant ballroom along with a group of guests. Guards dotted the room. They mingled with the brightly clad humans. She soaked in the splendor for a heartbeat before stealing into the dimly lit hallways. She needed to find a way up to the balcony. She tried to become one with the shadows as she patrolled the halls of the human castle.

"May I help you?" The woman wore a yellow dress that brought out the bright gold of her eyes. She was beautiful ... and strangely familiar.

Jade's fingers trailed the handle of a knife in her corset. "I've gotten turned around." And if the woman would turn around, Jade wouldn't have to see the terrible expression that would overtake her face when Jade's blade sunk deep.

"It happens to me all the time." A soft smile parted wide lips.

Jade's hand froze on her weapon at the woman's trusting expression. Again that sense of familiarity rocked her.

"I like your head scarf. I don't see that much here, but when I lived in the desert, people covered their heads all the time. Helped with the sun, and you didn't have to fix your hair." She gave Jade a conspiratorial grin.

"Yes. No one wants to see my *hair* at the moment."

"You'd get along with my son. He'd much prefer to wear his hair in a wild mane." She stopped talking, her eyes widening. "Excuse me if that came out wrong. You look lovely tonight. May I escort you back to the party?"

Jade dropped her fingers, glad she didn't have to kill this one … yet. She let the human lead her back toward the music and lights. The woman took Jade past a narrow spiral staircase. Just what she was looking for.

"Enjoy yourself tonight. Happy Lammas."

"Thank you," Jade said.

The moment after the woman sank into shadow, Jade followed. In seconds she was darting up the stairs. The stone steps opened to a narrow balcony overlooking the glittering ballroom. She stilled. A guard watched the scene below. He stood at full attention. She tiptoed back down the steps. She would have to kill him when it was time. She didn't allow one sliver of regret or remorse hack through the walls she'd built around her heart.

FORTY-SEVEN - IMPERSONATING THIRRO

The feather vest chafed. His breath steamed the helmet, leaving his cheeks unpleasantly moist.

"I'll do the talking," Thirro said.

Dara nodded. Gavriel didn't acknowledge the command. He was really grating on Thirro's nerves.

The performers they were impersonating had just entered the castle. Dara and Gavriel followed Thirro up the stone stairs. Thirro stepped carefully; he wasn't used to wearing shoes over his taloned feet. They didn't fit well.

"Looks like we are a bit late." Thirro enunciated the words—like the humans did.

The guard opened the door. Could it be that easy? Thirro took a step forward.

"Great costumes," the guard said. "Why do you get such good ones?"

"We are the main event." They certainly would be tonight.

Thirro jerked when a hand gripped his wing. Fingers tickled his feathers. He reached for his blade. No one touched his wings.

Dara's hand wrapped around his wrist, holding him back.

"These wings are incredible. So realistic. And enormous." The guard's voice was filled with awe. "How?"

Thirro turned, jerking his wings out of the man's dirty hands. He spoke through gritted teeth. "I'm a great hunter."

"We'd best catch up before our director has our heads," Gavriel said. He darted into the castle, black wings trailing in his wake.

Thirro stepped past the wide-eyed guard and followed, Dara's hand still holding his.

Killing the guard would surely raise the alarm.

FORTY-EIGHT - SEEN
JADE

*G*avriel, Thirro, and Dara would be at the castle soon. Jade should probably go hide and wait. Instead, she slipped into the celebration. People ate at long tables against the wall. Slaves darted around, serving steaming dishes. A throng of revelers had pushed back from their table and taken to the center of the floor. They swayed to high tinkling music. *He* was not among them. Jade prowled the perimeter.

"And who might you be?" The young man slurred the words as he blocked her path with his brightly clad bulk.

Her hand flew to her scarf, checking it. "Jasamine."

"Dance with me, Jasamine?"

Her smile was sweet as syrup. "Later." She flexed her wrists—ready. It was unnecessary.

He shrugged. "Something to look forward to." He moved aside.

She darted past, savoring the respect he'd shown her—even without seeing her knife. It made it so much harder to hate him. She pushed the feelings away. She had a mission to fulfill. She closed her mind to the injustice and cruelty she would bring here tonight.

That's when she saw him. Of course, he was at the king's table. Ferth stood like a statue, his deep-set eyes sad. She stared. He was dressed like the ridiculous humans, but he was not one of them. He shone with strength and power—even fallen, even as an abomination. Her heart pinged. Still her Ferth. No. He was not *her* Ferth. Sorrow bloomed over her breast. He offered his arm to the woman next to him, and she latched on. Jade blinked. The woman from the hall. She could see it now—the tan skin, the full mouth. The eyes. Her ribs squeezed. That was Ferth's human mother. He'd found her. And clearly, she loved him, even after all these years.

As Ferth guided his mother around the table, Jade thought of her own mother. Her hands went to her stomach. It would destroy her mother if she knew what Jade planned to do tonight. She was going to be sick. She shook her head, trying to dislodge everything from her heart. She swallowed hard, forcing her emotions and her weakness down, down, down.

Ferth looked up. She stood against the wall, ten yards away, but his stare struck her like an arrow. She froze. He froze. His gorgeous golden eyes gouged. She couldn't breathe. She should run. She should kill him.

His mouth formed one word. *Jade.*

Her chest twisted. Behind his human façade, her friend, her captain was still in there. Her heart reached for him.

He took a step toward her. And another.

She wanted to run into his arms.

He's a traitor. He's a traitor.

Belly churning, she whirled around and disappeared into the hall.

He was an abomination to the Draco Sang. He would die tonight. He had to. She sucked down air, her head dizzy and her chest riotous. But she couldn't shake the grief and loneliness she'd seen in his gaze. Even human, Ferth had power to speed her heart and draw her in. She should not have let him see her. Her hands shook. Her convictions wavered.

A guard stepped in her path. "No one's allowed past—"

She slit his throat.

FORTY-NINE - SPOTTED
FERTH

Jade.

Ferth stared at the spot where she'd stood— dressed as a human in a sleek gown and face make-up. He hadn't imagined her violet eyes this time. It was the touch of jackal in her gaze, the set of her jaw, the silk head-wrap hiding her fur and sharp ears that brought him crashing back to reality. Jade was here. In the castle. For a blink, he was happy to see her, but she could only be here for one reason ...

"Jade. She's here."

"Who else?" Rom asked, his thoughts paralleling Ferth's into dread.

Lyko and Rom flew out of Darius's gardens and toward the neighboring castle. They startled a couple on the street as they pounded past.

"We're about to find out." Ferth turned his mother to face him. "You need to leave." His voice was ice.

"You look like you've seen a ghost." Her voice soft with concern.

Worse. Panic rose. Not his mother. "There are Draco Sang here. Get out now."

She paled, and her body went still.

He clutched his chest as he swiveled his head side to side. *Great skies.* He didn't have his sword. "You there," he called to a nearby man with broad shoulders. "Come here." His voice had shifted into the commanding tone he'd used as a Draco army captain.

The man came.

"Quickly. Take this woman out of the castle now."

The man looked at his mother in confusion.

"But what about you?" Mira's brows furrowed.

"I'll be fine. You must go NOW." He thrust her into the man's arms and pushed them toward the doors. "Hurry."

The man started to jog, his hand on Mira's elbow.

Ferth scanned the room. Nothing seemed amiss. Guards still watched from the rafters. The king danced with a care-free smile on his face. Seven of the kingdom's twelve rajas mingled with the elite crowd. Almost the entire leadership of the nation was in this room. Twittering music played, grating on Ferth's rising stress. Darius was on the other side of the room, slowly turning circles with Angeline.

Ferth's pulse raced. Fear clutched. *"I've got to get them out of here."*

"We're coming," Lyko said, his southern accent sharpening in his anger.

"Keep your noses to the ground and your eyes open."

Ferth took a steadying breath and pushed through the crowd, his sights on Darius.

FIFTY - MURDER
THIRRO

"Quickly," Jade said. She'd appeared, seemingly out of nowhere, at Thirro's side. Her face was unusually pale and anxious. She darted down the hall, motioning them to follow. They sprinted past nine guards—each dead. Someone stepped into the hall in front of Jade. She didn't slow her pace. Didn't falter. The finely dressed woman died before she could even scream. Jade's knife dripped red along the marble floor.

Skies, she was good. When the time came, he'd have to aim true. Thirro's heart sped in excitement. Breathing hard, he jogged up a narrow set of stairs. A gurgling grunt greeted him at the balcony. Jade slowly lowered the dead guard to the floor. Thirro threw off his mask and ripped off his fake feathers. He peered over the balcony at the glittering party. Strong hands jerked him back.

"We can't be seen yet," Gavriel said.

Thirro twisted out of Gavriel's hands with a scowl. Dara smacked his bow against his chest, refocusing him. He strung it and selected an arrow. He ran his fingers over the fletching, his beautiful feathers. *Skotar's Arrow. King Killer.*

Jade sliced off her dress at the waist, leaving her in tight pants and a corset of knives. She accepted her bow from Dara and strung it.

Back pressed against a column, weapon ready in his palms, Thirro peered over the railing. He scanned the colorful crowd for the boy-king. So many targets. No one looked up.

Except one set of amber eyes.

He locked on the face. *Ferth.* Thirro's heart thudded, and he nearly dropped his bow. A feeling of connection snapped through Thirro. He gritted his teeth, hating that Ferth still had some power over him.

The music cut off.

A man with a red cloak shouted in a clear voice, "There is a dangerous threat in the castle. Please evacuate to the cream room. You will be safe there."

He spoke with authority. A raja to target, no doubt.

Thirro's gaze raked the room for the glint of a golden crown. The boy king was between four guards, head down, rushing toward the doors. Thirro cocked his arrow, but before he could let it fly, a bowstring twanged next to him. Jade's arrow slipped between two guards and hit the king in the back. A masterful shot. The boy fell forward.

Rage flared in Thirro, his vision blinking black. Jade had stolen his kill.

To Thirro's left, Gavriel fired. The whistle of his arrow silenced when it hit its target, a bearded old man in excessive velvet. A woman screamed. Pandemonium broke out, humans pushing and falling and shouting.

Metal reflected light near Ferth as the traitor's blade sailed through the air. Thirro grabbed Gavriel and threw him in front as a shield. The knife lodged in Gavriel's side. The traitor had no trouble firing at his old friend. So be it. Thirro dropped the groaning Draco raven.

"No!" Jade's lethal voice was aimed at Thirro. Her eyes turned to burning coals as she looked from the bleeding Gavriel to him.

Thirro leaped over the railing. He spread his wings, hovering near the high ceiling. Jade dropped to Gavriel's side. "Leave him," Thirro said.

Jade ignored his order as she pulled the knife out of Gavriel's side. He gasped and coughed. Thirro turned away from them with disgust. She was hindering the mission.

Human guards spread out from the dead king. Thirro hit one guard with an arrow through his throat—his favorite target. The next went down with an arrow in his heart.

"Take cover," Ferth yelled as he ran to a dead guard and took an unused sword out of a limp hand. "Throw anything you can find at them. Aim for his wings. Get soldiers to that balcony." Ferth pulled a small blade from his boot and threw it at Thirro. Thirro dodged, but the knife nicked his forearm. Fire seared up his nerves.

"Hello, traitor," Thirro's voice boomed as he trained his arrow on Ferth's neck. Ferth snapped up a plate from the table and twisted it in front of his face. Thirro's arrow cut into the metal and stopped halfway through.

"Come down and fight me like a warrior," Ferth yelled, still holding the punctured plate. The arrow tip hadn't even touched his pristine face. Ferth stepped in front of the raja with the red cloak and held up the cheap sword.

"A warrior?" Thirro sneered. "You were always claiming titles you didn't deserve."

"Is that why I always beat you in the squares?"

Thirro slammed his teeth together to hold back a petty retort. Ferth *had* always beaten him. But not tonight. He ducked and wove as silverware came at him from all directions. He fired into the crowd with practiced efficiency. Bodies scattered the ground, blood pooling and spreading like puddles in a storm. Panicking people made crisscrossing tracks of red on the white marble.

Dara dropped her bow, out of arrows, and flipped over the balcony. She scrambled down the drapes, leaping the last ten feet and pulling out her daggers. With a howl, she attacked. Gavriel appeared at the edge of the balcony, torso wrapped with his bloody tunic. With a grimace, he lifted Jade and ungracefully floated down to the main floor. The duo unsheathed their swords. Even injured, Gavriel cut down the crowd like harvesting wheat. The shrieking sound of fear and death filled the air. The humans didn't go quietly.

Thirro's jaw clenched against the ear-shattering screams. He aimed for the loudest prey, a large woman with an open mouth like a giant cave. His arrow went through her windpipe. She wouldn't be bothering him anymore. He swiveled back toward Ferth only to find Jade already stalking toward the traitor, twirling her short swords.

She would not be taking this prize from Thirro as well.

He hissed and pulled an arrow back. His sights shifted between Ferth and Jade. He trained his arrow on her back.

"Jade, drop!" Ferth's voice tore through the air as Thirro let his weapon fly.

Jade hit the ground and rolled. The arrow soared over her head and hit a slave in the leg. Thirro blinked. Ferth had protected her. And she'd trusted Ferth instinctively. Jade looked at Ferth, and Thirro saw the deep emotion that flashed across her face. She stifled it quickly, but it was too late. The violet-eyed coward still loved Ferth. Disgusting.

Thirro turned his last arrow on his true enemy. He aimed at the Draco brand that had slipped into view on Ferth's chest. He would get such enjoyment from seeing Jade suffer as she watched Ferth die. She would know that Thirro had been the one to conquer Ferth. And then he'd finally end her too. He could feel the beginning waves of pleasure rolled through his body as he pulled back on the string.

He gasped, his fingers suddenly paralyzed as icy pain speared his chest.

Ferth's eyes went wide as range targets as he stared up at Thirro. *Yes, traitor. This is the end for you. I've won.* Thirro inhaled to share his decree, but no air came. He looked down as the frost dug deeper into his breast. Jade's favorite knife stuck deep into his bare chest. Blood bubbled over his feathers. Thirro's arrow fell from his fingers and spiraled harmlessly towards the ground; his bow followed. His wings faltered. The cold turned to fire that blazed out from the hole in his chest where the hilt protruded; the black handle was splattered red. With effort, he lifted his gaze to Jade.

Her beautiful eyes burned as she watched him swoop lower. He saw no regret there, only an iron resolve. He'd lost. To a worthy opponent, but what did that matter now? He didn't feel pain when he landed on his wings. He didn't feel anything.

FIFTY-ONE - MISSION

FERTH

*F*erth didn't breathe. Jade killed Thirro. She'd killed him. The reality rooted his feet to the floor and sent his heart galloping.

Jade stood. She lifted her twin Dracosteel blades and faced him. A heavy emotion passed through her eyes as she looked at him, but in a flash she blinked it away, her face settling into cold lines. She'd lost her scarf and gloves. Jagged bits of green silk stuck out of the bottom of her corset above black pants. Gray and amber fur covered her arms and head. She still had a delicate nose and rosebud mouth, but she was no longer the underling he most often remembered her as. She was a terrifying Draco Sang. All innocent pretense had burned off her grim face.

She was here to kill him.

Blades lifted, she ran at him. He threw the arrow-embedded dinner plate shield at her. She slashed it down with her sword. It rang against the ground like a warning bell. He leaped over a groaning body. She silenced it by dragging her blade over his throat on her way past. Ferth stopped running and faced her.

The fighting around them subsided as Gavriel and Dara came to stand at Jade's back. The retreating humans and gathering guards turned to haze. He and Jade were the only people in this world.

"Jade." His voice was soft, but it carried through the room. "Don't do this." He spread his arms in supplication, but didn't get too close. The human sword in his hand was pointed down. "You don't want to fight me."

Her jaw jutted out, and she lifted her swords higher. "You are a traitor. It is my *duty*."

"This transformation isn't what we thought. I haven't fallen. I'm fre—"

"No talking." She shook her head as if she could shake out his voice. "You abandoned me. All of us. Your people." The pain and betrayal in her voice lanced his chest. She slashed forward. He lifted the borrowed sword to meet hers. The inadequate steel chipped under her blow. Never again would he leave his Dracosteel sword behind because Angeline said it *didn't go*.

He fought Jade off with practiced motions, but it wasn't as easy as it used to be. She was stronger now. Finally, he pushed her back, giving himself precious moments to speak. "I didn't mean to leave you. Not ever. It all happened so fast. I couldn't stay." He motioned to his human frame. "Not like this."

"Human now." She spat the words like a curse.

"No." Ferth was aware of every human in the room watching him. "I'm still a Draco Sang." He said it with pride, knowing, in this crowd of humans, he sealed his doom with this truth. "I'm still me, but *I am free*."

Jade shook her head.

"And I still care about you. You will never be my enemy."

A gasp rose from the corner of the room, but Ferth didn't look. He had only eyes for Jade, his friend, the closest thing he had to a sister. He missed her. "I don't know how to fix this, Jade." His sword lowered to his side. If even his Jade could aim to kill, how could he ever find home again? Loneliness and despair welled up inside his chest.

"You saved my life," she said.

"I would do it again."

She lowered her weapons, her eyes pink. "Now, we are even."

Relief flooded through him. Without thinking, he brought his fist over his head. He thumped his heart and sent the Draco Sang blessing over her.

A tear leaked down her check. She dashed it away, stiffening with a scowl. "Nice belly button." She turned to the room. Bodies covered the floor. People cowered under tables and fought to get through the doors.

"Let us leave and we won't kill anyone else. Stop us and we'll kill the last three remaining rajas." She pointed out Darius, Forsyth, and Nadab with fearful accuracy. "And we won't stop there."

Darius looked at Ferth in question. Ferth could kill Jade, but he didn't want to, and it would destroy his mind and soul in the process. And he couldn't do it before Dara and Gavriel murdered more innocent guests. And if all three attacked him at once, he was dead. Dara and Gavriel were obeying Jade. She was the commander here. Interesting. And Dara was looking at Ferth with unabashed regret. She was not sorry to leave him alive. The realization spread warmth through his chest.

Ferth nodded to Darius.

"No one will touch you until you are out of the building." Darius's voice held steady, but his fingers quivered.

"Fair enough," Jade said. "Good day." She gave a mocking bow. "Enjoy the few you have left before I return with an army." She looked tired and resigned as she said it. The crowd jerked apart, making a path. She stalked toward the door, stepping over corpses, blood smearing beneath her boots, Gavriel and Dara trailing along in her wake. She looked like a queen as she marched out. The doors slammed behind her.

Ferth's breath came rushing back and so did the clamor of panicked humans. Humans who now knew the truth.

"Secure the halls." Darius spoke to the last few surviving guards. "Get units four and five. Find them."

People clogged the doors, unable to leave. Everything had happened so fast.

"They're out here," Rom said. *"Across the yard. Gavriel is injured. We'll stop them."*

"No. Don't."

"They're nearly to the gates."

Rom and Lyko pounded toward the Dracos.

Ferth's command was iron. *"Stop. Let them go."*

Lyko whined as he drew to a halt next to Rom.

The three Dracos turned to face the wolves. Jade had her bow drawn, but she lowered it when the wolves stopped.

"Goodbye, Ferth," Jade said, her voice sad.

Rom barked. He wanted to run to her, to smell her sweet fragrance and walk by her side. He howled his mournful goodbye.

Lyko, still livid at all the Dracos in Laconius's camp for the death of Cal, clawed at the ground and bared his teeth.

"She spared my life," Ferth said.

Jade turned her back and walked away. Rom and Lyko watched her kill two human guards blocking her path before the three Draco Sang disappeared.

Ferth opened his eyes. The ballroom was too bright, the light illuminating terrible carnage. A moat of space lay around Thirro. Ferth closed the gap, dropping to one knee next to the familiar flyer. Red inked his outstretched wings, and Jade's knife stuck up like a flag. Death softened the hard lines of his face. They'd spent their childhood together—for the good and bad. They'd fought and challenged each other. Thirro never hid his jealousy or resentment well, but as children they'd always found each other at the end of the day. Ferth couldn't deny the sorrow that filled his breast. *Goodbye, brother.*

Ferth ripped Jade's knife free. He wondered if he'd have the chance to return it. He surprised himself with how much he wanted to. He pushed the desire away, knowing it was foolishness. He cleaned the blade against Thirro's thigh and secured it in the ridiculous ribbons that now hung loosely over his frame. His shirt gaped open, showing hard muscles and stark scars. It was a better look than before. Let them all see the truth. Ferth picked up Thirro's bow and unbuckled the quiver from between heavy wings. He'd be taking these too. Human weapons were not made like this.

Familiar barks rent the air. The sea of humans parted, and Rom and Lyko shot through. A guard lifted his sword and stepped forward.

"Don't," Ferth said, his voice molten iron. "They are *mine.*"

The guard stopped, but didn't lower his weapon.

"We should have been here," Rom said.

"I don't care who sees us. You aren't going anywhere without us again," Lyko said.

"Agreed," Ferth said.

Two strong wolves rammed into his chest. He wrapped his arms around their necks. Tears sprang to his eyes. They were safe.

"You let her get away." Lyko's voice was full of betrayal. His fresh wave of pain at losing Cal cut down their connection like a knife wound.

"Yes," Rom said it without apology.

Jade hadn't killed Cal. Tonight was another reminder that

all Draco Sang were not the same. Jade and Dara were not
Laconius.

Rom circled Thirro's body. *"What a waste."*

It was the abruptness that shook Ferth. That with the
flick of fingers and the snap of a wrist, Thirro's life was over.
The end of his story, whether it was finished or not.

Darius approached. "Are you hurt?" His face was hard—
the face of the leader Ferth had met at the border.

"No." Not in any ways he cared to admit.

"We haven't found any of them."

"Rom and Lyko saw the three Dracos escape."

"We'll keep hunting."

Ferth didn't expect them to find the Dracos. He couldn't
help but hope Jade and Dara remained safe. As he looked
over the room at what they had done, the thought
shamed him.

"You're okay." His mother tore through the crowd. She
slipped on blood, stumbling to catch herself. He jumped to
his feet, reaching out to steady her. Her blonde hair had
come loose, framing her fearful face like a wild swarm of
bees. She was shaking as she wrapped her arms around him.
She pulled back, looking him over for injury. Her touch was
warm honey.

She truly loved him.

A voice boomed across the blood-spattered ballroom.
"Traitor!"

Ferth's head swiveled.

Raja Forsyth's gray hair stuck out at sharp angles, and
rage reddened her face. Her fat finger pointed across the
room—at Ferth. "He's a Draco Sang. He's betrayed us to the
enemy. Guards!"

Lyko snarled, but Ferth silenced him with a hand on his
skull. Mira stepped in front of Ferth. It was a sweet gesture,
but he pulled her back against his side, in the protection of

his arm. The few uninjured guards still standing looked to Ferth and back to Forsyth. They didn't move toward him.

"He did not betray us," Darius said. "He saved many lives tonight. Yours and mine included."

Forsyth bristled. "That does not change the fact that he *lied* to us." She stepped forward, her beady gaze dropping pointedly to his exposed Draco Sang brand. "He made us believe he was one of us."

"He is here to fight for Elysium. And he proved that tonight."

"You've been housing him. Are you in on it too? You planned this so you would become king?" Forsyth held every eye in the room.

"Be careful what you say, Forsyth." Darius's tone was glacial. He hadn't moved from Ferth's side.

"Or what? You'll send your wolves after me?"

"I might," Ferth said. Anger swelled. This time both wolves snarled, underscoring the threat.

Forsyth had the decency to balk before straightening her spine with an offended scowl. She strode over to the dead king; the boy's body lay in a mound where he'd fallen. Forsyth plucked the crown off the young curls and set it squarely on her wrinkled brow.

"As head raja," Darius said, "I am now king of Elysium."

"Clearly the reason you staged this coup. And therefore, you forfeit the right."

Darius's jaw rippled, and his knuckles went white on the dinner knife he still held as a weapon. "Forsyth, you do not want to fight me now. I am not your enemy. Nor is Ferth. And you know it. You and I are both loyal to this country. You know I would never commit treason. I would have given my life for the king ... my nephew." His gaze was steady on Forsyth. "You will hand over the crown, or you will be arrested."

She wilted in defeat and lifted the crown.

Darius strode over and took it. He didn't put it on, just held it. "Anyone who touches Ferth or his wolves will be punished for disobeying the crown. Which, unfortunately, is my responsibility now."

"You use your power to protect the liar?" Forsyth hissed. "The son of our enemy?"

Darius opened his mouth, but another voice cut through the tension.

"We wake The Dragon with our quarrels." A tall thin man with a white beard down to his waist stepped forward. The crowd shrank away from his swaying gray robes. "He smells our weakness. He is hungry again."

"Raoul, get back and shut up," Forsyth said, shooing the man with both hands.

"Nogard wakes. With the North, he rises."

Ferth frowned. This was not helping.

"We must stop our petty arguments. We must kill The Dragon. We must hunt Nogard," Raoul said.

To Ferth's shock and dismay, the throng of people clung to the words, the dream. "Yes," they cried. "Kill the Dragon. Destroy the Draco Sang."

"This is madness," Rom said.

"We need to get out of here," Ferth said.

The chant gathered strength and volume. "Kill the Dragon. Destroy the Draco Sang. Kill the Dragon. Destroy the Draco Sang."

"Silence." Darius's voice was a clap.

The crowd quieted, but they leaned forward, toward their new king with desperation in their stricken faces. The ragged humans looked a puff away from toppling into the chasm of fear. They needed hope, and they looked to their new king for it.

"I agree with our royal scholar," Darius said. "Raoul has

studied every text on the subject. He has shown me the strangeness of the wind and the power that yet bleeds poison from the north. I've thought long and hard about our Draco Sang neighbors. To find peace, The Dragon must be found and killed."

The survivors relaxed slightly, except Mira, who tensed against Ferth's side. Forsyth folded her arms, managing to look both pouty and conniving.

"Who better to hunt the Dragon than one of his own? Ferth has Nogard's blood. He knows Skotar. We will send him to kill the Dragon."

"*Is he serious?*" Lyko asked.

Ferth did not want to answer that.

Darius speared Ferth with sharp eyes.

"*He looks deadly serious,*" Rom said.

"I have long watched for an opportunity to strike at the heart." Darius spoke to Ferth, but his voice carried over the room. "This is our chance. I trust you with this important mission. Do you accept?"

"*We do want out of here,*" Lyko said.

"*He's got me curious,*" Rom said. "*It doesn't seem so crazy when he says it.*"

"*Yes, it does. And what about the war?*" Ferth didn't say her name, but he thought of Suza. He wanted desperately to find out if she could really love him after he'd been condescending and cruel. Was it fair to ask it of her?

"*This is what the king of Elysium wants us to do,*" Rom said.

"*I think it's a waste of our skills and our time.*" Ferth stared at the raja as he talked to his wolves. "*And I hate that it feels like he's been planning this since the day we met. Lying in wait like a snake, watching for the opportunity to trap us into going on his stupid quest.*"

"*Are we soldiers for Elysium now?*" Rom asked. "*Do we still follow orders?*"

Ferth sighed. His mother's hands were warm on his side, strengthening him. "We accept the assignment. We will hunt for you."

Darius's shoulders lowered as he exhaled.

"Who will go with him?" Forsyth asked.

"We hunt alone."

"Accountability." She pointed an insufferable finger at him. "I do not trust you."

Then how could he be trusted to keep the poor volunteer alive?

She looked to Darius. "And as I am still a raja, I do have power here. I would ask that this *liar* have an Elysium-born *human* companion travel with him."

Silence reigned.

Ferth cringed when Darius finally nodded in acceptance of Forsyth's request.

The crowd shifted, and a young man stepped forward. A streak of blood smeared his hairless cheek. "I volunteer." The boy was thin and short ... and *weak*.

No. Please no.

Behind Darius, Raoul nodded in approval.

"Tobin. No." Forsyth's voice was firm. "You're fifteen, way too young." That was older than Tobin looked. "I forbid it."

Tobin lifted his chin defiantly. "I'm going, Mother. I listened when you refused to let me join the army, but I won't be held back now. I have studied with Raoul, and I agree with King Darius on the importance of this mission. I'm a good hunter. I can track anything. I will find this Dragon. I will help save our country." The fight in Tobin's jaw and the fire in his eyes changed Ferth's mind.

He'd do.

Forsyth scowled. "Fine. Then go. But do not return until you have succeeded." Her eyes were cold. "Bring us proof of The Dragon you think *you* can slay."

That would be impossible. Nogard died three hundred years ago.

Tobin lifted his chin. "I might not be able to carry such a big head home in my puny arms, but I'll bring you at least an eyeball."

Ferth grinned.

Rom chuckled.

Forsyth turned her back on her son, as if *he* were the disappointment.

Ferth let go of Mira and put a hand on Tobin's thin shoulder. When he squeezed, the wet sheen dried from Tobin's brown eyes. He looked up at Ferth with hope. Ferth forced himself not to recoil as the weight of responsibility slammed into him. He wouldn't be able to leave this boy at the next town. He wasn't as disappointed as he thought he'd be about it either. This boy had guts—even if it was the only thing he had. And Ferth couldn't leave him here with that terrible woman. Tobin's mouth curved up, showing small square teeth, a gap between the front ones.

"We have work to do," Darius said. "While *Commander* Ferth hunts in the north, we have an army to stop at our border. We have seen what the Draco Sang can do. We have seen their cruelty. We mourn the loss of our king. This night has been a great tragedy, but we will rise with vengeance. They will not have our lands. They will not have our families."

A cheer rose.

At least something good would come from this. It looked like the humans had just pulled together a defending army... and obtained a formidable king.

"Raja Forsyth will lead the armies north at dawn," Darius said.

Forsyth looked like a vein would pop in her brow. Her mouth worked sideways.

"May she return home victorious. Hail Raja Forsyth, captain of the armies."

"Hail Raja Forsyth." The room echoed the cheer. The mood lightened. The tension broke. People streamed away.

Forsyth stepped forward and spoke quietly to Darius. "You will lead the army north."

"You think I will let you stay here and get comfortable sitting in my seat?"

"I refuse to leave."

Darius's jaw worked. "You refuse a direct order of the crown?" He held up the gold band.

"I cannot lead an army. It is not the best way for me to serve this country."

Darius exhaled, obviously seeing the wisdom of her words. "Then I must go."

Forsyth let loose a satisfied smile. Ferth nearly punched her in the face.

"I will lead the troops and fight to defend our homes and families."

"Noble Darius." She failed to sound sincere.

"But I warn you." Darius's voice was a hiss. "When I return, and I *will* survive, the army will be at my back, and I will return as the rightful king of Elysium."

Forsyth grinned, showing a row of angry yellow teeth. "I hear the border is a dangerous place. I hope we will be welcoming you back very soon."

"Don't get too comfortable in my absence, *Regent* Forsyth."

She lifted her chin.

"Gather the raja heirs to the council room. We'll meet to appoint new rajas. It must be done tonight."

Forsyth nodded curtly before she turned and stormed away.

"New rajas who are watchful and loyal to me," Darius muttered. Ferth pumped his shoulder supportively.

Tobin stood at Ferth's elbow. The boy's eyes narrowed on the retreating woman's back. "Goodbye then, Mother."

"Meet me at the northern gates in one hour," Ferth said.

"Yes, sir." Tobin headed toward a door opposite the one Forsyth had taken.

Darius looked over the massacre.

"I'm sorry I couldn't stop them in time," Ferth said.

Bodies littered the floor. Red painted the scene in angry strokes. The smell of blood and tragedy hung thick in the air. "We lost this battle, but for the first time, I now have hope we can win this war. I never expected to be king, never sought it out. But I know that I will be a better war leader than Abner or Forsyth could ever be. There is a reason I have amassed so much land and wealth. I am fair, and I am good at this."

Ferth held up his hands. "You don't need to defend yourself to me. I see you. I know."

Darius exhaled, a sheepish look spreading over his face. "Sorry, I guess I was still in battle mode."

"I'm glad I'm on your side. And thank you for defending me."

"I am sorry to give up a powerful fighter at the border, but you will do Elysium a great service if you can bring down Nogard."

Ferth swallowed down a mocking laugh. How Darius thought there was an ancient dragon hiding somewhere in Skotar, and how Ferth had been roped into going after a ghost, he really had no idea. Of course, he also couldn't believe he'd faced Jade across blades tonight either. He hadn't hesitated to protect her from Thirro's arrow, and she'd walked away without the taint of Ferth's life on her heart. He might yet die in this war, but it would not be at her hand.

He'd seen it in her eyes—such a burden would have destroyed her.

"May the Mother be with you on your hunt. May you return victorious," Darius said. "There will be a place of honor here for you when you do."

"I don't belong here." Ferth didn't belong anywhere.

"You always have a place in my home. Give it a bit of time, then I hope you will return."

This kingdom would likely be destroyed by then. A Draco captain would be living in Darius's house. Ferth bowed. "Thank you for everything, Your Majesty."

Darius pursed his lips. "I'm not sure I can get used to that."

"You are the rightful king—the king this land needs."

His brow creased. He looked a decade older than this morning. "It is a hard road ahead."

"Race you to the border," Ferth said.

Darius cracked a small grin and put a hand on Ferth's shoulder. "Until we meet."

"Goodbye." His chest tightened. He would not be back.

His friend dipped his head to each wolf before he turned and walked away, the weight of a kingdom hunching his shoulders. Mira, Ferth, Rom, and Lyko padded out the opposite doors, ignoring the humans' hostile glares and the tang of fear in their whispers.

He stopped outside the gates to Darius's Azure Estate. "Please tell Grandpapi and Elssa and the others goodbye for me. Tell them thank you, and I'm sorry to leave them." He wrapped his ma in his arms. "But mostly, I'm sorry to leave you. I wish things were different."

She pulled back, her eyes gleaming in the lamplight. "I know. I do too. But you must go. I understand that. You were not made for the confines of these walls." She laid her hand over his heart and his Draco brand. "But promise me that no matter where you go or what you do, you will remember that I am thinking about you. I am wishing you well. I am loving you."

His insides went warm and soft, and he felt as if his face glowed. "I promise." He kissed her cheek. "I imagined you every day growing up, but you are better than I ever dreamed. I've always loved you, Ma."

She stepped back and kissed each wolf on his head as if in blessing. "Take care of each other."

The wolves nodded and purred.

Ferth's heart was a stone in his chest as he watched the mother he'd just found walk away.

Back at Darius's estate, he changed into black traveling clothes and strapped on his Dracosteel sword. He packed a bag of supplies from Darius's stores. He left a note for Titus. The next note was harder to write; Suza might not be happy to receive it, but it would be the best for her in the end. She deserved so much better than he. He left the letters on the desk, addressed and ready for delivery. He shouldered his pack and looked down at expectant faces.

"Let's go catch a dragon," Rom said.

"Or at least something worth finding," Lyko said.

"I'd like somewhere we no longer have to hide or pretend we fit in." Rom gave voice to Ferth's hope.

Shaking off the shackles of culture and expectation, Ferth ran out of the city gates and into the night, hunting fantasy, searching for freedom, and chasing dreams. A gray wolf loped at his heels, tongue lapping at the cool breeze. Up ahead, a white wolf howled at the stars. And at his side, a scrawny human boy struggled to keep up.

FIFTY-TWO - DEFEAT
SUZA

Suza wiped sweat off her brow and guzzled the sharp drink the boy gave her. Uriah retied some loose leather straps on her vest. She should be doing it; he was as tired as she. But she couldn't fight him about it or admit how much his careful attending gave her strength. Not when they were fighting the Draco Sang. And losing. These last weeks of battle had weakened and nearly bled dry the Elysium army. The humans clung to life and freedom by their blunt fingernails, waiting for reinforcements that didn't come. Ferth should have returned by now with the army he'd promised. Betrayal struck Suza harder than the Draco front line.

One of the Elysium soldiers in front of them dropped, his neck impaled by an enemy's curving sword. Suza lifted her twin blades. Rest time was over. She blinked out exhaustion and dizziness as she marched forward, into the slaughter.

"The Dracos have broken through the line on the east," Xandra said through the mental connection they shared.

Suza relayed the hawk's message to Uriah, commander of this center unit.

"Fall back," he yelled. The order traveled down the lines and with controlled reverse steps, the humans gave up precious ground.

Suza disengaged from her duel with a monkey Draco, slashing his furry forearm before jumping back. He looked down at the drip of red and then up at her, his eyes hungry and promising a painful retribution.

The human army shrank in on itself, backing away from the border that separated Skotar and Elysium. The Dracos fanned out, their swarm of soldiers no longer cramped by the narrow passage along the Rugit River delta.

Panic swirled through Suza. She could not become a slave again to these monsters; she could not lose the new freedom she'd barely gained. Who was she kidding? Laconius would never let her live. He'd kill every soldier here before plowing south through the defenseless humans to Mitera. She'd have to die fighting. Panting, she stepped back, over the bodies littering the ground. The Dracos moved forward slowly, catching their breath, savoring their victory.

Ferth hadn't returned from Mitera with reinforcements. No help was coming. Had Thirro succeeded? Was Ferth already dead? Today she would join him in the realm beyond the stars.

As the line reformed, Suza and Uriah lifted their bloodied blades, but a disturbance to the northwest had the Dracos turning around. Suza used the distraction to fold over her knees and suck down more air. Uriah killed a Draco—the better use of time.

"Slaves attacking from the rear," a Draco commander yelled. "Unit two, fall back and *deal* with it."

Suza craned her neck, her pulse a sudden roar. *The slaves.* Her friends. Her family for the last three years. She could see them across a sea of Dracos. Pearl and Kenji marched at the front. Pelussa and her raven stood at their side. She'd obviously snuck behind enemy lines and put herself at greater risk to help the slaves. Suza's respect for Pelussa grew. The blind woman looked like she knew what do with the jagged knife she held, but it would not be enough to save the band of rebels. Pelussa had the advantage of Draco blood. Only a precious few in that group of slaves had started out as Draco Sang underlings, and their weapons training was limited and long ago. No matter how much Kenji swung around his stolen sword in secret, he was not prepared to battle Draco warriors.

Suza turned to Uriah in panic. "We need to help them. We need to get them over here."

Uriah nodded, face bleak. "We can send word to tighten up the western edge, try to bring them around the side. There is no way we can punch a hole straight through to them." He didn't tell the truth written in his eyes; that it didn't matter. This was the end for the Lion's army. The Dracos would let the conquered citizens of Elysium live, but no one who'd lifted a weapon against them would survive their victory.

Suza looked back at her friends across the battlefield. Fear was a living thing in her breast. The Draco Sang pounded their chests and howled. The slaves' mutiny had incited a wave of violent impenetrable rage. Her brave, stupid friends had just condemned themselves to death along with the rest.

ACKNOWLEDGMENTS

Thank you to Monster Ivy Publishing. Mary Gray and Cammie Larsen are amazing to work with and say the kindest things about my story. Cammie's cover work is exceptional. Thank you to Rich Storrs for lending his editorial prowess to this project. Thank you to Adam for making the map of Elysium and Skotar. Thank you to my family, especially Mom, Katherine, and David for reading raw, early drafts, and Laura and Amy, who joined them for proofing rounds. Thank you to my husband and children for supporting me and thinking I'm cool for writing novels. Thanks to you, reader. Thank you for reading my book. And most importantly, thanks to God.

ABOUT THE AUTHOR

Mary Beesley believes humans are born to create, and promotes creativity in all its beautiful forms. She's learning calligraphy and watercolor. She loves exploring our magnificent planet and finding all the best places to eat around the world. But nothing beats coming home and sharing a pot of slow-simmered spaghetti Bolognese and homemade sourdough with  friends and family. If she's not in her writing chair, you'll probably find her hiking in the Utah mountains with her husband and four children. Find Mary at her website www.-marybeesley.com and on Instagram or Twitter @maryr-beesley.